DEDICATION

For Victor, who helped save me from me.

ACKNOWLEDGEMENTS

I would like to thank my wife Cindy for her love and support over the years, I adore you! To my children; Zach, Ian, Beth and Olivia you are my heart and my inspiration to love, live, and laugh at life and myself. To my Lord and Savior, thank you for these wonderful blessings and all you have graced me with.

Mike Lechette

Dear Charlie

A NOVEL

Edited by Mike Valentino
Salisbury, MA

Dear Charlie is a work of fiction. Names, characters, places and incidents either are the product of the author's imagination or are used fictitiously. Any resemblance to actual persons, living or dead, events, or locales is entirely coincidental.

Edited by Mike Valentino

Published in the United States.
CreateSpace, a DBA of On-Demand Publishing, LLC.

ISBN-13: 978-0615871462

ISBN-10: 0615871461

Cover design: Mike Lechette
Cover photograph: CreateSpace Cover Creator

DEAR CHARLIE

A Novel

PROLOGUE

There's so much we don't know about dying and death. What exactly does the person feel or think in those final hours and minutes? Are they coherent enough to know what's going on around them? Are they in pain? And probably the most controversial question of all, where does someone go after death? Do they just die or is there an afterlife like heaven or hell?

Raised Catholic, Chris had always believed there was a heaven and hell. He had imagined it was a sweet and peaceful transition. He would see the light and move on to a beautiful state of being called Heaven. As he felt his life slipping away, he second guessed himself at times becoming afraid and worried that maybe he wouldn't go to heaven or maybe there even wasn't such a place. He hoped there was.

Heaven was the ability to see and in some instances communicate with your loved ones, living and dead. As a Guardian Angel you were blessed to be a part of them for all eternity. You were allowed to throw Pennies from Heaven, that when found heads-up let your loved ones know you were okay.

Hell was the inability to see your loved ones and was spent in constant fear. The evil and demons man had become tormented and tortured you for all eternity. You roamed the world looking for comfort and companionship, in constant pain and never knowing anything about anyone you once loved. You could hear them, smell them, and sense them but you could never find them let alone communicate with them.

As he lay there comparing the possible options once again, Chris realized he was no longer in any physical pain, it had all but vanished. Just as suddenly as he noticed his physical pain was gone a strong and overwhelming emotional pain took its place. It was filled with a hurt and sorrow that overwhelmed him and he became frightened again. Hell?

ONE

She parked several blocks away from her target and pulled the hood on her dark blue sweatshirt up as she exited the car. The '89 Cavalier she drove would be easy to remember with its blown exhaust system and smoking tailpipe. As she walked down the final block in the housing area of Camp Lejeune the multitude of people was surprising. She had expected to see the normal garage sale crowd; the size of this one seemed remarkable. She flipped the half smoked Marlboro and exhaled her long drag. Creeping up to the first table she slipped the hoodie down on to her back. Her unkempt hair flared in all directions. The sweet smelling breeze blew through it as a kaleidoscope of colors peeked over the clouds on a beautiful North Carolina morning.

Rummaging through the tables lined with family treasures, bargain hunters haggled to save every possible dollar. She focused in on one in particular and discretely watched the Marine wife begin her assault.

"Devil dog, leatherneck, jarhead," are only a few of the vast number of monikers U.S. Marines are known by. With their incredibly well-built physique, rugged good looks and uncompromising integrity it's no wonder they're truly the few and the proud. So it's mind boggling to see a heavy unkempt woman who reared the kids with an iron fist and ruled her husband with threats and intimidation.

Most, if not all Marine wives were petite and attractive with bodies to match. They carried themselves very well and proudly showed off their trophy husband. The others like the troll in front of her was the stereotypical Marine wife. This is the one the public chose to see. Either way this woman gave all women a bad name at the expense of a child.

"Marcus, stop touching things or I'll swat you boy!" she shouted, her eyes never moving from her chubby fingers that manipulated everything on the table in front of her.

"Get that little butt over here, Mr. Man," she demanded. He complied without a fight. The fear of a whooping from a mother this hefty would frighten any child.

"How much is this?" she demanded. A large band of fat dangled from her arm as she thrust the lamp forward into the woman's face on the other side of the table. Her black tank top stretched upward revealing her pocked belly flesh.

"Eight dollars?"

"Will you take five?"

"Sure," the defeated voice answered. She dug into her bra and pulled out a clump of moistened weathered bills. Methodically she unraveled the wad and handed the home owner a crumpled twenty. As if she loathed touching the woman's hand the seller made change. The transaction was done.

The operative continued down the aisle and moved in beside Marcus. His big brown beautiful eyes met hers.

"Good morning, young man," she said greeting him with a smile. A needy grin appeared. Shyly, he attempted to wrap his arms around his mother's enormous leg as he smeared his snotty nose against her skirt.

"Get over here, boy!" she thundered, jerking him off one side and planting him on the other. The smile disappeared and his little brown face dropped, hollow and empty. She couldn't help but think of his future. Would his be like hers, forced to do awful things followed by the beatings and belittling? Maybe he'd have a childhood that she always wanted for her son, one full of love and laughter. Even though her life had improved, a black cloud seemed to follow her everywhere she went. Today was no different. The dark veil had caught up to her again. Marcus' crying brought her out of her trance. She looked down and sadly continued scanning the tables and boxes.

The large crowds may work in my favor, she thought. There were too many people lingering about for the merchant to watch everyone meaning the kill shot would in fact be delivered today. Just have patience.

Carefree, she walked around the displays picking up items and looking interested although she had no intent of buying anything. The mission remained simple, to deliver the package and get out. Even though she felt forced into doing it, the idea of finishing off the target was exciting, especially since it was him.

She was closer to the house now, the
final table in sight. She picked-up a hideous
misshapen red bowl obviously made in a
childhood art class. She flipped it over.
Carved into in to the bottom were the initials
C.M. partially obscured by a pink sticker
marked one dollar.

A dollar for this piece of shit? Are you
kidding me? A devilish smirk stretched across
her face growing bigger as she took in her use
of profanity. What a rebel. I should have been
in movies, action ones. Too much smile for
such a pretty girl she giggled to herself. With
cautious restraint she looked over her
shoulder. Her patience had paid off, the coast
was clear. With forced self-confidence, she
slipped through the door and into the kitchen.
Boxes spilled over the green counters and
brown tile floor making access difficult. The
recessed lights shined a bright sheen off the
urethane stained oak cabinets creating a
powerful glare. The bare walls had dusty
outlines of pictures and knick-knacks that at
one time jam-packed the living room. Some
nail holes had been filled in, but the deep
gashes in the twice painted over sheet rock still
waited for new life. The search was on to
pinpoint the perfect spot, not too hard to find
and not easy to miss. Up and down, back and
forth she scrutinized the kitchen. What's this, a
crisp ten dollar bill? I'll take that thank you,
stuffing it into her front pocket.

The quest continued. By what her mentor had told her, it was the son cleaning out boxes.

"He has to be the one to find it," was the order. There it was. It's perfect! This one had to be gone through. No responsible person could just toss a cash box out on the curb for the trash men to take. She lifted the box and set it on the counter. With a nervous smiled she removed the envelope from the pocket of her blue sweat shirt and carefully laid it in and closed the lid and locked it. "Perfect," she squealed with excitement. Directly to her right was a cardboard box filled with documents. Through the mounds of paper she found the bottom and set it in place. Mustn't be too easy to find she reminded herself.

"Who are you?" the small voice behind her beckoned. Fear froze her in place. The operation had been compromised. A flash of handcuffs, confessions and prison flashed through her mind. *Think you idiot!*

She inhaled deeply, dropped the box on the floor in the closet and turned around in slow motion. Before her stood a handsome young boy whose radiant blue eyes complimented his shiny blonde hair. Lie, and quickly, she told herself. She had done it so many times over the years. It was that ability to improvise that saved her from many a beatings and humiliation.

"Cheerio, little friend, you startled me just a bit," she cracked in a thick British accent though she had never stepped one foot outside of the U.S.

"My name is Clara."

"I'm Matt."

"Well, Matt, I seem to be lost. I was using your loo and on my way out—,"

"What's that?"

Seeming insulted and snobbish she slinked to his right. "Young man, in England we refer to the toilet as loo."

"It's over by the steps," he said, pointing towards the living room his eyes never leaving hers.

"Thank you I know. I've already used the facilities."

"Say, Matt," she purred drawing him in.

"Yeah?"

"I'm not feeling well. My stomach is a very upset and I……"

"You have diarrhea?"

"Um why yes, although ladies in no way discuss one's bathroom activities." She amazed herself by her ability to think of such gibberish.

"You talk funny."

"So do you, you little…."

"What?"

"…. handsome young man," she stammered. Her accent suddenly was very American. Struggling to regain her composure and her poorly faked British wit, she recomposed herself.

"Matt, I need your help to keep this our little secret. As a dignified lady, I'd hate for anyone other than you to know I have an upset tummy. In fact, I would be inclined to give you this new ten dollar bill if this was just our little secret." *Talk about burning a hole in your pocket,* she joked to herself.

"Wow, ten dollars, o....kay!" She passed the folded bill over. His face lit up as he stretched it between his two hands proudly.

"Thank you so much, Matt, bye now."

"You're welcome!"

Bribe time's over, time to go.

She left Matt admiring his new found wealth and approached the door far enough back to be hidden in the sun's glare. From the shadows she scanned the front lawn needing to escape as quietly as she had entered. The crowd seemed much bigger at the corner tables. Five or six bargain hunters had their backs to the exit when, Crash! The sound of shattering glass startled everyone. It was the perfect diversion. She couldn't have planned it better. Everyone's head shot around in unison and peered in the opposite direction. Heads bobbed left and right down the driveway to see the culprit who'd had broken one of the homeowner's prized possessions. The commotion played on and she slipped out into the mob overwhelmed with pride that the mission was complete. She had never been capable of doing something so daring a year ago. How she would love to see his face. She dreamed about his reaction and the turmoil it would create when an eager voice pressed her patience.

"Do you like this?"

Who was accosting her? "What?"

"Do you like it, the dish?"

"Um, sure." She hastily lifted the jewel as if caring. Her annoyance was evident.

"A dollar, huh?" She gauged the childish craftsmanship.

"Unless it's too much, then I'll....."

A charitable voice replaced her hostility.

"No, no a dollar's fine. I will in fact take this."

From her back pocket she retrieved her wallet, tore open the black Velcro and plucked out a single bill. She handed the meager sum to the small framed woman with a tired and somewhat gloomy face. You're not sad enough. Just wait until he opens the surprise.

"Thanks."

"No, I insist. Thank you!" Her voice was patronizing and cold. She turned and slipped back in to the population, her crime undetected.

TWO

He hated anything having to do with moving. By twenty-one, Jason had moved nine times during his father's twenty-two year naval career. This would be the final move for the Miller family, however Jason wouldn't be making this one. His father, Chris died five months ago and the family's time in base housing had come to an end. The move to a new life had begun. His stepmother, Sandy seemed more than ready to go and leave the memories of Camp Lejeune behind. He would visit her, more out of an obligation than anything. To visit his half-brothers Ryan and Matt though, would mean so much more.

Jason Miller joined the Navy three years before and was himself stationed at Marine Corps Base Camp Lejeune. His wife Kristy, a registered nurse had found a good job at Onslow Memorial Hospital so for now they called it home. With the Marine Corps Base expanding and the surrounding area of Onslow County growing, trade jobs and government jobs remained plentiful. Eastern Carolina seemed immune to the recession plaguing the rest of America.

Jason's mother Teresa died some years prior. She tried to cross Greenbay Road outside military housing in Great Lakes, Illinois on her way to the commissary. A guy in an old pick-up reached down into the passenger floorboards to pick-up his hat. He launched her small framed body airborne without even tapping the brake.

Jason recognized something had to be wrong that day because his dad never picked him up from school. In the living room on the old tan sofa is where he found out his mother had died. He heard his dad's voice but sat staring at him. He couldn't move. Minutes passed and they stared at one another.

"You okay, Sport?" Jason's mind spun out of control. He knew what he had said but couldn't seem to comprehend the news. Jason managed to nod and mumble, "Who will take care of me when you're away?"

His dad didn't answer. He bolted into the hall where his cries competed with the exhaust fan motor of the air conditioner. Jason stared at his reflection in the picture tube of the old RCA television left alone to understand his mother's unexpected death. The next few days came as a blur of people coming and going. The kitchen counters overflowed with cookies, cakes and pies. Lasagna and casseroles filled the fridge. As quick as the parade began, the rooms full of people came to an abrupt end. Finally he got the courage and asked his grandmother how she really died.

"She died instantly and had felt no pain," his grandmother told him later. Her overly soothing whispers emphasized 'instant' again and again as she spoke convincing only herself. When you're seven and only want your mom how long she took to die makes no difference.

A year later Chris met Sandy Wycheski at a bar called the Anchor Windless in North Chicago. Dad called The Anchor a dive and Jason got to experience the unique ambiance himself when he had gone to Boot Camp. The Anchor passed for more of a landfill chock full of the trashiest people in North Chicago.

"Sailors like the place," Dad bragged.

"The seedier the better."

They dated for six-months when they announced they planned to marry. Sandy had been married twice before both times to Navy men. She knew the bar scene or at least the seedy bar scene. She had a portly shaped face spotted with freckles, green emerald eyes and a double chin that highlighted her hyperthyroidism. Some people around town referred to her as loose. Chris seemed smitten with her and only his opinion mattered.

Sandy appeared okay at first; she never tried to take the place of Teresa. In fact that became part of the problem. She didn't try to be a mom at all let alone a friend. Jason felt tolerated; liked, not loved. She never came off as mean or hurtful, just plain Sandy. However, with Ryan and Matt life seemed different.

After years of fertility treatments she got pregnant with twins. The distance between him and Sandy grew even further. His relationship with has dad had tired within weeks of his mother's funeral so he accepted his new family as normal. He was never alone growing up, just unaccompanied.

His dad always treated the three kids equally but on occasion snuck Jason a few extras. Maybe guilt got the best of him or maybe because he knew Sandy often excluded him whether purposefully or not. They fought about Jason sometimes and Sandy would go out of her way to make sure he was included. She would take him to McDonalds or bake him a special dessert. After a week Jason would be right back in fourth place behind the two boys and his dad. Jason always knew his dad liked him, nonetheless he wondered at times if, like Sandy, he loved him. The one bright spot though was Ryan and Matt.

Kids have a special ability to overlook facades adults put up so Ryan and Matt knew early on that Jason had a different mom. They also knew Sandy treated him more coldly than them. They never took advantage and always needed their big brother. No one could deny the three Miller boys loved each other very much.

Sandy and the two boys had lived in the same old base house for five years. Jason had moved out after he finished his senior year at the Lejeune High School. He followed in his father's footsteps and at age 17 joined the Navy to become a Corpsman. He attended Field Medical Training Battalion at Camp Johnson right up the road from Camp Lejeune and wanted to go to 2nd Marine Division, then

Iraq. Instead he got orders right out of Corps School back to the Naval Hospital and assigned to work at Caron Clinic out at Courthouse Bay some ten miles from the main hospital. The clinic provides medical care and field support to the Marines attending the service schools as well as the 2nd Assault Amphibious Battalion. He couldn't work in the main hospital because his dad worked in the Administration Department as a Senior Enlisted Advisor. Jason had moved up the promotion ladder rather quickly to Second Class Petty Officer. A noteworthy accomplishment considering promotions in the Corpsman rating is pretty stagnant. He received his Associate's Degree in Allied Health Science at Coastal Carolina Community College and had landed a part-time job making some extra money at the nursing school, grading blood collection procedures. That is where he met Kristy. She was eighteen, pretty and dressed in tight jeans and a blue sweat shirt. From that first vision, Jason was hooked.

She arrived at the lab a senior in the Associate's Degree nursing program. Jason fell over himself making sure she drew his blood for her clinical phase. After a brief introduction their eyes met and the rest as they say is history. Although everyone said, "You're too young to get married," they made the determination to do it. Nine-months later on a crisp fall Carolina morning they celebrated in a small ceremony on base at St.

Francis Catholic Church. They rented a town house in Richlands, a small farming town in what seemed like a million miles away from Jacksonville and Camp Lejeune. Jason never had any special attachment to one place or another but with Kristy by his side he was intent on getting comfortable and have a home.

Chris had only been dead five months. However to Jason, Sandy appeared to forget about him as soon as she could. Her new life began the day he died when she wanted the hospital bed moved into the garage and the dining room table brought back in. The guy hadn't been dead twenty-four hours and she was rearranging the house? Jason tried to convince himself with little luck that this was part of the grieving process. He also tried to convince himself Sandy's grieving process included moving to Florida. She wanted to be closer to her sister but he didn't trust her. He believed she wanted be closer to Dave Walstad.

Chief Dave Walstad served as Chris's Casualty Assistance Calls Officer or CACO as they are more commonly known. He handled all of the funeral arrangements, death benefits, and military affairs when he had died. He seemed to spend an awful lot of time over-comforting Sandy until his transfer to Pensacola; the same town where coincidentally she had looked at condos. She claimed she hated breaking up the family by taking the boys to Florida. Jason thought deep down she couldn't wait to leave. He would miss his brothers a lot. He never used the word 'step' in describing them. He loved them, simple as that.

Jason pulled the last box from under the steps. As soon as he did, memories of his childhood flooded his mind in rapid succession. Christmas mornings with the smell and sounds of a fire crackling in the fireplace. Thanksgiving dinner and Dad falling asleep in his chair after gorging on turkey and pie and the huge Halloween costume parties that ended only when the base police showed up to shut it down. The memories would remain in the minds of those who lived them, but no longer in the house that created them. A new Marine or Navy family would move in after base maintenance cleaned and painted. Any new memories would be made by them. Kristy met him as she came through the kitchen door.

"The last one?" she asked nodding at the box in his hands.

"Yes, thank God."

"Well, here," she said as she moved a bunch of clutter from one side of the counter to the other.

"Set it down."

He lifted the box with a small grimace, his tired muscles struggling.

"Thanks, Baby. I'll be so happy when this is over. I hate this moving crap, but I hate going through this junk more than anything."

"Oh stop, these are her treasures."

"Treasures? I call it junk plain and simple. She's a pack rat and always has been. I wanted to rescue the real treasures that meant something. But no; she had a garage sale while we we're in Myrtle Beach. It's a bunch of bull if you ask me."

"Well it's her junk."

"Well, I'll be happy to go through 'her junk' and get out of here."

"Oh stop whining. Get some coffee, take a shower, go through the box and just chill out today."

"You mean why don't we go through the box and chill out today, right?" a puzzled Jason asked.

"No, I meant you, silly. Remember, Sandy, the boys and I are going to Cary for the day so she can spend time with her brother."

"Damn," Jason grumbled in disgust.

Sandy's loud and obnoxious brother Frank was one person Jason couldn't stand. He chain smoked Pall Malls one right after the other and his house smelled like dirty cat litter with rooms that resembled a dirty laundry room. He limped around the house from an injury he sustained in a car accident ten or so years before and hadn't worked since. He complained constantly of how his lawyer screwed him and of all the pain and suffering still lingering in his body. Funny how the pain never stopped him from going back and forth to the Hess-Wilco for smokes and Malt liquor every other day.

At the end of every visit he would hit somebody up for what he called a small loan, his code word for handout. Chris always had a soft spot for him and Frank leveraged his generosity to guilt him into giving him a few bucks. Jason had never given him any and wasn't starting now. Sandy was miffed Jason wasn't going although she seemed to have gotten over it. Kristy didn't care because she was going to visit with her mom and dad who lived in Raleigh, a short distance away.

"You'll have the whole day to yourself. You need to just sit and relax," Kristy implored. "Enjoy your quiet time. Lord knows you've earned a bit of time off," she said with a sense of envy in her voice.

"You're right I guess; just not used to being un-busy."

"Well you need to learn to. You did a remarkable job taking care of your dad and your brothers through all of this. Now you need to take some time for you. Okay?"

He hesitated, then said, "Okay, Babe."

Senior Chief Hospital Corpsman Chris Miller's life and twenty-two year naval career had come to an end five months before. He had spent five years as a Senior Medical Department Representative at the 2nd Marine Regiment. After his third tour in Iraq, the war had caught up to him physically and mentally. He had transferred to the Naval Hospital and worked in Administration for little more than a year. The flashbacks and the constant reminders of war's dark side seemed to follow him like a shadow follows your frame in the sun. Overwhelmed at times, he managed to hide his emotions well from almost everybody except Sandy and the kids. Being alone and drowning in a sea of Miller-Lite became his best medicine. He had alienated himself from family and friends and lashed out in anger almost daily for no apparent reason. The only time he couldn't hide his demons from anyone was when the wounded-warriors came by. They'd pass him in the hospital passage ways bandaged and bloodied, on crutches, in wheelchairs or with missing limbs. His mind played tricks on him constantly. He would visualize and hear things that he knew no one else could. His nightmares and night terrors drove him from the bedroom to the sofa after Sandy could no longer handle the screams in the middle of the night. They shook her nerves nearly as bad as his. He drank to forget everything about Iraq and the pain it caused him not realizing the pain he caused other people. The family learned to stay out of his way and to just leave Dad to himself. Jason never really wanted to notice the changes in his dad. He couldn't bring himself to view his father as an alcoholic or mentally ill.

Sandy had had enough, threatening to leave and take the boys. Finally given an ultimatum to get help or get out he begrudgingly began seeing a doctor up in the Mental Health Clinic. He never talked about it with anyone; family, peers, and especially the Marines who believed promotions and your career ended the second you walked into the Mental Health Clinic. Above all it was something no one ever felt comfortable asking or even talking about. Over time the therapy seemed to be helping. Ryan confided in Jason one day that Dad's nightmares all but disappeared as did his agitation. He did have relapses; bouts of insomnia, headaches, and what he described as funky migraines. At first, he attributed the symptoms as another relapse of anxiety and his Post-Traumatic Stress Disorder. But when he suffered a seizure at work, a CAT scan revealed something far more cruel; glioblastoma multiforme.

Also called spongioblastoma multiforme, this aggressive brain tumor grows quickly and once found is almost always fatal. In Chris, the cancer had already begun to metastasize throughout his body. He went quickly. Less than nine-months after his diagnoses he died, his lifespan six months more than originally estimated. Far too little time for such a young man.

Chris spent all of his final time but three days in Naval Hospital because he suffered such severe seizures. He died at home where he wanted to be with his family by his side. A hospice nurse had come in every day to check on him, his pain meds and to comfort the family that had gathered in vigil by his bedside. The cruel and hellish disease proved to be a difficult time for everyone, especially the two younger boys.

Ryan and Matt adored their father. His death hit them hard at that awkward age where a positive male influence is critical in lives of young boys. This reason alone fueled the anger in Jason that Sandy was taking them to Florida and out of their comfort zone. Jason knew he couldn't replace his father but believed he had the necessary tools to pass on values and morals every young boy needed. He had become the man of the family sooner than the title should pass from one generation to the next.

Jason had spent the last few days of his military leave going through boxes and separating things into the keep pile, the trash pile and the Goodwill pile. The arduous chore was passed to him since Sandy seemed too overwhelmed or too lazy to do. Jason thought the latter and resigned himself to an obligation to save as much as he could for the boys. *Finally, the last box. Thank God,* Jason thought.

"We're leaving," Kristy yelled from the bottom of the steps.

"Okay, I'll be right down."

"I put some left over spaghetti on a plate. Hit the reheat button on the microwave" Sandy yelled up the stairs as she jostled in front of Kristy.

"Thanks, Sandy," Jason said as he started down the steps. Her cooking tasted bland and mushy. Not to mention, who makes spaghetti sauce out of ketchup?

"Push reheat once or you'll burn the noodles."

"I know."

"I want to make sure. Oh, and make sure you feed Norman. He gets a half a can, and only a half a can. He has reflux and will vomit. Give him his pill, the red one, wrapped in a piece of the pre-made turkey bacon I bought or he won't chew the thing up."

Norman is the cat from hell. At fifteen-years old he was the animal matriarch of the family. Deaf and somewhat blind, he laid about with not a care in the world. The only time his hearing and vision seemed to function was meal time.

Kristy stood behind Sandy at the door, her smile stretched ear to ear as she lectured and instructed him like a thirteen year old on his fist baby-sitting assignment.

"I remember, Sandy. You covered all of this earlier."

"Oh, and don't forget to close the windows, rain's forecast."

"For the love of God, will you just go?"

"Don't be fresh with me in my house and don't use the Lord's name in vain. You'll go to hell."

No, he thought you go to hell. And technically the Marine Corps owns the house, you old witch.

Kristy moved past Sandy and stepped over to Jason, "You're so lucky," she whispered as she pressed her lips to Jason's.

"What I wouldn't give to stay here with you."

"Sorry, but you're pretty lucky too."

"Oh yeah?" she asked as she pulled her head back.

"You get her for four hours in a car!"

"Joy. I love you," she growled as she kissed him again.

"I love you too, baby. Remember; don't give that lazy slob one dime."

"Don't say things about my family. He's crippled," Sandy bellowed from the doorway heading towards the car. She didn't even turn around. Her back still faced the door.

"Yeah, yeah, yeah, you old windbag," he whispered.

After watching the car back out of the driveway, Jason headed up to the kitchen. He could finally clean out the last box in peace and quiet.

"Let's see what we got Norman shall we."

Norman purred in agreement from his perch on the counter oblivious to his surroundings. He unfolded the flaps of the box and peered inside to find bundles of old documents neatly arranged and firmly secured with rubber bands. He reached in and pulled one out. A tag on top in Sandy's hand writing read 'cell phone 2008-2010'. He began to thumb through the musty old paper. The pages zipped by his eyes and all he could think was packrat. He tossed the bundle across the room to the trash pile. The next bundle revealed some old tax returns, warranty cards, old pay statement and finally a few pictures of people Jason had never seen before. Had to be Sandy's side of the family, he thought. He went through the stack carefully and decided they all looked like thugs. Tattoos, long hair and beer cans filled every frame; each one taken in front of a single wide trailer. *What the hell were you thinking, Pop?* Jason asked himself. He initially glanced over to the trash can, but decided that Sandy would want them. Unlike her, he would give her a chance to claim things that meant something to her. He dropped them onto the counter for her to look at later.

He leaned over the box and found some old bank stubs dated three years earlier. $2,935.09 in savings; $3,754.11 in a Money Market; $1109.44 in checking. He tossed the statements in the trash. He reached in again and flipped a bundle on its side to get a better grip when he saw it, a metal box wedged under several other bundles.

"What do we have here?" he said aloud.

He wiggled the box from its paper grave as the mountain of old hoarded papers toppled to the floor. Maybe Sandy hid the money from the moving sale in here. Is she trying to lose the money? he wondered.

"Jesus, what next?" he complained aloud.

He walked over and placed the metal box on the kitchen table and pushed the release button. Locked. Frustrated, he picked up the seemingly light box and shook it vigorously back-and-forth. He could hear the sounds of something shifting.

It would need to wait a bit, he thought as he returned to the packing box and pulled out the remaining bundles. He looked intently as he worked but no key appeared. Where the hell could it be? Oh well, plan B.

The anticipation of finding hidden treasures enticed him. If the garage sale money was in there, he needed to make sure she had it for Ryan and Matt. If something different was found he might just keep it for himself. The last thing he wanted was Sandy to have his new found fortune. She had trashed everything else, this was his.

"Looks like were breaking in Norm," he said walking back to the counter. He opened the silverware drawer and grabbed a butter knife. Norman just sat on the counter his eyes still closed now facing backwards and purring like an old Model-T Ford. Jason chuckled and sat down at the table. He began to pry the edge on the box. After a few minutes of fidgeting he bent the top back enough that the lid popped open. His excitement built. He set the knife on the table and pulled the box towards him.

"Here goes nothing, Norm." Lifting the lid all the way back he looked in. The excitement quickly dissipated to disappointment; no money. In its place sat a plain white legal sized envelope. In blue-black ink across the front was a single name – Charlie – in crisp penmanship he immediately recognized. He reached in and lifted the envelope out and stared for a moment. He flipped it over; it wasn't sealed.

"Who the hell is Charlie?" Norman didn't answer him.

THREE

Jason set the envelope on the counter while he finished sorting the other papers. He had hesitated reading it not knowing what it could be. His mind raced with a half dozen different scenarios: an old love letter? A letter to an old friend? Maybe he had a lawyer named Charlie and it's a new will.

He finished rummaging through the box. There was nothing worth saving. He picked up the bundles he had dropped on the floor and flung them into the trash pile without even looking at them. The cash box was quickly double wrapped in old Wal-Mart bags and put into the bottom of the trash can out front. The last thing he needed was Sandy bitching he'd broken something. After all of his chores were done, Jason returned to the kitchen and looked at the letter. Well let's see what we got. No one will ever know he convinced himself.

Jason reached into the fridge and dug out a Diet Coke. He grabbed the envelope and headed for the sectional sofa in the living room. With his hands full, he kicked a few boxes that were stacked along the corner and they tumbled to the floor.

Sinking down in the chair he set the letter on his lap. He popped the top on the ice cold can as several droplets of condensation dripped on his shirt. He took a long sip and set it on the table. Anticipation swirled in his stomach as he picked up the envelope flipped it over and pulled out the neatly folded cream colored papers. He tossed the envelope aside and unfolded the papers. It was neatly written in his dad's distinct handwriting:

January 6th

Dear Charlie,

It seems like an odd way to start a letter to you rather than Hi sweetie or Hey Kiddo. I guess a more formal introduction lets you know how little I know about you, but don't let it confuse you with how much I love you. I'm writing this snuggled in an uncomfortable hospital bed wrapped in blankets with a scarf around my neck. I am wearing the old blue sweater someone knitted for me so many birthdays ago I can't remember who made it. I am at peace since the odds are fully against me and medical science has finally done all it can. The Grim Reaper has caught up to me and is standing outside my window. I know I am dying and I hope to be at peace very soon. Funny, I knew all along I was dying and nothing could be done. The way you feel physically, not to mention the way people talk to you. I guess its best described as a living wake. People are falling all over you and kissing your ass, telling you how much you meant to them. Why they didn't tell me sooner, I'll never know. Maybe it's because I haven't been too approachable these last years I don't know. More on that later.

Anyway, the nurses seem nicer but kind of on edge when they come in to see me. When I ring them at night and ask for a ginger-ale they rush

right in, and with ice no less. If I was here for a
hernia or anything else they'd bring me a ginger-ale
but warm, with no ice, and about three hours after I
had asked for it. When the Corpsman wheels me by
the nurses' station I can hear them whisper 'there he
goes', or 'I feel so bad for him', and I even got a 'he's
so cute all bundled up like that.' Dying but cute,
huh? I just nod and smile at them. I can tell their
smile is forced and uncomfortable. They never say
anything directly to me only about me. Maybe they
think I'll get upset or begin to cry. Knowing
myself, they're probably right although I only cry
alone at night when no one can see or hear me.
Either way I wish they'd just talk to me, rather than
at me.

I have decided that since I'm alone most of
the day and have really nothing to do, I would take
this final step and write this letter. I'm going to try
like hell to take all the years I've bottled up inside
me and put them into words for you. I never really
share my thoughts with anyone so the diary I kept
in my mind of your life's events I'll try to put on
paper. I'll just write what comes to mind and hope
I can share with you how much I truly loved you all
of my forty one or hopefully forty two years of my
life. My life?

It's been like any Sailors who has sailed
many seas; some days were calm others were
stormy. I look at myself as a regular man with
seemingly regular thoughts but who's lived a very
irregular life. As I set out on my final sail I want to
stay on course and feel the breeze on my face every
second of every day right up to the very end. I
want quality days at sea on this trip, not quantity.

Some of the greatest emotions, events, and dreams were the shortest lived. I am learning that now.

I'm back! I just spent twenty minutes with the doctors. They were here giving me all the ins and outs of radiation and chemo. I told them thanks but no thanks I'll pass. I know it's their job but I can't see be being sick for three months to get one more month of life, and that's if I'm lucky. I have already lived longer than originally thought. I can't understand people going through this treatment and that treatment to get that one extra day. I know my life is going to end and with this letter I hope to be at peace.

Jason felt the blood drain from his face and the uneasiness of disbelief sink into his stomach. Oh my God, Dad had another kid? He felt nauseous. How could he? How could he do this? He was overwhelmed with emotion, his heart hammering faster and faster in his chest like the wings of a humming bird. Just like his father, he was always good at hiding his emotions but he could not hide the fact that he was actually feeling physically ill.

"Okay, okay relax," he repeated trying to calm himself. It didn't work.

I can't believe this, Jason thought his emotions getting the best of him again. The memories he had of his father were slipping from his mind and anger and betrayal started to fill the void. He took a deep breath, "Give him the benefit of the doubt. Or, at least try too," he whispered.

FOUR

The ringing phone broke him from his trance. He dashed into the kitchen dodging boxes along the way. He picked it up on the fourth ring. Or was it the fifth?

"Hello?"

"Hey, Babe," a cheerful Kristy chimed from the other end. "What's wrong? Took you a while to answer."

"Nothing, you just caught me off guard."

"Oh, okay, you sound funny. Everything okay?" she asked.

"Yeah, fine. How was your ride?"

"Okay, I guess. The ice lady said nothing for 130 miles which was fine with me. They're over at Uncle Frank's and I'm sitting here at Mom's. You sure you're okay?"

"Yeah, just tired."

"Well get some rest, enjoy your quiet time cause when I get back there you're going to need all the energy you can muster."

"Oh really?" he asked suddenly more attentive.

"Really," Kristy purred.

"I'll call you when we're on our way back, okay?"

"Sounds good, Babe. Tell your mom and dad I said hi."

"Will do, I love you."

"Me too."

Jason hung up the phone and focused his attention back on the letter. He walked over and stared at it. He took a deep breath, picked it up and sat back down on the chaise and began reading where he left off:

January 8th
　　　　Hey, I'm back. I needed a blood transfusion. I was feeling like hell and I guess my platelets were low. At this point they could tell me anything, what the hell do I know?

Jason stopped and thought back to that night; Man, he was sick. I sat with him for hours talking and reassuring him. He looked so frail and weak. I went to the staff bathroom locked the door and cried for a long time that night. I think that's when I truly accepted the fact he was going to die. He looked back down at the letter:

　　　　Seemed like I was getting weaker, but a little bit of blood put some pep in my step! I just got done reading over the letter again, I'm trying not to leave anything out, but since I don't know what to put in, I guess I'm doing okay. I was thinking about what questions you may have for me so I am going to answer what I think I would ask if I were you.
　　　　Probably one of the biggest questions you have is what happened between your mom and me. Well Faith--

Jason sat up. Faith? Dad's secret lover?

--she was the most beautiful woman I ever met! The first time I saw her, I couldn't even talk. I was eating lunch and happened to look up as she walked past me. The cafeteria was packed and I knew she was looking for a place to sit. I was sitting alone but I could tell right away I was the last person she wanted to sit with. I hid behind my mystery meat and watched her move from table to table trying to find a place to sit. Finally she gave in. When she asked if she could sit down I just stared at her like an idiot. Finally, I just blurted out, "Hell yeah!" I scared the heck out of her I'm sure. She sat down and never once looked up at me. She even asked for the salt without looking up. I was so nervous that I knocked her soda right into her lap. She let out a scream and the whole cafeteria looked over at us. I kind of freaked out and grabbed a stack full of napkins and started stuttering, "I'm sorry, I'm sorry." I reached over and began to dab her lap. I wasn't trying to cop a feel, but it was like my brain had fallen out my head. She smacked my hand away. I kept saying, "I'm so sorry," over and over again. She didn't say a thing. She pulled away and angrily reached down to pick up the cup that I knocked on the floor. Only problem was I was reaching for it too. We bumped heads like two cymbals at the symphony. We sat up dazed, looked at each other and began to laugh. The rest they say is history. We were inseparable from that day on. We talked and laughed almost all of the time. I can't tell you how happy she made me. We spent a lot of time together and I think it was love at first sight. As time went on and we got more and more

serious, it became hard to control our feelings and our bodies. It was tough. We had to maintain separate lives and keep our relationship secret. It's complicated and even more so today with everything going on in the world. Then one day our secret got out because you came along!

I want you to know first and foremost what a special part of my life you were, right from the very beginning. My wildest dreams came true when I discovered that you were growing inside of your mom. What a beautiful surprise you were! She was scared at first at how I would react. I was scared – for a split second. Then fear turned to surprise, which turned to joy. Instantly, I was the happiest man in the world. Like I said, I was scared because I knew how to take care of me and how to love your mom but I had no clue on how to take care of a baby. Not to mention we were living these secret lives.

Again, it sounds so lame to tell you it's complicated, but it is even to this day. You'd think after all these years I could explain it better. I guess that's why I'm here; to write about it and maybe get my head fixed. I'm going to sign off for now, I'm pretty tired so I'll write more later.

Jason's mind raced. Head fixed? His cancer was terminal, how could he get his head fixed? Jason took a deep breath and closed his eyes; he needed a few minutes to refocus; what the hell was going on?

FIVE

As Chris came into the shock trauma room, copious amounts of blood were dripping off the table. Standing in the thick of it were a group of doctors, nurses, and Corpsman all trying to save a life. Tubes crisscrossed the body; wires were connected to various machines that chimed with each passing second.

"We need to open the chest," the surgeon pleaded.

The words echoed in the room and the team scrambled to cut into the young body. The clicking of the rib spreader drowned out the mumbled words spoken by the staff. Chris stood across the room and watched the angels of life fend off the angel of death. A young nurse stood at the patient's head and gently rubbed her hand across the pale ashen face that blended into nothingness. She gently stroked the face and calmly whispered, "It's okay, baby, shhhhh, and I'm here. We love you and it's going to be okay; you're going to be okay. If you want to go it's okay, you can. You can go now. It's okay. You can go now if you want to." She slowly raised her head from the table and turned and looked directly at Chris. With her bloodied glove, she slid the light blue surgical mask down and said, "You can go now."

"What?" Chris asked confused.

"You can go now," she repeated.

"Go where?"

Slowly and methodically each member of surgical team turned and faced Chris. Standing around the pallid corpse they turned and pulled down their surgical masks. Covered in blood, they too repeated the ominous verse; "You can go now, you can go now."

Chris' heart started beating faster and faster, he could taste the acid from his stomach rise painfully through his chest and seep into his mouth. They repeated it over and over again, "You can go now, you can go now." It was getting louder and the echo of their chant resonated in his head.

"What are you doing?" he implored. "What's going on?"

The group ignored his pleas. They moved in unison and parted as the patient rose from the table; chest open, heart beating. Sliding off the table and on to the bloody floor, the group began moving towards him; almost floating across the room.

Fear overcame him and Chris tried to move; tried to turn and get away but his feet were fixed to the floor. The thickened blood held him captive to the floor. The figures pressed on. The patient was leading the way; no face, no genitals, and no structures to differentiate who or what it was. It became more obscured in the glare of the operating room lights. Moving closer, Chris could hear those words again, "You can go now, you can go now." No mouth, no lips, no face but yet a distinctive voice that passed through the room into Chris' head.

"Oh my God! It's you! Charlie? Charlie is that you?"

"Chaaaarrrrliiiieeeee!"

The scream for his child echoed the halls of the third floor of the Naval Hospital's multi-service ward. Chris sat straight up as reached for the bedrail. Sweat poured over his face and chest as a corpsman and nurse came barreling through the door. The light came on as the nurse called out,

"Are you okay, Senior?" the nurse asked. There was dullness in her voice since she had been through this a few times before.

"Fine, I'm fine," he snapped.

"Another nightmare?"

"Yeah, same one."

"Same one, again? Would you like something to help you sleep?" she asked hoping he'd say yes so she could finish watching Judge Judy.

"Why, my nightmares keeping you away from your game of solitaire?'

"No, Judge Judy. And that's my business Senior Chief."

"Doesn't someone need an enema or something?"

Lieutenant Carol Shriver and Senior Chief Chris Miller had never gotten along. Ever since he called her out for having junior enlisted pick-up her dry cleaning and walk her dog, she had despised him. The Director of Nursing Services went through the roof when Chris told her what was going on and demanded it end. And end it did; Lieutenant Shriver was given a poor fitness report that pretty much would end her naval career. She was biding her time until she got out working the night shift. Now that he was her patient, Chris was on his toes and never took any meds from her when she worked. He thought she'd try to OD him or worse.

"You know I don't need this from you tonight," she quipped.

"Why, got a dog to walk?"

"That's totally uncalled for Senior Chief!"

"Oh, go clean a bed pan," Chris snapped at her.

The young corpsman smiled as Shriver turned to leave. "Ring the station if you need something," she said walking out the door.

"Thank you nurse fuzzy-wuzzy, please come again," Chris yelled.

The corpsman busted out laughing. "Senior, you crack me up, man."

"Well, I'm glad I could be of service to you, young man."

"Do you need anything?"

"A cure for cancer if you have one, but I'll settle for a ginger-ale and maybe you could help me sit up a bit better?"

"The cure for cancer I can't do unfortunately, but I can do the soda and the seating arrangement."

"Thanks," Chris said as the corpsman raised the head on the electric bed.

"How's that?"

"Much better, my man."

"I'll be right back with that soda."

"Thanks."

Chris got himself situated and all snuggled in. He was so cold tonight and his head was pounding. Damn tumor, he thought. He hadn't been this cold since his tour in Great Lakes.

"I got your soda, Senior," the Corpsman said as he bounced through the door.

"Thanks so much, man," Chris said sincerely.

"Hey, by the way what's your name?"

"Oh, I'm HA Louis Santos."

"Well, hey there Louis. I'm Senior Chief Miller. You can call me Senior."

"Louis laughed. I know who you are; you're like a legend up her getting Shriver off our case and getting us out from doing her work."

"Well, make sure you learn from it and when you make Chief someday take care of your sailors the same way. Okay?"

"Okay, Senior, you got a deal."

Louis and Chris talked for hours that night and for many other nights thereafter. Anytime Louis worked the ward, he always asked to take care of Chris. His own father had died of cancer when he was very young and taking care of Chris gave him the closure he needed. He would sometimes close his eyes and pretend that care he gave Chris he was actually him caring for his dad. It closed a wound that had lingered for many, many years.

One night, after watching the Carolina Hurricanes get beat up by the Philadelphia Flyers, Chris posed one of the most important questions he ever had to his new found friend.

"Hey, Louis. Do you think you could do me a favor? Nothing big but as you can see I'm in no position to go for a stroll through the hospital. I just need something taken care of."

"Sure, Senior whatever you need."

It would still be several days until it was ready; however Chris began to explain to Louis exactly what he needed him to do.

SIX

Jason opened his eyes to Norman standing in front of him on the chaise. How he got there without so much as a creak in the floor was strange, this cat was strange. Norman was purring and started rubbing his face across Jason's legs. What a pain, he thought. He raised the letter up and continued reading:

I'm back. I had that nightmare again. It just keeps playing over and over and I just can't seem to get it out of my head, but I'll keep trying. I know Lucien will want me too, and I need to.

Who the hell is Lucien? Jason wondered.

When our families found out about you, all hell broke loose. It seemed like. . .

Jason flipped the page over, "Seemed like what? What do you mean seemed like?" he shouted. He flipped the letter over, back and forth multiple times looking for the answer. The back of the page was blank. Where's the rest of the letter? What the hell. He quickly ran through all of the pages. There has to be more he said to himself as a panic set in. There has to be more. Where's is the rest of the letter? Jason's heart sank. *How am I going to figure this out?* he pondered. Who and where is Charlie? He looked down.

Norman continued to rub his face along Jason's legs.

"Come on, Norman, damn it," he said hopping up off the chaise. Norman jumped off the chaise and came running in behind Jason into the kitchen. Funny how he heard that but nothing else. It seemed the only time this half dead feline ever moved was when his internal feed clock went off. Norman was not like most cats where you could leave food down all the time. He would gorge and eat until he got sick so he had to be fed twice a day.

Jason got Norman a can of food, or was it a half a can? He couldn't remember so Norman got a whole can and a red pill wrapped in ham, or was it bacon? Jason's mind was so consumed by his dad's letter that Norman was the least of his worries. Norman's dinner was interrupted as Ryan and Matt bounced through the door.

"Hey, Bro," said Matt.

"Hi guys. Have fun at Franks?" a startled Jason asked.

"Not really, he smells funny," said Ryan.

Jason smiled. "We're back," Kristy yelled out.

"Jason, where are you?"

"In the living room," he said as he slipped into the room and gathered up the letter. He stuffed them in his back pack.

"What are you doing?"

"Nothing babe, just getting my stuff together so we can go home."

"How was your trip?"

"Not bad; not bad at all."

"Oh, BS!" Sandy blurted out as she stormed in the living room.

"I thought you said no cussing?" Jason asked just to antagonize her.

"BS is not a bad word, smarty pants. The drive was terrible. There were all kinds of traffic and congestion. It was hot too. I damn near sweat to death."

"I told you to turn on the a/c," Kristy said.

"You told me to but you didn't want me to, there's a difference."

"Okay, well you know what? It's all over, you're home now and we can all have a nice evening before we have to go home."

Sandy kept walking, head down into the kitchen and mumbled something as she walked by. Kristy and Jason smiled at one another and rolled their eyes.

Jason spoke up, "Did Uncle Frank-Frank hit you up for a loan?"

"No, in fact he didn't this time."

"Wow, I'm impressed," Jason said.

"Don't be, Ryan told me Sandy gave him two-hundred dollars or something."

"What a lazy ass," Jason said with a hint of anger in his voice.

"Oh no!" Sandy screamed from the kitchen. Her voice startled Jason and Kristy.

"What's wrong?" Kristy yelled back hearing the fear in Sandy's voice.

"It's Norman, he's throwing up, he's really sick looking. My poor little man."

"Damn," Jason blurted out. "We got to go," he said tugging on Kristy's arm.

"Well, Sandy since you have a lot going on we're going to get on our way home. Thanks for letting us help you clean up. I took care of that last box. Ah, we'll see you and the boys this week for dinner some time. Yeah, um call me if you need anything." Kristy looked puzzled as Jason grabbed their belongings and gestured to her with his head that they move towards the door.

"Bye, boys, love you," Kristy yelled as Jason pushed her out the door ahead of him.

"Love you guys too," they yelled back the X-Box holding their attention.

Jason and Kristy made it through the door and hastily headed out to the walk.

"Oh my God no! Is that ham? He can't have pork," were the last words Jason heard as he slammed the door shut and fast walked to the car.

"How can he be allergic to pork?" Kristy asked.

"Who the hell knows? She's a nut-bag," Jason said.

"Did you give him ham?" Kristy asked.

"Maybe, by accident." He smiled back.

Jason pulled out of Tarawa Terrace II and on to highway 24. As they approached Western Boulevard, Kristy broke the silence.

"So what did you do while we were gone besides try to kill Norman? Get any sleep?"

Jason smiled. "Nah just chilled." He was hesitant to tell Kristy about the letter. He had always told her everything. But this was different. He didn't want anyone to put his dad down any further than he had.

"Did you find anything interesting in the box?"

"Some old bank statements, papers, and stuff. Nothing big."

"Well, that's good. I'm glad it's over and everything is done."

"Me too," Jason said.

"Now maybe we can get some normalcy back. It's been a long few months, but I'm sure it's been longer and harder on you."

"It has, but I could never have done it without you. Thank you so much for helping me, especially with the nut-job of a step mom I have."

"That's why I'm here. Remember? . . . for better or for worse?"

"The words cut deep inside Jason's heart. He knew he had to tell her. She was his soul mate. And that's what soul mates did.

"Well, the whole for worse part. You mean that?" he asked.

"Of course, why?"

"Well, I sort of left something out. I actually did find something."

"What?"

"Well, it was a cash box...."

"You found money!?" Kristy exclaimed in excitement.

"No, Babe."

"Oh," she said obviously disappointed. "Well, than what?"

"I found a letter from my dad."

"Oh, okay?" a hint of confusion in her voice.

"It's written to someone named Charlie."

"Charlie who?"

"Well, from what I can gather my dad had another kid named Charlie."

"What, you're kidding?"

"No, I wish I was," he said solemnly. He stared straight ahead.

"Did you read it? What did it say?" she asked

"Well rather than have me explain it, why don't you read it."

"You have it?"

"I do. I have to admit I was afraid to tell you at first, embarrassed I guess. I just don't want you to think bad about him. Hell knows I already do."

"First of all, Jason, I would never judge him. Second of all I have never not told you anything or hid anything from you, and third if you can't talk to me, who can you talk too?"

Jason knew she was right. Honesty was very important to Kristy.

"You're right, I'm sorry. That's why I'm telling you now. No secrets."

"The truth always comes out, Jason. You've got to trust me. Okay?"

"Okay, I'm sorry." Jason leaned over the center console and puckered his lips for a make-up kiss. Kristy smiled and leaned into him. A short but sweet kiss and it was over.

"No more secrets," she hissed.

"Scout's honor, no more secrets. So, do you want to read it?"

"Yeah, where is it?"

"It's in my bag."

Kristy reached into the back seat and pulled out the letter. It was all wrinkled from Jason's hasty exit from the house. Kristy flattened it out and began to read it as they merged onto the highway 24 bypass. She read the letter as they crossed route 53, highway 111, and Briarneck Road on their way into Richland's. As they pulled on to Main Street, Kristy finished. She began flipping pages and rummaging through the bag.

"Where's the rest of it?" she asked with the same anxiousness as Jason.

"That's it, there is no more"

"No more? Are you sure?"

"I'm sure. That's it, that's all there was. There may not even be anymore. He might have died before he finished it. Hell I don't even know how a letter that was written a month or two before he died wound up in a box with three and four year old bank statements. So your guess is as good as mine."

"So what's the plan, what are going to do?"

"Whoa. Plan, what plan? There is no plan. I mean it's not like we can just go knock on a door someplace to find Charlie and Faith. And where the hell would we look? Honestly I have no interest in it. My dad lied to all of us. He lived a secret life. I don't want to find anymore skeletons. Let it go."

This wasn't really true. Deep down Jason wanted to know and needed to know.

"Let it go? No way!" Kristy snapped. "We're not letting anything go. There's a kid out there whose father died and who needs to know that. By what's written in this letter, they don't know. Not to mention you have more family than you thought."

"I know, but....."

"But nothing, Jason. You've told me more than once that you've felt like an outsider in your own family. The only person you ever felt somewhat close to was your dad. I have no idea why he never told you or anyone else about this but he seemed to have his reasons."

"How could he hide this from us, though?"

"I don't know. The fact is he did what he did. Let's not judge him just yet."

"Easy for you to say, he's not your dad."

"That's not fair." Jason heard the pain in her voice. "I was there from the beginning; from his diagnosis till the end like everyone else. I nursed him, helped him, and loved him just as much as you. Don't ever compare dads to me. He was just as much to me as he was to you. It looks to me that not only did he love you, but he loved Charlie too. And, maybe Charlie's in the same boat as you. There are no buts Jason. You need to find them."

Jason turned the car off; they gathered their belongings and headed into the house. It was well past dark and Kristy fumbled for the light switch.

"Home sweet home," she said as she finally found the switch. Jason knew he had upset her. She had been there for him and his dad.

Kristy began to clean. Whenever Kristy got upset she cleaned; kitchen, bathrooms, and bedroom you name it. If she was on a cleaning binge, she was not happy. If she broke out the carpet shampooer she was pissed. He knew this routine and he knew the best thing to do was stay clear until she got over it. The last thing he wanted was a fight. He was tired and mentally drained. Out of the corner of his eye he caught the light blinking on the answering machine. He checked the caller I.D. It was his grandmother.

The message was a simple one; "How are you, how's Kristy? Please call, I'd love to hear from you. . . " and so on. Jason deleted the message and went up to the bedroom. Kristy was already in bed, blankets pulled up and facing the wall away from Jason. She had been cleaning. All of the clothes were put away; she had rearranged the towels in the bathroom, and even cleared off her dresser. Again, he knew to stay clear. Never try for make-up sex. That was a big no-no with her. Jason brushed his teeth, slipped of his jeans, and slid into bed. He reached over, turned off the light and rolled over on his side, his head facing the opposite direction of Kristy's.

"Good night," she whispered after a long pause, her words competing with the hum of the central air.

"Good night," Jason said. Never go to bed mad. That's what his dad always said.

"Hey, Kristy?"

"What?"

"I love you."

"I love you too."

The steady hum of the central air continued. Kristy spoke up.

"Want to fool around?"

"Who, me?"

"No, the other guy lying beside me."

"Well, I guess if I have to."

"Why, you little creep," Kristy shrieked as she sprang up and hit Jason with her pillow.

Jason let out a belly laugh rolled over and grabbed the pillow as Kristy followed through on her next swat. She fell on him still giggling. They caught each other's eye for a brief moment and passion came over them. She pressed her lips on Jason's and they kissed deep and strong. He lifted her tee-shirt over her head exposing her soft supple skin. He flipped her over onto her back and they consumed each another like only young lovers can.

With the passion and excitement engulfing them, Jason found himself thinking that this make-up sex he always thought was a no-no actually was a yes-yes.

Damn, marriage is complicated.

SEVEN

On Sunday mornings Jason and Kristy had a routine they loved to follow. They would get up early, about six-thirty, have coffee and read the paper. They'd shower and then they'd head out to Lowes, Wal-Mart, and then Kettle Diner for some brunch.

On this Sunday morning however, it was well after nine before they got up and going. They had been up late the night before and all of their built up tension had been burned up. Ah, young lovers.

They showered and dressed in silence. Their tiny smiles and the hidden glances said all that was needed to be said. They knew they had an incredible love and they could feel it throughout their bodies and minds. They spent the day holding hands walking through the Jacksonville Mall and then over to Lowe's and the Home Depot. They picked out a few hanging baskets that were on sale and picked up some fresh fruit at Wal-Mart. They finished the day with dinner at the Marina Café. Over a bottle of red wine, they talked about life, love, and each other and watched the sun disappear behind the Carolina Pines. It was a bright colorful sunset over the New River. They never once mentioned Sandy, Dad, the boys, or Charlie. They didn't need to; Charlie was there. No matter what they did or where they went that day Charlie was there. They passed a park with kids on the swings; Charlie was there. They saw an ice cream cone handed to a baby; Charlie was there. A crying baby in a cart at Wal-Mart; Charlie was there. Every face was a hint pushing them closer to find the truth.

It would be these thoughts, the constant reminders that would propel them deeper into a mystery that might never be solved.

He had practically broken the key off in the old front door dead bolt that needed replacing and dove to answer the phone.

"Hello?"

"Well hello, dear," a cheerful voice came for the other end.

"Hi, Gram."

"Did you get my message?"

"Yes, I did. I am sorry I didn't call back sooner. We were at Sandy's helping her clean out the house. We got home late last night, and we've been out shopping all day."

"That's okay, dear. How is the ice-queen?" Gram never liked Sandy.

"As good as she can be."

"I guess that means she's still moving to Florida?"

"Yeah, in a couple of weeks after the boys finish summer school."

"It's such a shame. If your dad was alive he'd never stand for this."

"Gram, if Dad were alive this wouldn't even be an issue."

"You're right, I just miss him."

"We all do, Gram."

"Well, most of us anyway," she said taking another jab at Sandy.

Florence Barker Miller lived in Lansdowne, Pennsylvania, where Chris was originally from. He had one brother and one sister and was very close to all of them. His dad had died at a young age but Florence never gave one thought to dating, let alone re-marriage. She believed that when you were married it was until death do you part for both of you. She had been single for thirty-seven years. Not one date, one flirt, one anything. This belief added to her dislike of Sandy. She felt mixing a marriage and adding children created hostilities and insecurities that were not fair to anyone. Jason always believed that's why Gram went the extra mile for him. An extra twenty - dollar bill for birthdays, or she'd slide him ten dollars for vacuuming her car when he visited. She'd always say, "This is your special treat, between you and I, okay?"

"No problem, Gram, he'd say." She loved Ryan and Matt just as much as Jason but as her first grandchild, she had a special place in her heart for him.

They talked for over an hour catching up on the family news and gossip. Uncle Paul, Chris's brother had gotten a promotion with SEPTA; the Southeastern Pennsylvania Transportation Authority. He was a trolley driver in the suburbs but was now a supervisor. He liked the hours better, but a lot of his friends were mad and had cut ties with him since they were big in the union. They felt Paul had stabbed them in the back by crossing over to management. The union did not like management and vice versa. Paul said it was an adjustment and those guys really weren't friends anyway if they let it bother them. Plus, he liked the extra money. Paul's greatest notoriety in the Miller family was that he was the first openly gay Miller. He had been in a stable relationship for twenty-one years with Alex and although it was never discussed Alex was accepted and loved by the entire family. Gram refused to believe Paul was gay, even when he told her. She simply replied she did not know what that meant other than being happy. So if he was happy so was she. She accepted Alex as Paul's friend and roommate. She never said so, but she loved him just as much as her own children.

Aunt Maria, Chris's sister was great. She always seemed to attract drama. Chris called her a soup sandwich, always falling apart. She was married to a nice guy named Bill who had a bit of a gambling problem. Gram would bail them out after Bill would blow his paycheck on the races. Then Maria would get upset and shop out her frustrations and stressors at Bloomingdales. Back and forth, back and forth. If it wasn't one it was the other. They were a perfect match and very much in love, but had addictions that they could not control. One fed on the other. They had two kids, Kelsey and Billy Jr. They were okay considering their parents were a mess at times. You had to credit Gram for that; she always had a way of making everything better.

As the conversation dragged on, Jason brought her up to date on everything that was going on in North Carolina. She tried to hide her dislike of the situation but her tone told the story. As the phone call drew to an end and the uncomfortable silences started gaining momentum, Jason noticed Kristy carrying the letter from his dad into the living room. She had taken it from the kitchen counter where it had sat since the night before. As Gram was saying her good-byes Jason interrupted.

"Hey Gram, I have a quick question."

"What is it?"

"Well, did Dad ever mention someone named Charlie to you?"

Kristy stopped in her tracks, the blood drained from her face. He's lost his mind. "No, no that I recall. Who is it?"

"I'm not sure. I found this letter when I was cleaning out a box and it's written from Dad to someone named Charlie. It goes on to talk about Charlie and his mother, Faith.

"Faith?" Gram's tenor changed. Jason sensed the tone of hostility in her voice.

"Who told you about her? Did that witch, Sandy tell you? We don't talk about her." Jason was stunned, his grandmother had never yelled at him, ever.

"Who is she?" he asked.

"That's not important. It's ancient news and conjures up old memories that we need not get into. You should let your father rest in peace and leave this nonsense alone. I have no idea who this Charlie person is, but as far as Faith goes, it's over and done with."

And with that for the first time ever in his life Jason was hung up on by none other than his Grammy.

"Well that didn't go as expected," he said hitting the off button on his cordless phone.

"What the hell got into you? Asking the big question out of the blue like that," a still stunned Kristy asked.

"I'm not sure; it just seemed to come out. I saw you and I saw the letter in your hand and thought what the hell."

"What the hell is right? Is she pissed?"

"Just a tad, she hung up on me and I'm not sure why. She's never talked to me like that and never freaked out like that. Weird."

"Well, what did she say?" Jason gave her the condensed version.

"I think she knows something," Kristy said.

"Knows what?" Jason asked.

"Who Charlie and Faith are and even better, where they are."

"You're crazy," he said.

"Am I? Think about it, she got pissed over two names that no one has ever mentioned before. If they meant nothing she wouldn't have gotten in such a tizzy."

Jason thought a moment. "You really think so?" he asked unconvinced.

"Yeah. I do. And I think you do too, deep down inside. I think you know she knows something"

"Maybe you're right. But why would she freak out like that?"

"She could be embarrassed; like you the other day," she teased.

"Very funny."

"Maybe your dad hid it from her and she didn't find out until later. I don't know. But you know Jason; you could always call her back and ask her. Or, better yet call Sandy."

"No, not right now. She needs time to cool off, and I need time to figure things out. Plus, Sandy thinks I tried to kill Norman so I need to give her a day or two more to get over that drama."

They were deep into discussions, theories, and motives that the sudden ring of the phone startled both of them. Jason checked the caller I.D.

"It's Gram," he said.

"Good, she's probably calling to apologize," Kristy said.

"Should I answer it?"

"Of course," she said cocking her head to the side in a sarcastic but playful tone.

"Smartass!"

Kristy smiled.

"Hello?"

"Jason?"

"Aunt Maria?"

"Yeah, listen about that call you and Gram just had…"

Jason could feel the ass chewing for upsetting the matriarch of the family. Standby he thought.

"I only got a minute. I'm upstairs at Gram's and I'm supposed to be in the bathroom. If she finds out I'm calling you, she'll kill me."

"Okay," he replied.

"Look, I heard what she was saying about Faith."

"Faith!?"

Jason sat up and slid forward on the couch. He glanced at Kristy in shock. She shimmied over beside him pressing her ear against the receiver to listen in.

"Yeah, who is she?" Jason leaned away to the left and shooed Kristy from his side. She gave a playful frown and ran into the kitchen and picked up the extension. Jason could hear the refrigerator motor grinding in the background.

"What can you tell me about her?"

"All I know is your dad and her were big in love and one day, poof: they were broken up somehow."

"When?"

"Years ago, in high school before he was in the Navy. The family doesn't talk about it. It's real hush, hush for some reason."

"Well I found this letter from my dad and he mentions her. But the letters addressed to Charlie."

"Who's Charlie?" Maria asked confused.

"I'm thinking they had a baby."

"A baby?"

"Yeah, he talks about being this great dad and how he loved Faith. Then the letter just ends, like there're pages missing or he just couldn't keep writing because he was so sick. I don't know."

"Jason, I don't know anything about any Charlie. Are you sure you got it right?

"Yeah. I have the letter and it says in a roundabout way this all happened before the Navy. I could be wrong, but I don't think so."

"Wow, that's strange."

"Tell me about it."

"Ya know this Charlie kid would have to be at least like 23 or 24 by now."

"I know."

"You sure about all this?"

"Not one-hundred percent," he said. "Do know where she could be, this Faith girl?"

"No clue, but she had to be from around here. Oh I gotta go, Jason. One of the babies has followed me upstairs. I can't even take a pee without your baby cousins following me."

"But, you're not peeing, Aunt Maria."

"No kidding, really? Look, call me if you need me and I'll call you back if I hear anymore or can find out anything, okay?"

"Okay, Au….."

"Mommy, who be talking to on dat pone?" a toddler's voice boomed over the receiver.

"Got to go, love you Jason. Bye." The line went dead before Jason got out his, "Bye, Marie."

Jason and Kristy hung up. Jason sat back more confused than ever. She walked over and snuggled in beside him. He took her under his arm.

"Wow. This just keeps getting better and better," she said.

"Sure does. It's just so weird."

"I know, right? One thing I do know is that your Gram knows more than she's telling. You need to talk to her."

"I tried, she hung up on me."

"Then go up there and see her. Ask her face to face."

"My leave is up. I have to go back to work tomorrow."

"Call your Chief; ask for two or three extra days. We'll go up first thing in the morning."

"We'll go?" he asked.

"Of course. You don't think I'd let you go alone. Plus, I love road trips. You get to eat all that fattening highway food!"

"I don't know, babe. I just don't know what to do. I feel weird calling for more leave. I have taken so much time, Dad dying, the funeral, the pack-out. It's so much to deal with." He sat forward, rubbing his hands over his face.

Kristy got serious. "You know what, Jason?"

"What?"

"I will never begin to know what you're feeling. You have all of these emotions swirling around in your head with your dad dying, Sandy taking your brothers and moving, and now finding this letter. It's so much, so soon. One thing I do know is that you are very smart and very caring. You want to know and you need to know. It will kill you forever if you don't ever take the chance to know. You need to do this."

He knew she was right.

She brushed her hand down his back. She moved closer to him. They embraced. Jason knew what had to be done.

He thumbed through his briefcase and found his recall bill. Chief Sutton's number was on page four. He was the Leading Chief Petty Officer of the Caron Clinic. He liked Jason and it didn't hurt that Jason's dad had initiated him into the mess either. After only a few minutes of explanation, Jason had a three day extension on his leave. He called Aunt Maria's cell phone and told her he was coming.

"The light is always on. You know that, sweetie," she said.

Jason loved his Aunt Maria. Although her and Bill had some issues, she was always there for him. Jason and Kristy packed an overnight bag, took a shower, and jumped in the car. It was a nine hour drive to Lansdowne. They'd be at Aunt Maria's by eight a.m., traffic permitting.

EIGHT

They arrived in Lansdowne a little before nine. Traffic through Washington, D.C. had slowed them down, not to mention Kristy needed her highway food fix. They had stopped at a Denny's off of I-95 to get a bite to eat and then stopped again outside Fort A.P. Hill, Virginia at the very first Wawa convenience store. In Jason's mind Wawa coffee was best coffee in the world. He even liked it better than Dunkin Donuts. Anytime he went north he made numerous trips to Wawa. He'd stock up on their coffee and haul it back to North Carolina.

Aunt Maria greeted Jason and Kristy with big warm hugs. They made the customary small talk; the ride up, their stops, traffic, and the price of gas. But what Jason really wanted to talk about was Charlie and Faith.

"Like I told you last night, I don't know anything else and Lord knows your grandmother wasn't talking."

"Does Gram know I'm here?" Jason asked her.

"Yeah, I told her. She's looking forward to seeing you, but don't expect much in the way of the Faith thing. She's still pretty upset and says that if you're coming up here for just that reason, you're wasting your time."

"Great, Gram thinks it's a waste of time too."

"Who thinks it's a waste of time?" asked Maria.

"He does," Kristy said pointing over at Jason.

"Well, I don't think it's too much of a waste of time if I'm here," he shot back.

"Alright, so where do we start?" Kristy asked.

"How about the high school?" Maria chimed in. "Go through some old yearbooks and see if there's a Faith in there. If she was in school with him, she'd be there, right?"

"Oh my God you're right. Let's get cleaned up and go," he said excitedly.

"You sure? You need some sleep, you look beat," Maria said.

Jason let out a big stretch; arms up over his head. "Yeah, you're right. Night-night."

After several hours of sleep and a hot shower Jason slipped into the kitchen and made himself something to eat. Aunt Maria went into work late. Bill had been there since six a.m. Kristy joined him and they ate in silence; the only noise in the kitchen was coming from the cars that whizzed by on Marshall Road. After putting their plates and knives in the dishwasher, Jason grabbed a lemon flavored Propel from the fridge and he and Kristy headed out the door.

Upper Darby High School was on Lansdowne Avenue at the top of the hill. Founded in 1895, it's the oldest High School in Delaware County, Pennsylvania. It's one of largest campuses in the state with more than 3,900 students and an annual graduating class of 1,100. Over thirty-five famous celebrities, athletes, inventors, and businessman had graduated or attended Upper Darby High School. They included Tina Fey (Class of 88') who was the first female head writer for Saturday Night Live, two time Academy Award winner Alvin Sargent (Class of '45), singer-song writer Jim Croce (class of 60'), and 1992 NBA Basketball Hall of Famer Jason Ramsey (class of 42'). Over the years it had toughened up and while still a good school it had its fair share of behavior problems.

Chris had started at Upper Darby High School but dropped out in the ninth grade. He had always told Jason that he hated school, school hated him and the best thing for him to do was quit and join the Navy. Gram was devastated and had a hard time accepting his decision. However, as his military career took off and as his personal accomplishments increased her devastation turned to pride and patriotism.

They entered the building on the first floor and headed into the main office. A pleasant woman greeted them from behind the counter.

"May I help you?"

"Yes, Ma'am." Jason had that Southern male politeness about him.

"I'm trying to get some information on a student that may have attended here in 1986 or 1987. I only know her first name; Faith."

"Well, I can't really help you with that here. We only keep current students records here on the campus. Old records are sent to the main office for archiving."

"Well, do you by chance have any old yearbooks we can look through?" Kristy asked.

She hesitated. "Before we go any further," she said, "May I ask what this is about and who you might be?"

"Oh, I'm sorry, ma'am, my name is Jason Miller and this is my wife Kristy. My daddy went to school here in the late eighties and knew this woman Faith. To make a long story short, he died last year—"

"Oh, I'm so sorry," she said interrupting.

"Thank you, I appreciate that. Like I was saying, he died and it appears that my dad and this Faith person might have had a baby together. I'm just trying to find out if it's true."

"Oh." Her genuine smile and kindliness turned judgmental.

"What year did he graduate?" she asked.

"He didn't." Her face seemed to get a bit colder.

"I see." Jason knew he was losing her to the moralities department.

"Ma'am," Jason said pleadingly. "My dad was a good man. He made some mistakes in life but he joined the Navy, did three tours in Iraq, and managed to make a good life for me and my brothers. I even joined the Navy. I only have three days of leave left to try to find out about this Faith person and whether or not I have a sister or brother I've never met. Please, will you help me?"

Jason hated playing the military - dead dad card, but he needed her help. She stared at him for a moment. Her facial expression softened and she seemed to loosen up. Jason had dropped his line in the pool called heart strings and she was ready to be reeled in.

"Well, we do keep a copy of all of the old yearbooks in the Library. Come on, I'll take you over there. You can sit and go through them if you like."

"Thank you so much, ma'am," Jason said.

She filled out two visitor passes and handed them over. Jason handed them over to Kristy with a wink and she put them in her purse.

"Follow me, please."

They walked down the brightly lit hallways peering into classrooms as they walked. They kept going through mazes of twists and turns of the enormous campus until they reached the library. Once inside, she took them over to shelf holding the yearbooks. Before leaving she turned to Jason.

"Thank you and thank you to your father for all you've done in service and sacrifice." Her demeanor was warm and heartfelt and with that she slipped out the door.

They pulled down 1985, 1986, 1987, and 1988. The carried them to a table, spread them out and sat down.

"These were all of the years my dad would have attended. I think he dropped out midway through '86. He had to repeat his freshman year. We'll start earlier just in case and see what happens."

Jason stared thumbing through '85 while Kristy grabbed the '88. "Anything?" he asked as he scrolled through the pictures.

"Nothing" she said.

"I got nothing here either." He grabbed the '86 and started thumbing through the names and pictures.

"Man, they had some big hair back then," he said to Kristy.

"I know. Some of these girls, it's like their hair would just explode in a fire ball with all of the hairspray that had to have used."

"Bingo!" Jason exclaimed. "We have a Faith, no two of them; Faith Rider and Faith Sterns."

"I have them too, class of '88. Looks like they did graduate from here."

"Cool, now we just got to find them."

"Let's ask Dex."

"Who?"

"You'll see," he said with a wink getting up from the table.

"Excuse me, ma'am, do you by chance have a phone book?"

"Do you have a hall pass?" the librarian asked as she peered down her nose at him, sizing Jason up and down.

"Ah, no ma'am, but...."

"But nothing," she snapped. "No hall pass, no help!"

"Ma'am, I'm not a student."

"Oh," she huffed. "Who are you?"

Jason went through the whole story again and motioned for Kristy to hand over their visitor passes.

"You should have these passes visible," she said tearing off two pieces of scotch tape with her free hand.

"Thank you, you're right," was the bothered reply as they pressed the tape passes onto their shirts.

The librarian looked at them curiously. "A phonebook?"

"Yes, a phonebook," Jason said even more bothered.

She sat down the folder she was holding, walked behind the counter and returned. She handed the phonebook to Jason. Without saying a word she picked up her folder and went back to what she was doing.

No wonder librarians live alone, he thought. He turned and went back to the table. He plopped down beside her and they opened to the R's.

"Rider. . .Rider. . .Rider" Jason read aloud as his finger slid down the page.

"No, Faith, just a Frank Rider," he said.

"Here, what's the number?" Kristy asked as she pulled out her cell phone.

As the phone rang Jason could feel his pulse in his throat.

"Yes, Sir, I am trying to reach a Faith Rider?" she asked.

"Oh, I see. Any idea where a Faith Rider might be?"

"No, I don't think you're a phone book," she said and balked. "But, I do think you're a jerk!" Kristy slammed her phone shut.

"Take it that wasn't her?"

"What gave it away?"

"Okay, well let's try Sterns." Jason flipped through the phone book and scanned for Sterns.

"Nothing. Damn," he said dejected "I give up. Come on, let's go." They returned the boxes to the shelf, making sure they were back in numerical order. They walked towards the door hand and hand.

Kristy grabbed his arm. "Facebook!" she shouted.

"What?" Jason asked.

"Facebook! When some women join Facebook they add their maiden name if their married this way old friends can find them."

"And you know this how?" Jason asked.

"Cause I've done it along with a trillion other women."

"Excuse me?" she asked a young girl walking by.

"Yes?"

"Is there a computer lab here?"

"Right over there," she said pointing to the other end of the library.

Kristy hurried over, Jason in tow and sat down at an empty computer. She typed Facebook into the search engine.

Blocked. The school had blocked social networking sites.

"I got ya," a deep voice resonated from behind. A gigantic teenager came over and slipped over Kristy's shoulders, his arms resting on her shoulders as he typed away uninvited. His massive frame blocked Jason out of the way. He thought it odd but Jason was struck by how handsome he was.

"You need to circumvent the server by diverting the I.P. address through the...."

"Look, Hercules, thanks for the Cisco lesson, but can you just help us out?" Jason blurted out a bit overawed by the uninvited guest.

"Sure, old man," he said turning to Jason. "Anything to help a lady," he said as he flashed a flirtatious wink at Kristy. Jason just stood there.

Old man, he thought. *I'm twenty-one for Christ sake.*

"There ya go, you're in," he said standing up. "Anything else?"

"No thanks. Me and the old man got it from here." Kristy smiled.

"I'll be over here if you need me; I have study hall this period."

Jason moved closer to Kristy, trying to squeeze his medium sized frame in front of the giant's view.

"Old man?" he asked.

Kristy laughed and logged in to Facebook. In the search space she entered Faith Sterns. Nothing. No Faith Sterns anywhere. She backspaced and added Rider. Four Faith Rider's came up. One in Maine, one in New York, One in California and one in Upper Darby, Pennsylvania.

"Holy crap, Jason. I think we found her!"

Butterflies circled Jason's stomach, he swallowed hard. A large lump still stuck in his throat.

Kristy opened a new window and did reverse white pages and came up with an address.

"You cannot be on there!" the frantic and hurried voice of the librarian squeaked as she reached for Kristy's hands on the keyboard.

"Don't touch me!" she growled.

"Excuse me?"

"No excuse me. I'm not some little kid you can bully, I'm a grown woman. You want respect? You need to show respect. We were just leaving anyway," Kristy said, closing out the screens.

"You go, girl!" came the deep engaging voice of the giant, his hormones raging.

"At ease, Hercules," Jason mumbled as they scooted out the library door and into the maze of hallways.

Kristy was never one to back down and she certainly did not like to be disrespected. Respect was earned, not given. She had little patience for anyone who was rude or bossy.

They headed out the main entrance and jumped into the car.

"Where to?" Jason asked.

"Twenty nine Overhill Road."

"I know exactly where that's at," Jason said as he pulled on to Lansdowne Avenue and punched the accelerator.

NINE

As Jason drove up Market Street and past the 69th Street terminal he couldn't help but notice how dilapidated the area seemed since he last visited here. His dad had grown up here on Marlborough Road and always said what a great place it was to grow up. Back then it was a mixed neighborhood of Italians, Greeks, and Irish. Now it looked like a crime ridden ghetto. Jason wondered what it must have been like growing up here and what his father might have been like as a kid.

They had to go up Marlborough Road to get back down to Overhill. Jason stopped in front of his dad's old house; number 41.

"That's where Pop grew up," he said pointing to the old twin.

"Wow. It looks like a dump."

"Today it does. But when he was a kid he said it was awesome. In some of the pictures he showed me it really looked nice."

He inched the car forward slowly until they were far enough past his dad's old homestead then he drove on. He turned right on Chestnut and then on to Overhill. Weathered old row homes with oxidized metal siding and chipped paint lined both sides of the block. He found 29 and parked on the right side of the street.

"Here goes nothing," he said to Kristy and he opened the door.

"Think positive." They walked up the path towards the front door. The grass had been recently mowed and the lawn was nicely manicured. The smell of new mown grass filled the air and the squeals of a few kids playing in the street echoed of the old homes. I wonder why they aren't in school.

He rang the doorbell and waited.

A few minutes passed and the old wooden door opened. A woman cautiously looked out.

"If you're selling something, I own it. If I don't I'm still not interested," she said.

"No ma'am, were not,' Kristy said.

"What do you want then?"

"Ma'am my name is Jason Miller. My dad, Chris Miller might have gone to school with you."

"So?" she asked.

"Well, we're looking for a friend of his named Faith Rider."

"The woman just looked at them. "Your Chris's boy?" she asked cautiously.

"Yes, ma'am, I am. And this is my wife, Kristy."

"Well today's your lucky day; I'm Faith Rider. She undid the locks on the screen door and opened it. She smiled.

"My, my, I never thought Chris would have a boy so handsome and with a wife no less. Come in, come in," she said.

"Thanks' ma'am." Jason and Kristy stepped through the door on to the porch. She pushed the doors closed behind them, turned the dead bolts and locked them in.

"Don't mind me locking the doors. Twenty-five years ago my mom and dad never locked this door. But times have changed and so has the neighborhood. Come in, come in," she said waving them through the enclosed porch and in to the living room.

"How is Chris?" she asked.

Uneasy Kristy and Jason looked at one another.

"He died last year, cancer."

"Oh, I'm sorry to hear that." Faith sat down in an old recliner and stared off to the window on the left.

"He was a good guy. I always liked him. He was one of the funniest guys you'd ever meet. And helpful! Chris would do anything for you even if he didn't like you. That's just the kind of guy he was. Ah, memories," she said looking distant.

Without warning, she snapped her head around, "So anyway, what brings you here?"

The quick change in her demeanor caught Jason off guard.

"Well, ma'am, after my dad died I found this letter. In it he talks about being in love with a girl by the name of Faith. We checked all of the yearbooks and found two; you and a girl by the name Faith Stern. He alludes to the fact the he might have had a baby with her or for that matter, you," he said uneasily. He felt his face heat up and knew it was beat red.

Faith laughed. "Oh dear it couldn't be me. I never dated your dad. He was a great guy and all but I had no interest in boys back then. In fact I've had no interest in boys unless of course they're part of the community."

"The community?"

"She laughed again. Yes, sweetie. The community; the gay community. I was born a dyke and I'll die a dyke."

Kristy burst out laughing and quickly regained her composure so as not to offend. Faith smiled at them.

"I see one of you got sense of humor."

Jason squirmed in his seat, and felt even redder. Faith sensed his uneasiness.

"It's okay, I get that a lot, the laughs and the fidgets," she said smiling.

"No, no, it's not that," Jason quickly replied. "It's just I was hoping—"

"Hoping I was the Faith you were looking for?"

"Yeah," he said.

"Well, I'm sorry I'm not."

Just then a woman came though the dining room. "Faith who's there?" the voice asked.

"It's Chris Miller's boy."

"Chris Miller's boy!" she exclaimed. A rather masculine looking woman entered the living room. Jason stood to greet her.

"Jason Miller, this is my wife, Kristy," he said extending his hand.

"Gene Allred," she said giving his hand a solid squeeze. "It's Gene with a G, not a J. Boy you're a cutie," she said smiling at Kristy

"Thank you, you're very kind."

She turned her attention back to Jason. "Man your dad was awesome. How is he?"

"Dead," Faith replied matter-of-factly as she lit a cigarette. She took a deep drag and let it out slowly. Smoke filled the small living room.

"That blows. How'd he croak?" Her somewhat straight forward approach caught Jason by surprise. Kristy loved it.

"Cancer," Faith answered for them.

"That blows," Gene replied.

"Hey, sweetie?" Faith asked tapping Gene on the hand.

"Yes?"

"Could you grab these kids some tea or lemonade?"

"Oh sure. Where are my manners, I'll be right back."

As she left the living room Faith leaned forward. With a cigarette dangling from her mouth she had motioned Jason and Kristy forward.

"She gives lesbians a bad name with all that butch act. I love her but if I wanted a man I'd get one!"

Kristy sat back and busted out laughing again, this time not regaining any composure.

Jason smiled broadly. The ice was officially broken.

Faith told some stories about Chris as they sipped really bad tasting lemonade. Jason found himself thinking about how much he missed his dad. It was great hearing that he was such a nice guy and so well liked in school. As the minutes turned to more than an hour, Jason knew she could talk all day if he let her. But he wanted to get to the job at hand.

"Faith, by chance did you know another Faith? This one named Faith Stern?"

"Oh yeah. But she died in '91. Or was it '92? Drunk driver or was it suicide? Hell, I can't remember. Anyway I think it was an aneurysm. I think." She looked at the ceiling, her head cocked to one side, thinking.

"Faith, please," Jason interjected.

"Oh, yeah. Um I don't think it could have been her because she dated some jock all through high school and then went off to college out of state. That's where she died or was killed or something."

"I think they're looking for Fathiya," Gene hollered from the kitchen.

"Who?"

"Fathiya; the girl he was dating, her name was Fathiya."

"Who the hell was that?" Faith yelled.

"Stop yelling at me," Gene fired back.

"Well get your ass out here so I don't have to."

Kristy laughed again, pressing her hand across her broad smile. Faith smiled and flashed them a wink.

"Oh, for God's sake," Gene moaned as she stormed in the living room.

"Her name was Fathiya. She was some foreign girl from Iran, or Pakistan, or some-where-a-stan, or some place. I don't know for sure. We called her Faith because no one could pronounce her name right. I am pretty sure that's who it was."

"I remember now. She was real cute."

"You'd remember more if you'd stop smoking all that funny stuff."

"Oh go marry a man," was the playful reply.

Gene stuck her tongue out at Faith. "Blaaaaa!"

"Blaaaaa," yourself Faith said laughing back at her.

Jason wanted to throw-up.

"Do you know where I can find her? Where she lives?"

"Dead, I think," Gene said.

Wow these girls had a way with just throwing it out there with little empathy he thought.

"Murdered is more like it," said Faith.

"No one could ever prove that."

"Well it doesn't take a rocket scientist to figure it out."

"Who are you, Perry Mason?"

"Oh, hush you."

"Ladies, please." Jason raised his voice and caught himself in disbelief. They both whipped their head around and looked at Jason.

"I mean, I'm sorry but what happened to her?"

"Hell, no one's called me a lady since Sister Mary What's her nuts did during my first holy communion," Gene said. "I like you, you got balls." She reached over and smacked Jason on the back and smiled.

Kristy kept laughing and enjoyed the show.

"Thanks, but what happened to Fathiya."

"I heard she died of some kind of infection; blood or something. A lot of people think that her old man killed her."

"Why?" asked Kristy.

"She got knocked up," Gene said. "Well that was the rumor anyway."

"Gene!" Faith exclaimed.

"Well, that's what I heard. And he's looking for a kid right? So it makes sense."

"No one could prove it," Faith insisted trying to ease the enormity of what Jason was hearing.

"I can, or at least I think I can prove part of it," he replied.

"What? That the old man killed her?" Jason had their full attention.

"Nah, this is the first I heard of that. My dad wrote a letter to someone named Charlie and kept referring to as the woman that he loved and I guess had a baby with."

"And you think that this Charlie is their kid?" Gene asked.

"Yeah, I do. Were there any rumors about a baby being born before she died?"

"No, not that I remember."

"Me either," replied Gene. "I never heard anything. We ran with a different group."

"Right, the community?" asked Kristy smiling.

"That's right, give that girl a prize!"

"I'm sorry we can't help you anymore."

"That's okay, you've helped a lot," said Jason.

"You could always go ask her old man."

"What?" Jason said shocked.

"Her family has owned the same dump of a store down on Long Lane since grass was green. Or is it Market Street actually?"

Oh, not this again Jason thought.

"Anyway, it's the old Chevy dealership on the corner. He bought it a hundred years ago and made it a beer and lottery place. It's called the Lotto-Beer. Stupid name if you ask me. It's like two blocks up," Faith said

"I know exactly where it's at."

"I wish we could be more help," apologized Gene.

"You've been more help than you'll ever know."

"Come on, Babe" he said looking over to Kristy. "Let's run down there, maybe we can catch Mr., Any idea their name?"

"No clue," said Faith. Probably some weird jargon that sounds like your saying All Beer Money Clip Holder with Chiclets in your mouth."

Kristy shrieked out a laugh. Embarrassed at her squeal, she quickly covered her mouth.

"You're such a lady," said Faith.

"That's what he said," Gene said pointing at Jason. "But don't tell my guy-no-cologist."

Kristy laughed out loud again and Faith threw them another wink.

These two could be a lot of fun, or a lot of trouble with a few beers in them, Jason thought.

"Well, on that note, I wish you the best and hope you find what you're looking for."

"So do I. Thanks to both of you for all of your help."

"You're welcome, sweetie. And hey, if you ever want to come back and give us the rest of the story we love gossip; hell we love company," said Gene.

"We'll keep that in mind," Jason said with a smile. He liked Gene and Faith both, especially Gene. She said what she wanted and didn't really care what people thought. She was who she was. He liked that about people.

They stepped out and down the three steps leading on to the path up to the sidewalk.

"Bye-now," said Kristy.

"Bye," the smiling face of a new friend grinned. The door closed and the sounds of locks sprang repeatedly.

"Well, looks like we're headed to buy some beer."

"And lottery," Kristy reminded him. "Plus, I need a good drink." She slammed the passenger door closed and they were on their way.

TEN

Jason swung their little red Honda Accord into the parking lot of the Lotto-Beer. He and Kristy had rehearsed what they might say and how they might say it in an effort to calm their nerves. It wasn't working. They walked in and the infrared buzzer alerted the clerk that someone had entered the store.

"May I help you?" a small voice from behind the counter solicited. A very pretty woman obviously of Middle Eastern descent was standing there with a smile.

Jason approached the counter as Kristy peeled off to the beer displays. "Yes ma'am, I am looking for the owner."

"We are not hiring right now," she said in a thick accent.

"Oh no, ma'am, I'm not looking for a job, just some information."

"What information?" she asked cautiously.

"I am looking for any information about a girl named Fathiya. She was a friend of my father's."

The woman hesitated and then spoke sheepishly. "She was my aunt. I never met her; she left a long time ago way before I came to America. I don't think we can help you."

"Maybe someone else can?" Jason pressed.

She hesitated again, a look of fear on her face. "I am not sure. My grandfather may speak to you; Fathiya was his first daughter. He does not speak of her for it is rude to speak of ones children. I will see if he will come and speak to you. Please wait here." Wanting to end the conversation she turned to go through a small doorway covered with a multi-colored sheet, when he stopped her.

"Ma'am, before you go what is or was her last name?"

"Why do you ask?"

"I would like to be respectful when I meet him. I need to know what to call him." She seemed pleased at his attempt to be kind.

"Her full name was Fathiya Tahzib Umar. Grandfather's name is Abdullah Ibn Umar. Wait here please," and through the sheet she went.

Several minutes passed and Kristy walked up to the counter with a twelve pack of Rocky Raccoon's Honey Lager. She set it up on the counter. The condensation had already begun to sweat the bottles.

"Any luck?"

"I don't know. She's getting the grandfather who is supposed to be Fathiya's dad."

"Really?"

"Yeah so we'll see."

"I think to play it safe we should call her Fathiya and not Faith. At least here anyway."

"You're right," he agreed.

Suddenly, a loud commotion could be heard coming from the back room the young girl has disappeared into. The voices were getting louder as they approached the front of the store. Thick Arabic accents and several voices zipped back and forth. An older man barreled through the curtain separating the back room from the service counter.

He was a short man, maybe five foot-three. He had a rather large pot belly, which was partially covered by a brown sweater vest and a checkered long sleeve shirt. His perfectly combed hair and neatly shaved face complemented his big salt and pepper moustache. Anger showed on his face; his eye brows were pressed down and in and he approached the counter aggressively so much so Jason and Kristy took a step back. For a small man, he was very intimidating.

"What do you want? Who are you?" he asked in an angry thick Middle Eastern accent.

"Mr. Umar?" Jason asked.

"My name is Abdullah, now what do you want from me?"

"Okay, I'm sorry. Mr. Abdullah I was hoping to get some information about Fathiya?"

"Why? What business of this is yours? She has been gone a very long time. We do not discuss such things. This is none of your business." He seemed irrational and bitter.

"What do you want?" His black and gray eyebrows scrunched down even further over his scowling face.

"Sir, my dad, Chris Miller and your daughter may have been dating."

"And?"

"You!" he erupted. "You are the bastard of that man?"

The anger and disdain he was displaying overcame the entire room. Words escaped him. He had no chance to speak or defend his father as Abdullah continued.

"He destroyed my daughter. He made her impure and defiled her in the eyes of Allah. She brought shame to her family. No decent Muslim man would want her after he touched her. You have the nerve to come here and ask about her? Get out of here, and never come back."

"Now wait just a minute," Jason began, finally given his opportunity to get a word in. "I didn't mean to come here and upset you. My dad died...."

"Good, he should burn in hell with all of the infidels."

"Look, I just want to know if she had a baby."

"How dare you!" he screamed. His rage swelled and erupted like a percolating volcano.

"She is gone away and she will not be back, now get out!"

His face purpled and a large vein bulged from his forehead. He began to scream and yell in Arabic, pointing his finger deeper and deeper into Jason's face. Spit spewed from his mouth. Just then two young men came through the curtain carrying sticks, they too were screaming in Arabic. One smashed a stick down on the counter. A loud crash startled everyone including the old man.

"Jason we need to go," Kristy said, her voice shaking.

"Wait!"

"No, Jason, we're going now!"

"Listen to your woman and get out," one of the younger men said in English.

"You mean my wife?' Jason snapped back overcoming his fear.

"Let's go, Jason, please!"

He came to his senses. He would never win a fight three against one, especially when they had weapons. He couldn't risk Kristy getting hurt either. But who the hell was this guy to bad mouthing his father and his wife?

"Okay, we're going. Just relax," Jason said backing out of the store.

"Do not come back, ever," one of the younger men yelled escorting them with his stick. They moved to the relative safety of their car as the other man followed them out stick in hand.

Kristy locked the doors and Jason started the engine as quickly as he could, considering he was fumbling around nervously with the keys. He finally got it started and backed out onto Long Lane. He watched through the rear view mirror, his eyes and those of the young man came together as he drove away.

"Damn it, Jason. Could you have been anymore tactful?" Kristy asked.

"Whoa, wait just a dog-gone minute. What the hell was I supposed to say? Excuse me; did my dad knock up your daughter? I had no idea how he'd react. And considering he was getting more and more pissed I couldn't have asked him anything before getting smacked upside the head with that damn stick. Jesus, Kristy!"

They rode in silence for a few minutes. "We're no closer to finding Charlie then we we're three days ago."

"Sure we are," reassured Kristy. "We have connected some lot of dots but the big one still needs connecting."

"What dot would that be?" Jason asked.

"You grandmother," she said. "You need to talk to her."

"We need to wait until tomorrow. It's already after five, I'm tired and I'm hungry. Let's go back to Maria's and start fresh in the morning."

"Sounds good to me," Kristy said. Now stop at the next bar and let's get a six pack! I need a drink!"

They stopped at Danny's Corner Tavern and got a six pack of Miller Lite. Not exactly the Rocky Raccoon Lager Kristy wanted, but it would do. Back at Maria's they had dinner and then sat and talked for a few hours, Kristy reliving the afternoon with her new lesbian friends and the crazy Arabs they had met. By nine o'clock they were both ready for bed and excused themselves for the night. They tried to sleep but the sounds of Maria and Bill having sex prevented that for the first hour.

"God, hurry up and finish," Kristy grumbled.

"Want to fool around too?" he cooed.

"Don't touch me I'm sleeping," she joked.

Jason smiled and let out a chuckle.

Maria let out a final scream and a door slammed, presumably their bedroom door. The house went silent.

Finally, sleep.

ELEVEN

Jason arrived at his grandmother's at eight o'clock. Kristy had decided to stay at the house and surf the net to see if she could find out more about Fathiya or Charlie.

"It's simple," Jason said. "She went back to Pakistan and had the baby. She's not dead, just banished. Leave it alone, it's a waste of time."

Waste of time or not, Kristy wanted to know more.

"Fine. I'm going to Grams; I'll catch up with you later."

Grammie had always been a late sleeper. She stayed up late and watched David Letterman and the all of the infomercials. She bought more crap than she knew what to do with and most of it wound up as gifts she showered on Jason. He loved his Flavor-Wave but wished she'd save her money or at least spend it something more useful.

Jason came in through the back door. The old rusted spring let out a tired weak stretch that did not stop it from slamming shut.

"Who's there?" a small voice called from the dining room.

"It's Jason, Gram."

"Oh, come in. I have been waiting for you. I thought you would come last night." She rose from her chair to meet him at the doorway. She was still in her house coat, her hair neatly wrapped in a scarf.

"Sorry, we got tied up."

"Where's Kristy?" she asked in disappointment struggling to see past his much bigger frame.

"At Maria's. She's not feeling well." The lies had begun.

"Is it serious? Morning sickness, maybe? Hopefully?" she asked with a smile.

"Good God no, Gram, that's the last thing I need right now."

"You say that now but before you know it, the pitter-patter of little feet will be upon you. Hopefully before I die."

"You're not going to die, Gram."

"You never know, they could tell me tomorrow I have cancer."

Gram caught herself in her own words and sat down mortified.

"That didn't come out right, dear. I'm sorry."

"It's okay, Gram, I knew what you meant. You want some coffee?"

"Please."

She followed Jason into the kitchen so he could pour a cup of coffee. The Mr. Coffee machine had developed yellow and brown tinges from years of use. The old pot sat in the same spot for all the years Jason could remember. She had used gray duct tape to hold the dry rot cracks that covered the handle.

"Why don't you buy a new one next time you're watching QVC," he said extending the pot towards her so she could see it.

"Why? It still works," she said, grabbing the creamer from the fridge.

"Well, because this looks like it's growing tomaine poison."

"At least I'll die drinking Folgers."

They both smiled as he topped off her cup. They finished stirring their cups and headed back into the dining room making small talk along the way; the weather, the condition of the old house, and all of the same things they had covered a few nights before on the phone. Jason could feel himself getting tense, a lump building in his throat. He needed to ask. They sat in the old wing back chairs facing one another.

"Gram, about the other night, I…"

"It's okay. I shouldn't have been so abrupt. There are just some things we don't discuss, and she's one of them."

"Why?" he asked. He could feel the sweat pool on his brow and the hot flashes form over his head. His pulse pounded in his throat.

"It's just not something I care to talk about."

"Gram, please," he implored.

"Why are you so interested in bringing up the past?" she asked, her voice gaining volume. "Your dad is dead, let it go. Don't destroy your memories of him."

"Gram, I can't. If he didn't want us to know he never would have written that letter and set it in a place where he'd figure we would find it."

"Oh how could he put a letter away, he was bedridden? Not to mention, you said it wasn't even finished. Now who would hide a half written letter?" she said.

"I don't know the answers to any of those questions. Truth is, there are more questions than answers and that's why I'm here. If I have a brother or sister somewhere, I'd like to know."

There was a long silence between them; only the sound of old pendulum swinging back and forth on the grandfather clock filled the air. Grammie stared down at the newspaper in front of her on the coffee table. Jason couldn't tell if she was reading or thinking, or both. The muscles on her old weathered face clenched back and forth. Her wrinkled and spot covered fingers tapped away on her cup.

"Jason," she said softly, "I will never talk about this again, ever." She turned to face him, her bottom lip quivering.

"Gram, I..."

"No, listen," she interrupted as she lifted a single slightly bent finger to her lips.

"When your dad started the ninth grade, for the second time I might add, he met her."

"Faith you mean?"

"Yes." She again lifted her finger to her lips.

"Sorry."

"At first I saw no harm in it. I thought she was Italian or something. Never once did I suspect she was one of them."

"You mean Muslim?"

"Yes. I'm not a bigot mind you but the whole Middle East thing was still brewing. We had gone through the Libya mess and Iran hostage crisis. There was a lot of anger and resentment towards foreigners, especially middle easterners. The country was scared and I admit I was too. Your father didn't care, though. He was so happy when he found out she was pregnant and I suspect he thought I'd be too. But then again I was born in a different time when those types of things didn't happen. If you got pregnant out of wed lock it was taboo. He was very angry at me when I told him how disappointed I was. And I was very angry at her because I felt she was trapping him. He didn't care. He was going to marry her and show the world what a good father he could be and how wrong we all were. Maybe because his grandfather had died so early in his life, he needed to prove something to me. I don't know."

She set her cup on the small cherry colored table beside her.

"It wasn't to be. After her father found out, all heavens broke loose."

"You mean hell; all hell broke loose."

She gave Jason a stern look, "Yes dear, hell. I'm not that old."

"Sorry."

"Anyway, your dad thought she would feel the same way and run away with him. Her father would have none of it. He was very angry. Like any father I guess would be. Your dad wouldn't relent, and kept after her. He began to threaten your dad and told him he would kill him if he came near her. Your dad didn't care. He loved her, and wanted to be with her. He would go to her house at night and wait to see if she would come out. Her dad pulled her out of school and basically hid her from the world. Several weeks later a man came to the house. He said he was an uncle of hers and wanted to talk to your dad. I was afraid they would start fighting so I wouldn't let him in. Your dad snuck out the back door, came around the front and confronted him on the porch. He wanted to know where she was. He told your dad that Faith, I can't believe I am saying her name, he came to say that Faith had been sent back to..."

"Pakistan?"

Annoyed, she replied, "Yes, Pakistan. Stop interrupting me."

"The man said it was a waste of time trying to find her; he never would. He wanted your father to leave his family alone or, there would be consequences. What that meant I don't know, but I thought it meant he'd hurt your dad. He told her she was gone, and gone forever. Your dad exploded in a fit of rage I had never seen before. He began to yell and scream at the man and grabbed him. Mr. Wilcox from next door came running over and grabbed him off of the man. The police came; it was a mess. No one was arrested or anything however we soon became the talk of the neighborhood. I was so embarrassed and I guess ashamed. The police told your dad to stay away and the family got a restraining order. He was devastated. That's when he joined the Navy; up and out of the blue. I always believed he joined thinking he could use the Navy as a way of finding her. Silly, huh? I guess no one can answer that one now," she said with a smile.

"I guess, Gram. Or maybe he joined because he was upset or..."

"Or mad at me?" she asked, her tone already divulging the answer.

Jason nodded an agreeable yes.

"I thought that too, and I guess I still do in a way. It was only later that we started hearing rumors that she never left the country, was here the whole time, hidden in the house away from your dad and the rest of the world. Rumors went back and forth for years and years that she had secretly had the baby and given it away to a family member somewhere. Other rumors were she died during child birth, but no records or anything were ever found; your dad searched and searched. Nothing. Not a death certificate or a birth certificate or anyone for that matter. One rumor was she had a girl, another rumor was a boy. Some people said that horrible man secretly raised the child as his. I never knew. No one does I guess except for the Lord our God and those vile people. Your dad was devastated. As time went on your dad was never himself again. It didn't help that no one would say where she was, if she was dead or alive. If she died there wasn't so much as an obituary. What kinds of people don't write an obituary? Savages, all of them. Don't get me wrong, I'm not a bigot, just honest."

"So no one ever saw Charlie."

"Jason, I don't even know if there was nor even is a Charlie. And honestly, after what they did to your dad and to this family I don't care."

"You don't care if you have another grandson or granddaughter?" Jason asked in disbelief. Wouldn't you like to know?"

"No," she said coldly. "Not after what they did. I guess if it had happened some other way or maybe if I wasn't still so angry it would be different. I just don't know. Your grandfather used to say, 'You don't know what you don't know.' In this case, he couldn't have been any wiser."

She looked at Jason intently. He looked so much like his father she thought. She actually felt relief; she had held that story in for so many years, never sharing it with anyone. As much as she didn't want to at first, she was glad she had.

"I'm so sorry Jason for all of this; for your dad dying, your mom dying, Faith, Sandy, and my crazy foolishness. I'm sorry too if I let you down, if I'm not the grandmother that maybe you thought I was."

"It's okay, Gram, you did the best you could with what you knew. Mom and Dad dying is not your fault or anyone else's. You don't know, what you don't know. Right?"

"I guess you're right." She smiled at Jason. Tiny tears welled in her eyes, made more visible by the missing eyelashes that father time had claimed over her many years.

She reached over to him and he rose to accept her hand. He reached down over her tiny frame and whispered, "I love you Gram."

"I love you oh so much too, Dear," a small whimper in her voice. Clearing her throat, she pulled back.

"Now let's stop this nonsense," she said abruptly pulling away playfully. I'm an old woman and I don't need this stress," she said, her voice now prim and proper.

"You're right, Gram. What you need is an omelet from the Lansdowne Diner."

"I'll get my coat.'

"You're still in your nightgown."

"Well just tell them you checked me out for the day."

"Yeah, right, Gram," he said with a laugh. "You think the family was at the top of the gossip list back then? You haven't seen anything yet, if I take you drooling in there!"

Gram chuckled as she turned and walked briskly through the living room.

"I'll be right down."

Gram glided up the steps and changed into a polyester leisure suit popular among the older generation. Lime green was not Jason's color, but she was happy.

They spent the rest of the morning over breakfast and telling old stories about Chris. There was no need for small talk. Jason and Gram could talk for hours unforced and made up. They laughed over all of the funny things he did as a kid and as a young father. Later, she took Jason's' arm as they strolled down Lansdowne Avenue and window shopped at the old store fronts. The windows were filled with sale signs announcing the spring and summer sales. They side stepped the authentic gas lanterns and cobblestone pavers as they walked. Gram taking cautious baby steps, her beige heels avoiding cracks in the pavement. She loved being out and spending time with her grandson. The only living link to the man she had borne and then had to bury. It was a feat no parent ever wants to think of, let alone do.

When Jason dropped her off at her house late that afternoon, they shared a long warm embrace. The bond between grandmother and grandson had not been broken with this morning's earlier events. In fact, it had been shored up with the bricks and

mortar called family and solidified with its
main ingredient; love.

TWELVE

Jason heard an unfamiliar voice as he came into the house, a man's voice. Company? He came through the living room and rounded the corner into the kitchen. An older man, maybe in his early sixties sat across from Kristy. He was in a blue sports coat, gray slacks, white shirt, and a blue and gray stripped tie. His hair was thinning but neatly combed without the comb-over. He had gold rimmed glasses and his skin was a rosy red. His weathered hands clutched a mug filled with coffee.

Kristy saw him first, "Oh, this is my husband, Jason," she announced proudly as she got up to greet him with a kiss.

The stranger stood up, and flashed a pleasant nod hello. Jason saw the gun and badge on his waist. His somewhat large belly obscured the guns handle.

"How's Gram?" she asked following her kiss up with a hug.

Distracted by the stranger, Jason responded, "Good, we had a nice talk."

He changed direction. "And you are?"

"Hi Jason, I am Detective Anthony Loza, Upper Darby Police. Your wife's told me a lot about you. Thank you for your service to our country."

"Oh," the surprise of his new guest's presence was noticeable. He managed a polite, "Thanks" as he stood facing Loza.

Kristy sensed Jason's trepidation.

"Detective Loza is working the cold cases. He took over Fathiya's case since the original detective retired. I found his name on-line and called him to see what information there was about her. I told you I was going to do some research on her," Kristy said a bit uneasily. "That's what led me to the detective here. I called him after reading about some of the case on-line."

"Why is she a cold case? I thought she went back to Pakistan?"

"We don't know where she is."

"And don't you need a crime to have a cold case?"

"We don't even know if there's a crime. All's we have is a missing persons report filed by your dad and a truancy slip from her high school. And since the family has never cooperated one way or another, we shelved it with only the bit of information we had. Normally we don't hang on to these types of reports but it just didn't feel right to the original detective."

"I didn't think there was much information, period?" Jason replied.

"Well, there isn't. That's why when your wife called me I came right over to see if between us there was any new information. I have to be honest; I never thought I'd hear anything else about this case. I read about it several years ago and like my predecessor, I don't feel right just closing it."

"Information about what? She's gone, right?"

"We have no idea if she's gone away, dead or not to be honest and no evidence to say one way or another. Trying to track a kid half way around the world especially in a country that is as dysfunctional as Pakistan is hard. The story the family gave us is unverifiable and they refuse to cooperate."

"What about plane or immigration records?" Kristy asked.

"We checked; nothing in the US. However, the old man claimed she didn't leave from here and wouldn't tell us where she left from. And at the time you could cross into Canada or Mexico with no passport. Checked Canada; nothing.

"And Mexico?" Jason asked disgusted.

"The main cities, the big ones have good records, the small places shoddy at best. You're lucky if someone will answer the phone down there. So theoretically she could have flown out of some hole in Mexico and there'd be no way to verify it. I heard all the rumors; she's in hiding, she's living with family, and so on. There were even some rumors that maybe the old man killed her because she got pregnant. By the way, it was your dad that impregnated her right?"

"Saying it like that seems a little deviant, don't you think?" Jason responded, his tone defensive.

"I'm sorry, that came out wrong."

"Damn right."

"Jason Miller!" Kristy exclaimed. "What's wrong with you? Stop it."

"It's okay, Mrs. Miller, Jason's just standing up for his father. A trait I am sure he was proud of."

Jason ignored his subtle try at redemption.

Kristy was eager to move on. "Detective, what do you think; was she killed, missing, or murdered?"

"Well, unfortunately rumors don't solve crimes and here we have a lot of rumors about the old man and his old ways. Honor killing, shit like that. Oh, sorry," he said nodding at Kristy.

Kristy smiled. "It's all right, I've heard worse. I'm married to a sailor."

Detective Loza smiled back at her.

"You were saying?" an impatient Jason pressed.

"Because of their religious beliefs, Muslim I believe," he said looking down at his note pad, "there were all these internal policy rules for proceeding. They really tied my hands; since the Muslim religion was seemingly new to this country and people were still hung up on Iran and such the ACLU was all about religious freedom, blah, blah, blah. Like I said, we have no proof a crime was committed."

"Explain to me, Detective how is it in this country we can't do anything because we may upset the Muslim religion or any other for that matter?"

"Jason, I feel your pain."

"No, I don't think you do."

Detective Loza changed posture; he became very irritated. "Look guy, I don't write the laws, make the laws, or even think half of the laws we have are worth a rat's ass. But I enforce them and that's what I'm trying to do. What happened, what policy was, and what politics is going on now or umpteen years ago isn't my problem. Today and today's laws are. So you can be pissed, miserable, and cocky all you want, to a point. After that it needs to be about justice. As for the Muslim religion or any other; you're comparing apples to oranges. And for the record, I do feel your pain. I lost someone to a violent crime. My daughter was raped and murdered six years, four months, and twelve days ago. That's why I do cold cases. So don't you ever tell me what I do and don't feel." His stare cut through Jason who looked away slowly in shame. His over reactions had gotten the best of him.

A painful quiet came over the room. It was the pain only a father could feel for the loss of child and it was palpable.

"I am so, so sorry," Kristy empathized. "It must be so difficult."

"It is. I lost Karen and with her part of me. But I keep going, praying that someone will find the animal that did it. Like you, Jason, I want answers and I want justice. But being pissed, miserable, and cocky clouds your ability to see it objectively so you can win. Letting it consume you only lets them win. Don't let them win."

"I'm sorry," Jason pleaded sincerely.

"Apology accepted, now let's get back to business. I really want to help if I can, okay?'

"Okay."

"Detective, why not just go get Mr. Umar and ask him again what happened to her?" Kristy asked. "I mean, we talked to him."

"You did?" he pried eagerly.

"We met yesterday. He was not as eager to meet us when we introduced ourselves," Kristy replied.

"Pissed, huh?"

Jason spoke up. "Major league. Started yelling how my dad made her impure and stuff. Then guys came out with sticks yelling and screaming, hitting the counter. It was wild."

"Scary is more like it," Kristy clarified.

"Well, we simply have no evidence that a crime was committed, just a hunch. And it's not a crime to not want to talk to the police. So the fact the old man won't, can't be challenged. Unlike TV we just can't go and sweep folks up off the street. I'd like to. Factor in the country is at war, the anti this and anti that when it comes to the Muslim people and religion, and you have a recipe for a CNN nightmare. The last thing the UDP needs is news trucks camped out on West Chester Pike. Politics and law that's what it boils down to. At my level it's about solving crimes so we need to keep it on the down low until we have something concrete." Loza turned to Jason, "I was hoping that maybe I'd find some new information in that letter you found. While compelling, it didn't give me much more than I knew."

Jason looked at Kristy with a slight glare. He wasn't mad, just taken aback. He hadn't figured she'd shown him the letter. He hesitated and wasn't sure why. Maybe he was afraid Loza would judge his dad.

"Hey, Jason I'm not the enemy here and I'm not here to judge anyone. Your wife doesn't seem like she is either. I'm trying to find the truth. I understand your apprehension, but you need to trust me."

He looked at Loza, "It's just I don't want my dad to look bad."

"For what? For loving a woman that seemed to fall off the planet? Because you're looking for a child he may have had with her? Come on Jason, you're a smart guy. No one here, and I'm sure anywhere, would judge him other than what he was: a victim. I'm only trying to help."

Jason thought for a minute as he stared into the eyes of a man quite a bit older than his dad. He felt the apprehension in his body slowly lift and sensed the sincerity Loza had shown him.

"I'm sorry, Detective. I don't mean to be an ass and sorry for what I said earlier. It's been a long week."

"No problem. Like I said, I really do understand," he said. He moved right along, "So, what were you able to find out from your grandmother?" he asked.

Jason retold Grams story. Kristy sat captivated on every word of the love story.

"Did you guys ever talk to her?" he asked as he finished telling his tale.

"Yeah, we did. She just told me about all of the rumors; the baby, her dying, going to Pakistan, disappearing. It's so frustrating that no one outside of the Umar family seems to know anything."

"Detective?" Kristy asked.

"Yes?"

"What does your gut tell you?"

"Honestly, and this is off the record...." Jason and Kristy nodded their heads eagerly.

"I think the old man killed her and dumped her someplace."

"You do?"

"Sadly yes. I searched airlines around the world and immigration records the Feds have access to; nothing. I have searched every possible public information web site and every law enforcement database; nothing; I even made a special trip to Harrisburg and talked to a woman in vital statistics, nothing. No birth or death certificate was ever issued for a Charlie or Charles Ibn Umar or Fathiya Umar.

She has seemingly fallen off the face of the earth."

"Could it be that Charlie had a Muslim name? What if Charlie is a pseudo name for a more traditional Muslim name? I mean it's possible."

"We tried that angle and struck out there too."

"So, I guess what you're saying is Charlie doesn't exist?" Jason asked.

"Well at least not according to any records in fifty states or territories. But then again, there was a lot of inner circle pressure on her dad. He's old school, hard line Muslim. So it could be he hid her in the house, she delivered at home and somehow got the kid out of the state or country. Hell she could have had a miscarriage and went back to Pakistan. Or like my gut's telling me, he killed her and dumped her. The brother is some sort of home schooled doctor, so if she delivered, had an abortion, died, was murdered whatever; he was knee deep in it too and he could have provided the medical care. Maybe with asking questions and shaking the trees over there something new will come up. Hopefully we can get this solved and find the answers and closure you need."

"We'll see." The reply was unconvincing. "Thanks for all you're doing, we appreciate it."

"No, thank you for calling me. I was surprised as hell. I haven't heard the name

Fathiya in a long time. If you hear anything more, could you let me know?"

"Sure," Kristy replied. "We'd love to help if we can."

Loza slid a card over the table to Kristy and she picked it up and glanced over it. She handed it to Jason and he did the same.

"Well if that will be all, I'll let you two kids get back to your day," he said straining to squeeze his large body out from the chair.

"Take care, and thanks again for your service to our country," he said extending a hand to Jason.

They shook hands. "Thank you too for the information. And about what I said earlier, I'm really…."

"No need to say anything more, thanks." Jason could tell he was uneasy talking any more about the reference to his daughter.

Kristy walked Detective Loza to the door. Jason stayed behind in the kitchen. He was no closer to finding Charlie than he was two days ago. Now finding out that the UDP thought she was dead made his mind spin out of control. He opened the fridge door and grabbed a beer. It was Miller time he thought. No pun intended.

THIRTEEN

Jason lay on the futon staring at the ceiling, the morning sun peeking through the blinds. He had not slept well the night before. The metal bars that ran across the frame of the futon dug in to his back through the flimsy mattress. It was a little after six a.m. and he could hear his little cousins playing around. Bill and Maria where scurrying around the house preparing to leave for work. They had said their good-byes the night before at a family dinner Maria had quickly pulled together.

Everyone was there, Gram, Paul, and Alex. They had a wonderful evening laughing, talking and of course drinking. Kristy and Alex started making mojitos and by midnight were feeling pretty good. Those two were always coming up with a new drink special whenever they got together. Kristy was sleeping soundly. She was lying on her back with her left arm swathed up over her eyes. Her right arm was draped across her chest rising and falling with the rhythmic motions of her breathing. Too many mojitos. He smiled. You deserve to let your hair down too he thought as he looked over to her. They were going to sleep in and leave around lunch time to head back to North Carolina. He went back to work on Thursday and had an overnight duty, Kristy on Friday starting 12-hour nights for three weeks.

He was too tired to sleep and hadn't been able to find a good deep sleep that refreshed and made him whole again. He had given up on that type of sleep when his father was diagnosed with cancer spending day after day at the hospital, at the house, and in his own self-pity. Good sleep wasn't an option and wasn't on the priority list. He suffered through his insomnia with his mind spinning like the rainbow colored pinwheels he blew on as a child. He was going back to North Carolina with far more questions than answers. He wished he had been able to find out more about Fathiya and Charlie; however he had come to the end of the line. Maybe it's time to put it behind you, he thought.

The gray and black clouds parted as they drove through Rocky Mount. Rays of brilliant sunshine broke through and provided a bright golden sheen on the wet concrete highway, I-95 was unusually empty of traffic. The array of cars and trucks that plagued the roadway was nowhere to be found. Jason argued with himself as to whether it was because of the rain or the gas prices that now topped $3.94. He flip-flopped back and forth. It was an argument he couldn't win one way or another but it kept him busy; and awake. Kristy had slept almost all the way home nursing her hangover. When she finally woke-up she had a small snack, chatted with Jason and then buried her face in a P.J. Parrish paperback. Jason wanted to get home as quickly as possible and Kristy had no appetite so they didn't stop for the customary highway diner food. Nine hours after their journey began Jason swung the Honda in to the parking lot. He got out of the car and stretched his stiff and tired body and looked over at the windshield covered in multicolored moth parts blown flat by the rushing air. He'd need to run it through the wash in the next day or two or the hot North Carolina sun would bake it in making it nearly impossible to get off.

He was dreading the long night ahead of him. He needed to get his uniform washed and ironed and then pack an overnight bag with fresh clothes for Friday's work day. Duty was not his favorite part of being in the military however it was something that had to be done. At most hospital commands, everyone enlisted stood duty until you made Senior Chief. Officers had a similar hierarchy. They stood duty until they reached the rank of Commander; unless they were line officers in which case they had their own way of doing things. At times it seemed like busy work that could be done by hiring one or two civilian employees who liked working nights.

Jason stood the Mate-of-the Day watch. A big fancy title for phone answerer. He had his four hours answering the phone on the Quarterdeck until his relief arrived. He liked the first watch from 2000 until 2400. This way he could get five or six solid hours of sleep until reveille. The mid watch, 0001 until 0400 sucked. It was like being up all night. It was up to the Chief-of the Day to make the schedule. Some were fairer than others who played favorites. Jason never used his father's name, rank or status in the command to get any special treatment. If he felt like he was getting it, he backed off or recused himself. Conversely, if he felt he was getting screwed because of his father's name, he addressed it with equal furor.

It was well after two a.m. before Jason finally fell into bed. The soft white sheets and the comfort of the memory foam wrapped him in a cocoon of pleasure. Every part of his body relaxed. The tension in his muscles slowly slipped away. He snuggled up behind Kristy who had gone to bed a few hours before, the effects of her mojito mixology lesson still lingering. He kissed the back of her neck.

"I love you, kitten," he whispered. His usual insomnia would not be a concern tonight. Within minutes he was fast asleep.

FOURTEEN

As he came over the bridge in Sneads Ferry to the back gate, the entrance to the base was deserted. That was one benefit of working out at Court House Bay, little to no traffic in the mornings. The main gate on highway 24 was a mad dash of traffic and congestion that could back up all the way to the Jacksonville by-pass, some two miles away.

The young Marine waved him through the gate and he drove along the winding road to the clinic.

"Welcome back, stranger," was the greeting Chief Sutton gave him.

"Good to see you. Get everything worked out?"

"I guess, Chief." Jason didn't believe his own lie, but it was easier than trying to explain the past week's events. "Thanks for the extra couple of days, it really helped out."

"No sweat," he shot back.

Jason knew deep down that it really wasn't a help. It turned out to be more of a problem with so many more unanswered questions and new emotions to deal with.

"Just let me know if you need anything else, okay."

"Yes, Chief, I will."

The day dragged on and on. Every Marine that came into the clinic seemed to talk slower and slower. Their mouths moved and the words hung on the thick dry air blowing from the vents of the old air conditioner that never cooled the clinic even in the mild mid-May heat. Finally 1500 came and he was on the road to duty. He drove the twelve miles to the main hospital and snaked up and down the multiple rows of the parking lot until he finally landed a space in staff parking.

He checked in at the Quarter Deck and checked the duty roster. The Chief-of-the Day was Chief Daniels.

Chief Evan Daniels was one of the junior sailor's favorite senior enlisted. He worked in Patient Administration Department and oversaw almost every aspect of the administration of the hospital. He had been to Iraq with Jason's dad and they had been friends right up to the end. He was a fair but firm Chief. He believed that rules were written in black and white, but we lived in color so decisions were made with a more common sense approach. There was always a need for Navy regulations, but he also understood that you needed to view every situation separately and to their own merits.

Jason scrolled down the roster. He had the 0001 to 0400 watch. Could this day get any worse he thought? He sat around the Quarter Deck until muster at 1600. He gave Kristy a quick call to see how she was feeling.

"Fine. I think I am finally alcohol free," she said giggling. "Just getting my scrubs ready for tomorrow night. Sure wish you were home."

"Me too, Baby. But we have all day tomorrow."

At 1600 on the dot, the duty crew lined up for muster, and Chief Daniels went over the day's events, the threat condition, and any inclement weather advisories.

"All clear and all quiet," he reported. "Let's keep it that way."

"Aye-aye, Chief," was chorused from the sailors standing by.

Jason was off until his mid watch. He could go to bed, read a book, study for advancement; pretty much anything except leave the hospital compound. On this day he decided dinner was in order.

He headed down to the galley. As he approached the galley doors he stopped and read the menu posted on the door; Swiss steak. One of his favorites. This day wasn't so bad after all.

He grabbed a tray and asked for the Swiss steak. The butter scotched colored caramelized onions, the dark brown gravy smothered over the mashed potatoes, and a heaping spoonful of green beans rounded out his meal. He poured a glass of milk, paid the $3.25 for his meal and headed to an open table. There was a group of civilian employees sitting across the galley laughing and talking loudly. Jason was immediately annoyed. Couldn't they keep it down so he could enjoy his meal? He grabbed the remote control off the table beside him and turned on the television. Scrolling through the channels he found News 14-Carolina, the local twenty-four hour news channel. Weather on the ones was their big promotion although the weather forecast was usually wrong.

Jason settled back into his dinner and the noise from the other side of the galley slowly faded away. His focus was on the news and what was going on around the crystal coast, until that name caught his attention.

"You can bet yourself on that, Lucien!"

Jason froze. That name, I know that name. It was in the letter. Lucien. That was his name. He scanned the room trying to find one of his missing links. His eyes stopped at the entrance to the galley. Standing right outside the galley door was a tall slender black man. He was wearing checkered polyester pants, and white shirt stained with food and a starched white apron. He had a chef's cap on with tufts of gray and black hair spiking out on either side. He was laughing and waving down the hall.

"I'll see you tomorrow, man," he said again as he waved his arms frantically.

Jason sprang from his seat and charged through the door. He ran into the hall and heard the sound of sliding metal as the elevators closed.

He turned to the slender man, "Excuse me, who we're you just talking to?"

The man was caught off guard at Jason's demanding and abrupt approach.

"The man, who is he?"

"Whoa, whoa, slow down. What do you want, man?"

"Who were you talking to?" Jason demanded.

"Who the hell are you?"

"That name you just yelled; Lucien, who is it?"

"Hey man, why don't you mind your own damn business and stay out of peoples conversations?"

"I just need to know who it was. It's really important. I'm not trying to start anything, I just really need to know," he pleaded.

The cook looked at him judging his honesty. "It was Dr. Wilton."

"Dr. Wilton?"

"Yeah, man, Dr. Lucien Wilton. He works up on the nut-hut."

"The Mental Health Clinic?"

"The one and the same."

"Thanks, man. Thanks a lot," Jason fired back as he turned and sprang down the hall.

"You're welcome," he mumbled in confusion.

Jason hurried with a sense of urgency. He needed to get up to the third floor and find Dr. Wilton. Has another dot been connected? Was Dr. Wilton the psychiatrist Dad had been seeing? Maybe he knows something about Charlie. More questions than answers.

He got to the elevator and pressed the button. That uneasy feeling when he gets anxious came over him again. The same one he had reading the letter for the first time. His heart started pounding and he felt his throat tighten. He swallowed hard trying to force his throat open. He needed to calm down and catch his breath even though he didn't think he could.

"Come on damn it!" he yelled out, pressing the button several times in rapid succession. The ding-ding of the elevator arriving slowed his impatient anger. The doors opened and he shot in and hit the third floor button with the same ferocity as he did the call button.

The elevator took its time and was in no need to rush. Jason paced back and forth trying to calm himself and keep his heart from exploding. It felt as if like hundreds of questions were flooding his mind and he couldn't just grab one out of the air to ask. The door opened and he hustled out to the left. Most of the overhead florescent lights had been turned off; only every third one was lit in an effort to save energy. Up ahead he saw a figure pass under the yellow flicker of a dying lamp.

"Dr. Wilton?" He gulped hard, his tight throat preventing a louder question to be yelled out.

Jason cleared his throat. "Dr. Wilton?" This time his voice was distinct and much louder.

The figure stopped and turned around slowly. "Yes, that's me," he let out with a heavy uninterested sigh.

Jason was walking briskly to catch up.

"Can I help you?" an agitated voice uttered from the shadow.

"Yes, Sir, I'm sorry. My name is HM2 Miller. My da....:

"Was Senior Chief Miller, right?'

Jason was caught off guard. It was as though he was expecting him or something. He slowed his approach and asked cautiously, "So you knew him?'

"I'd like to think I knew him well."

"I was hoping to talk to you about him."

"Walk with me."

"Okay."

They started down the hall towards the Clinic.

"What can I help you with?" he asked. His tone was therapeutic and comforting. It was a complete opposite of their brief introduction a few moments before.

"I was hoping to get some information on my dad?"

"What kind of information?"

"Well, I was wondering what he may have told you about my family."

"HM2, your father told me a lot of things. And you, more than anyone should know I can't tell you anything because of privacy laws, HIPAA specifically."

HIPPA, better known as the Health Insurance Portability and Accountability Act enacted in 1996, places strict guidelines on the release of an individual's medical information even after death.

"Well I figured since he passed away you could talk to me about him."

"Sorry. The only person I can speak to or release information to would be the next-of-kin or executor of the estate. Do you know who that is?"

Jason sure did. It was the one person who was never going to give Jason access to the information; Sandy. And he couldn't go asking because she may not know anything about Faith and Charlie.

"Yes, it's my step mom."

"Well, she's the only one I can talk to unless she signs off on your access. I'm sorry."

"I don't see her giving me access. We don't really see eye-to-eye."

"So, I've heard."

"But, it's more complicated than that," Jason pleaded.

"Then I suggest you both go to counseling and work out your differences," he scoffed. He reached the solid wood door to the Clinic. Looking down at the speckled white floor, he pulled hard. Its heavy weight pulled back against him as he struggled to squeeze himself through and end his conversation with Jason.

"Did he ever talk to you about Charlie? Does the fact that he had another child interest you?" Jason sputtered out. He once again felt his throat squeeze shut with anger and fear. "I found this letter and I need help figuring it out."

Dr. Wilton stopped solid in place. His jaw clenched. The letter. He raised his head and looked forward leaving his back to Jason. He stared at the front counter that had recently been fortified with security glass.

"I am interested. Where is this letter?" he asked intrigued.

"So you know about it?"

"I do. Where is it?" his voice more annoyed.

"First, what did he tell you?" Jason's confidence level was rising. The reaction from Dr. Wilton signaled he knew more, a lot more.

"If you want my help, I'll need to see the letter."

Jason thought for a moment. What leverage would he have if he showed him the letter? He could read it and still tell him nothing. He hesitated; it was a risk he had to take.

"It's at my house."

"And what does it say?"

"It written to someone named Charlie. Then it goes on to talk about a girl named Faith, short for Fathyia and…."

"What did you say?" Dr. Wilton burst out. He swung around his lips pursed and eagerly moved towards Jason.

Jason backed up. His voice cracked in fear, "I said Fathiya his girlfriend, and I think their kid, Charlie."

"Relax HM2. I'm sorry if my reaction startled you. It's just that I haven't heard the name Fathiya for a while. Normally she was referred to as Faith.

"Your dad —," he paused trying to find the right words. "He was a complicated man. We discussed a great number of things, but none seemed more important than his issues with Faith and Charlie.

"What issues?"

Dr. Wilton realized he had said too much, "I told you, I can't talk to you about that."

"Then what the hell can you tell me?" Jason lashed out steeping towards the doctor.

"Hold it right there HM2! Calm down!"

"Calm down! Are you kidding me?" he hollered. His voice bounced off the empty walls and echoed down the lowly passageway.

"A minute ago you're acting like I found the Holy Grail of letters and now once again you're telling me, 'I can't tell you.' Do you realize what I have been through the last four days? I found a letter to a kid I didn't know existed. I went to Philadelphia and found out Faith was actually Fathyia, almost got my head bashed in by her militant father and his friends, and finally discovered who the hell my dad referred to as Lucien in the same letter. And you're telling me to calm down? No, Doc! Screw that. I'm sick and tired of calming down, not getting answers and getting the run-around."

"My, my you've been a busy boy this week," Dr. Wilton said somewhat sarcastically.

"Don't patronize me, Doc."

"Look," Dr. Wilton began "I'm not patronizing you. I'm actually giving you credit. It's refreshing to see someone try to find the truth. Most people accept things at face value because it's easy. They don't want to upset the balance of things in their life. Maybe it's because you're in the unique situation of being on active duty and serving at the same duty station as your father; maybe not. Either way I give you credit. However, you're going about this the wrong way."

"Oh really?"

"Really."

"Then what the hell is the right way?" he begged.

"Go to your step-mom, tell her what you told me and give her the opportunity to allow you consent to look at the records or at the very least give permission for me to tell you what you need to know. You may be surprised."

"She won't," Jason replied with confidence.

"Have you asked her?"

"I just found all this out, I haven't had time."

"Well find time. That's the only way you'll get any information out of this Clinic or me, period."

"I can't believe this," Jason said with a sneer. The idea was stupid. Sandy would never tell him anything.

"HM2, I will tell you this. There's a lot more to this story and a lot more to your father. I am not telling you he had anymore secrets or was a bad guy. On the contrary, he was a very good and noble man who stood up for more than you could imagine. And it cost him dearly in ways I can't tell you about right now. I will tell you that he died with a clear conscience and lightened, not heavy, heart. He was able to forgive himself for things he had no control over. And he died with a great love and affection for you, your mom, Sandy and your two half-brothers. Go home, HM2 and...."

"I have duty."

"Fine, go back to duty. Take some time to think about what I'm telling you and go talk to your stepmom. You have the power to fix this."

"What exactly am I trying to fix?" Jason said pouting.

"Your relationship with your stepmom; or lack thereof. And this feeling you have of betrayal and anger towards your father. He was a man you admired and loved your whole life. Now you've uncovered a secret and you're pissed at him."

"Your damn right I am!"

"Then fix it. Take my advice and find the answers you want or just need. I will not give you the answers. Part of my job is helping people identify what the problem is and guiding them so they fix it."

"So now you're analyzing me?"

"I guess if I need to. And given your reaction, it may not be a bad idea especially in a time where you could be called to deploy at a moment's notice."

"What does deploying have to do with it?'

"A lot. Do you really want to take all of the anger and hostility you have in your heart and on your mind into combat? Maybe fixing things here and now will prevent a tragedy later on."

"What the hell are you talking about?" Jason asked perplexed.

"Like I said, my job is helping people identify what the problem is and guiding them into finding answers. In your case, and that of so many others, it should be done now rather than later."

"Well thanks for the offer, but no." Jason turned around and stepped to the fire exit and pushed the panic bar hard. The door flung open and crashed into the door stop.

"Good night," Wilton said.

He never looked back at the man who held all the answers but refused to reveal them. His mind raced as he muttered aloud, "Damn it Dad why did you do this to me?"

FIFTEEN

Jason spent the rest of his duty night in deep thought. Although he hated the mid-watch, he welcomed the peace and quiet that came with it this night. His mind revolved around what Dr. Wilton had said, ". . . you have the power to fix this." Fix what he kept asking himself? The way Jason saw it; Dr. Wilton had the power to fix it, solve it even.

Just answer my damn questions, he thought. The phone rang. Jason's groggy voice recited the customary greeting; "Naval Hospital Quarter Deck, HM2 Miller speaking. How may I help you, Sir or Ma'am?" The wife of a young Marine wanted to know if her husband was in the ER. He had cut his hand and needed stitches.

"One second, ma'am, I'll transfer you," he said. He pushed the flash button and dialed the ERs extension. When he heard it ring he hung up. Transfer complete. He returned to his racing mind rehashing the previous day's events and trying to find a way, any way around talking to Sandy about it. Maybe he could forge her signature or just tell her she needed to sign some papers so the hospital could achieve Dad's medical records. The hospital was a year or more behind on achieving records, so that wouldn't work. He ran every scheming possibility through his mind. He had to get the information he needed to finally put his mind and heart at ease.

Records? Oh my God he thought sitting straight up in his chair. That's it. His medical records. Why didn't he think of this before? He could go down to the records vault and see if his dad's record was there. What an idiot he thought. Why didn't you think of this sooner?

He knew a few Corpsman who worked in records and thought he could get a hook up. He grabbed the duty roster and scanned who was working in the Admissions Department on the night shift. They had access to the records vault. "Come on, come on," he muttered aloud. Bingo! HN Wade was working. *There is a God,* Jason thought.

He logged on to CHCS and looked up his dad's social security number; he'd need that to find the record. The Composite Health Care System is the Navy and Marine Corps electronic medical record. This was highly unethical not to mention highly illegal but at this point he didn't really care. Now to get a hold of Wade.

Brian Wade and Jason got along really well. He used to work at Caron Clinic with him and they'd work-out and have lunch together from time to time. He suddenly was wide awake, his internal battery recharged. Four-a.m. could not come sooner. Jason's brilliant idea supercharged him even though the simplicity of it seemed too good to be true.

A little after four-a.m., HN Johnson showed up on the Quarter-Deck to assume the watch. Jason had never seen a black guy with bed-head before and was taken aback by the contorted afro. His hair was pushed in on one side; flattened with the impression of the vinyl pillow. The other side looked like a fine black Brillo pad with the same wiry and wrinkled texture. His uniform looked like he slept in it and his tie was dangling too low, minus a tie tack. His belt buckle was all scratched up and his web belt had frayed ends spiking out of the end. HN Johnson was the first impression you got of the Naval Hospital when you came across the Quarter Deck. No wonder some people thought the hospital was a dump and a meat shop.

"What's up, man? Sleep well?" Jason asked.

"Terrible. Those racks are lumpy as hell. It was sleeping on a bag of dirty ass sneakers. I hate this place, man," Johnson said shaking his head.

"Could be worse, could be in a sand trap in Iraq," Jason wisecracked.

"I'll take it. No duty there," Johnson said walking over to the desk.

"But you get shot at."

"Touché."

"Hey, man could you do me a favor?"

"Wuz up?"

"Could you page the Admissions clerk to medical records, I have to pick up something."

"Sure, HM2, done."

"Thanks, man, have a good one," Jason said hurrying away.

"You too, bro," he grumbled, the sleep still apparent in his voice.

He walked briskly down the hall past the mini exchange and the Lighthouse café. He made a left and proceeded past the empty offices. The fresh scent of cleanser caught his nose. The cleaning crews had been busy throughout the night refreshing the stale air and vacuuming away the previous day's dirt from the commercial grade carpet in the offices and clinics. He came to the end of the long hall and made a right into the Medical Records Department. It was brightly lit, but eerily quiet. He walked over to the counter and peered in; no one.

"Can I help you?" was the inquiry from behind.

Startled, Jason turned quickly to see HN Wade sashay in the door. "What's up Wade?" he acknowledged.

"Hey, what's up, Jason? Did you page me?"

"I did. How you've been, man?"

"Good, man. You?"

"Alright I guess; working nights, going to school over at Coastal during the day."

"That's cool, that's where I graduated from. What are you studying?'

"Just an AA in Allied Health; only one semester to go."

"That's awesome, man."

"So what can I do ya for?"

"Well I need a hook-up."

"Okay," he asked cautiously.

"I need to see if my dad's medical record is still here. I need to take a look at it."

"Oh, man that's a big favor."

Jason had rehearsed his lie.

"I just got back some test results from New Hanover and it looks like I may have some kind of genetic disorder." Telling Wade the results were from an outside hospital meant Wade couldn't look it up in CHCS to check out his story. "I was hoping to see if Dad had it. Kristy is kind of freaking out thinking I could pass it on."

"She pregnant?"

"Nah, not yet, man. That's why I need to check. She wants to wait until I know for sure. And you know my step mom and I are on the outs, so if I waited for her to get it for me I'd be retired."

"I want to help you but I don't know, man. I don't want to get in trouble."

"I don't want to either. How's this; what if you just unlock the door and I'll do the rest. You just go on your merry way. If anyone asks, I'll tell them the door was open and I helped myself. I'll take the heat man I promise. Plus who's around? It's like four thirty in the morning."

Wade thought a minute weighing his options.

"All right, man. Just promise me if you get caught it's on you."

"You got my word, dude, I promise."

Wade pulled the key from his pocket and walked over to the door. "You owe me big time for this, man," as he slid the key into the lock. With a swift turn to the left, the door opened. With the same urgency, he withdrew it and turned away. As he walked briskly out of the records Department he reiterated to Jason, "Remember, you found it this way."

"It's all good, man," Jason reassured him as Wade disappeared into the hall.

Jason moved the door inward and slipped into the records vault. He closed it behind him turning the knob so the bolt mechanism didn't strike the plate. With the door secure, Jason pulled a strip of paper from his pocket. On it, he had written the last four digits of his dad's social security number he had looked up on CHCS earlier.

He walked through the throngs of records. At any given time there were more than 30,000 records on the shelf. Active duty, retired, and family members all crammed on eight mechanical shelves that ran the entire length of the room. He approached the center aisle and pushed the button. The sleeping motor came alive and the shelf slowly inched open. The wheels squeaked on the old rusty track and the sound amplified a hundred times louder. It was like opening a cellophane bag in a movie theater; it just echoed no matter how hard you tried to keep it quiet.

Jason got scared and thought about leaving. Once again, his nerves started to get the best of him. His heart was fluttering and his throat tensed up. He had come this far, no turning back. The wheels stopped automatically when the shelf was fully extended. Jason wandered in between the cabinets and scanned for 6865. "Come out, come out where ever you are," he whispered under his breath. He found it. There were several of them. Military medical records are stored by color based on the second to last number of the social security number. Since the second to the last number was six, these records were white. He reached in and pulled out one record at a time. On the third try he found it: Miller, Christopher A. It hadn't been archived yet. Glad they're behind on archiving he thought.

He pulled it down and stared at it for a brief second. He didn't have the time to get nostalgic; he had to get what he came for and get the hell out of there. He couldn't take the record with him that would be worse than just looking through it. He flipped it open and started scanning the SF-600's.

The Standard Form 600 is the Chronological Record of medical care. It was opened at boot camp in Great Lakes, IL and closed when you died, separated from the Navy, or retired. It was then archived to the repository in St. Louis, Missouri basically forever. That was of course if the military hospital did what they were supposed to do by regulation and archive it. He looked over the top page; flu, sinus infection, nothing from Mental Health. He picked up a stack and fanned through them stopping in no particular place. He glanced over the page, again nothing.

"What the hell are you doing?" came the authoritative voice.

Jason slammed the record shut and dropped it to his side clutching it tightly.

Chief Daniels was standing at the head of the row, looking down the row at him. "I said what the hell are you doing here at o-dark-thirty in the morning?"

"Nothing." How stupid of an answer was that he thought.

"Nothing?" the Chief corrected giving Jason an out.

"Actually, I was looking at a record."

"Who's?"

Jason hesitated. It did not matter if he told him now or in thirty seconds, the wrath would probably be the same.

"My dad's, Chief."

"Cough it up, Bonehead," he ordered raising his hand and snapping his fingers.

Jason walked over to him; he didn't expect the Chief to come to him.

"Here ya go, Chief."

"Go to my office, HM2," the stern voice ordered.

"Yes, Chief." Jason walked by Chief Daniels, his throat narrowing more and more and the end of his Naval career flashed before his eyes. Kristy is going to kill me was his last thought as the Chief's door closed behind them, Jason standing in front of his desk.

SIXTEEN

"So, what's going on?" Chief Daniels asked as he placed the record down on his desk and sat down opposite Jason. Jason just stood there looking at him; he was at a complete loss for words. A hot flash engulfed his head and then he felt it; a torrent of emotions so overwhelming he could feel his eyes begin to well and his upper lip quiver.

'No he thought, no, not now. You can't do this. Get a grip, please.' It was no use though, it was going to happen. A single tear ran down his face, then another, and another. Suddenly and uncontrollably he began to cry. All of the emotions he had hidden deep down in places he never talked about began to flood from his body. He had not had a good cry in many years. He didn't even really cry when his dad died, maybe because he was expecting it. He had never cried like this in front of strangers, ever. He never allowed himself to lose control in public only in private.

When his father died Jason stood stoically at his bedside as the last breath left his body. He hid in the bathroom right after that and cried alone. Later, he looked over the shoulder of the Funeral Director as the visitation waged on for three hours without losing it and he ignored the playing of Taps as the flag draped coffin was saluted for the final time. After he got home and stood in the shower, he cried for the man he loved; alone.

How could he let this happen now? He tried to stop himself, it was no use. He raised his hands and buried his face into them. Chief Daniels sighed and sat back in his big leather chair.

"Sit down, Jason" he said. Jason lowered his hands and stepped back a few steps to the blue sofa lined against the wall. It had a sheet, two blankets, and a pillow stacked on it.

"Try not to snot on my bed," Daniels insisted as he tossed Jason a box tissue. "They're the Light House for the Blind brand so they'll scrape the skin right off your face."

Jason caught the box and pulled four out in quick succession. He set the bland blue box beside him on the couch, and dragged the tissue through his eyes. He blew hard into the wad collecting snot in a steady flow. His sobbing continued.

The events of the past week had taken their toll. Thoughts of his mom, Sandy, and the two boys who wouldn't know their father added more intensity to his cry. He cried for his own self destructive behavior that had overtaken him this past week. Memories good and bad, old and new raced through his mind. Why is this happening to me now? After what seemed like an eternity, he reached for another handful of tissue from the box on his lap. He wiped his face.

"These things are like sandpaper." He snorted.

"Told you those things will rip the skin right off your face. What I never understood was how a blind person could figure out how to make a tissue or work the machines. No wonder they burn; they're working in a sand paper factory and don't know it," Daniels joked trying to put Jason at ease.

Jason smiled. He was feeling better and very relieved, even though he knew he could be in some serious trouble.

"You alright?" Daniels asked.

"Yes. No. I don't know, Chief."

"Alright then. So what's going on? Obviously this is coming from some place and not just because I found you looking at your dad's records."

Jason let out a deep breath. He spent the next hour methodically taking Chief Daniels through the whole story from the letter; to the brain storm he had hours before. When he was done, they both sat in silence. Chief Daniels thought for a moment taking in everything Jason had told him. He spoke with a sense of purpose.

"First thing is I kind of agree and disagree with Doc Wilton; you should talk to your stepmom. She may know, she may not, and you may or may not find out one way or another. It's not for you to tell her. Would you want to know your dead wife had a love child twenty-something years ago?"

"No."

"But on the flip side it's not about a love child, it's about missing family. If you really are serious about finding the truth, then go and talk to her. Nothing has ever been accomplished in silence."

"Second, what I do know is that you are driving yourself crazy and putting the hard work you've put into your career in jeopardy because you're not thinking straight. You're driving hard to the wall on a hunch. And third, when you took the advancement exam for HM2 or HM3 for that matter, did you have a section on health records?"

Confused by the last question, Jason answered meekly, "Yes, why?"

"Do you remember if you scored well?"

"I don't remember, Chief."

"Well I'm guessing you didn't, you boob," he cracked. "If you had you would have known that mental health notes are not kept in the permanent medical record, they're kept in a secondary record maintained in the clinic." He pointed to his desk where his dad's record sat.

"There's nothing in that record except blank 600's that just say he showed up and talked to them. The actual objective findings from the wizard are not kept in there."

"Oh. I guess I forgot about that," a dejected Jason admitted. How could he have been so stupid he thought?

"See what I mean? This whole mess is clogging your judgment and I'm telling you if you don't get a handle on it, it's going to screw up you career, your marriage, and what remains of your family." Daniels leaned across the desk and spoke with personal sincerity. "Jason, I've known you a long time, even before you came into the Navy. I loved your dad like a brother. He was one of the best mentors and friends a guy could ask for. He would smack you silly up if he knew you were acting this dumb." He sat back, his tone more professional. "So, this is the deal; this event never happened. It's between you and me. No one will ever know but us. If there's one thing I learned from your old man is everyone makes a shit-sandwich now and then but the trick is not to eat it. So throw your sandwich away and get yourself together. Go see your stepmom if you really need to. See what she knows and try to come to an agreement on you seeing his records or talking to the doc. In the meantime, I'll throw some feelers out and see what I can do to get you some access should all else fail. No promises, but I'll see what I can do. Okay?"

"Yes, Chief. Thank you so much, I really appreciate it. And I'm sorry about the whole record thing, crying, all of it."

"That's what I'm here for. You've had a rough time with a lot to take on. It's all good. If you need anything else come find me. I'm always here as you can see," he declared awkwardly as he swooped the room with his arm.

"I'm sort of living here. I have my own crap-sandwich I'm trying to throw out...."

"I'm sorry again, Chief."

"Don't be, it's all good. Gretchen and I don't see eye to eye when it comes to believing whether PTSD exists. Obviously since I don't and she does, I get to live out of my office. A long story for another time and another pay grade," he said taping the anchors on his collar.

Jason knew that Chiefs don't share much with anyone other than fellow Chiefs. He needed to wait many more years to get the chance to join the world's most selective fraternity; that of the Chief Petty Officer.

"Now get out of here. Go get cleaned up and get to muster, duty ends in about an hour." Daniels told him as he stood from his chair. "Then get your butt home and enjoy your day off."

Jason stood up and reached his hand out. Daniels took it. "Thanks again"

"Like I said it's all good. Someday I'll need something, and you'll help me out, just like the mob. Except we don't break legs, we just give you a terrible evil," he said, grinning.

Jason smiled and shook his hand. Chief Daniels had saved him. He spent time listening, giving advice, and not criticizing him. While he did point out Jason's stupid mistakes, he seemed more interested in helping him. He was a genuine Chief and Jason felt it. It reminded him of his dad and how at times they could talk about anything. Even if his dad didn't agree he always told Jason what he thought without condemning him or patronizing him. Maybe their relationship wasn't the Father Knows Best type, but it was better than most.

Jason left the office and headed out the door. The hall was coming to life with sailors and civilians that worked in the hospital. He dodged people left and right and headed down the passageway until he got to the staff locker room. Once inside he looked at himself in the mirror. His eyes were puffy; his face was red. Anyone with sense could tell he had been crying. Jason didn't care. Although he looked like hell he felt reborn in a way. The cry had done him some good and was maybe a fresh start since he always hid how he really felt about everything:

He never made love; he was intimate,
he never hated; he disliked,
he never cried, he wept and so on.

This sudden feeling of liberation scared him a bit. Maybe because it was new and a passing feeling that would wear off or because it made him more vulnerable, he wasn't sure. What he did know is that he wanted to continue on the ride the words of Chief Daniels; *"Get yourself together, Jason."*

He showered, shaved, and put on a fresh uniform and reported to morning muster. When he was done he walked to his car and went home. He wanted to spend the day with

Kristy before she started her night shift at the hospital. He wanted to tell her about everything that had happened the night before and wanted her opinion about the records, about talking to Sandy, and about him. Chief Daniels had given him a lot to think about, now he needed to. But he also needed Kristy's advice. Was he thinking right? Was he in too deep? Was he hurting his dad? There was no one better than Kristy to tell him the truth.

He pulled into the driveway and headed for his reserved spot. He gathered up his dirty uniform and his shaving kit. At the front door he propped himself in the door jam and fumbled for the key. Before he could get all the way through the door, he dropped his uniforms and spilled his shaving kit.

"For the love of Pete!" he hollered. He picked up his mess and balanced it to the sofa where he dumped it. He walked down the hall and flicked the switch to his left that brought the small kitchen to life. Dirty dishes were piled in the sink along with the remnants of a half-eaten frozen pizza. Kristy had probably been up late so she could sleep longer into the day. This way when she started her shift at seven p.m., she could stay awake all night. After loading the dishwasher and wiping down all of the counters, he took the trash out to the dumpster. Back in the house, he grabbed a Sunny Delight and headed upstairs to check on Kristy.

Kristy was snuggled in bed with the new blue comforter entangling her body. She was in a deep sleep. Jason stopped in the doorway and watched her sleep. She was so beautiful, her skin so clear and soft, her body so perfectly sculpted. He wondered why she chose him when she could have any man. How did he get so lucky? He tiptoed in around the bed behind her, set his drink on the side table and slid into bed behind her spooning her warm skin. Her limp body came alive and she reached her arm back and stroked Jason's leg.

"You better hurry up and get out of here before my husband gets home," she teased.

"I think he'll be late, traffic's a mess on Western Boulevard. Maybe I could sneak a kiss?"

"Oh all right," she purred rolling over to embrace him. They shared a passionate kiss with the intense passion two young lovers.

"Whoa, where did that come from?" she said as she began to kiss his chest.

"I've been saving it for a rainy day," he said.

"Then bring on hurricane season!" she exclaimed. "Man I love your kisses so much!"

"I love you, Kristy."

"I love you too, my darling," she whispered squeezing his body. "How was your duty?"

"Interesting?"

"Really?"

"Yeah, a lot went on."

"Like what?" she asked.

Jason told her about the previous night's events and the grand finale with Chief Daniels finding him rooting through the records. He was hesitant to tell her about his emotional meltdown since he rarely, if ever showed that type of emotion. In the end though he decided to tell her. He wanted her to know everything even if that meant exposing his vulnerabilities and his poor judgment. He finished talking, proud of himself that he could be so open. They both lay still and silent, their breaths in sync.

"Sounds like it was an interesting night," Kristy said breaking the stillness of the room.

"It was. So what do you think?"

"Well," she began, "I think you do want a relationship with Sandy even if you won't admit it. I also think you need to know what that doctor knows about your dad, and I think I am very proud of you for finally letting someone in."

This was not the reaction Jason thought he'd get. At the very least he thought Kristy would be somewhat pissed he had almost lost his career. Instead she seemed happy with him.

"I'm not going to lie," she continued, "I wish it had been me that you first opened up too, rather than the Chief but I'm glad you finally did."

"I'm opening up to you now, though," he said.

"Yeah I know. It's a girl thing I guess and a wife thing. I wanted it to be me. Either way I'm happy you did."

"Are you mad?" Jason questioned.

"No, no, baby. I'm proud of you; I guess I'm being a bit selfish. Like I said, it's a girl thing. I think this whole Charlie thing, the talk with your Grandmother, Sandy and the kids moving, and so on, has been a lot on you. But I also think it's been good for you and good for us."

"Good for us how?"

"Here we are; we're telling each our feelings and sharing with each other our deep thoughts. Like I said it's a girl thing."

"Well how is it been good for me?"

"Again, you're sharing so much and I guess I feel more connected, more inside your head."

"What do you mean, more connected?" Jason asked abruptly as he sat up. Kristy slid off his chest and sat up too, holding the sheet up over her breasts. "Relax, babe."

"No, what do you mean more connected? You weren't before?"

"Yes, I was. But I always knew you had a side to you no one, not even I, have ever been allowed in to. It's not a bad thing, Jason. It's a good thing."

He realized he was being defensive. His old ways of paranoia and self-doubt were still very much there.

"I'm sorry, I just thought you meant you weren't happy with me," he said.

"Quite the contrary, I am so much in love with you and I couldn't be happier." She stroked his cheek with her left hand, her soft fingers against his face.

"You mean everything to me. I love you."

"I love you too, I'm sorry I over reacted."

"It's okay."

They snuggled back down under the sheets, Kristy pressed firmly against Jason's body. They drifted off to sleep with the womp, womp, womp of the ceiling fan singing them a lullaby. Around ten-o'clock Kristy slid out of bed and into the shower, the sound of her hair dryer woke Jason. He staggered into the bathroom and faced the toilet. Ah the first morning void he thought as his bladder emptied turning the blue toilet water to green.

"Now that's love," Kristy said smiling. "When you can pee if front of your spouse you know you've found your true love."

"What if I were pooping?"

"Oh well that's a soul mate," she chided back.

Jason smiled as he slipped off his boxers and stepped into the shower. Even though he had showered at the hospital, he needed to wash the sleep off his body and freshen up. He looked forward to spending the day with Kristy.

He stepped out of the shower and reached for a towel and dried off and wiped the steam off the mirror. His face looked normal, no puffy crying eyes. He finished drying off and stepped into the bedroom and got dressed. Downstairs Kristy was flipping over a pancake.

"Want one?"

"Sure, if you don't mind."

"Not at all, my love," she said as a ladleful of batter sizzled on the grill.

They made small talk over brunch. There was a passionate chemistry between them. Each smile, every wink and hand gesture just solidified more and more Jason's new feeling of love he had for this woman.

"So when do you want to go?" came the question as Kristy cut into her cantaloupe wedge.

"Go where? Jason asked a mystified look on his face.

"To see Sandy," she replied matter of fact.

"Sandy?" he asked caught off guard.

"Yeah. Why wait?"

"Well I......"

"Well nothing. You need to do this."

SEVENTEEN

Jason succeeded in his quest not to complain as they drove over to Sandy's. This is not how he envisioned his day off with Kristy. As they drove out of Richlands and headed towards Camp Lejeune he made small talk to mask his fear of confrontation. The cry that had spurned his rebirth this morning had diminished. He knew he had to talk to Sandy but he thought he could wait a few days, formulate a plan and approach it in a more methodical way. However, Kristy believed in getting things done right away. That's what he loved about her and that's what drove him crazy about her. But this is why he told her everything; she would know what to do. She also knew Jason had serious bouts of indecision.

As they approached the main gate at base housing Jason felt his throat tighten. He pulled out his I.D. card, presented it to the Marine sentry and was waved through. As he drove through Tarawa Terrace he began to relax. He felt different. There was no longer a tightness in his throat and his hands were not as sweaty. He could feel his pulse, albeit it more subdued. He felt somewhat calm, although not confident. The usual basket case feeling he had was gone and replaced by a sense of responsibility. Or was it maturity? Either way he felt different.

With base schools closed for teacher in-service training, his attention shifted to the swarms of kids who ran and played along the rows and rows of perfectly manicured lawns in military housing. He remembered doing the same thing at bases all over the world. He had made friends in five or more different countries and had been fortunate enough to visit a dozen more. Maybe if he was lucky enough, his kids could enjoy the privilege of living the life of a military brat.

Kristy was rubbing his right thigh as they drove down Tarawa Boulevard. He turned right on Inchon Street and stopped in front of the house. He put the car in park, shut off the engine and sat silent for a minute.

She reassured him. "Jason, you can do this, it's okay."

"I know. And I know I need to. I guess it's need more than want to."

"But you want to know, right?"

"Yeah."

"Well then let's go," she said as she opened the car door."

They got to the front door and rang the bell.

"I got it." Matt ran over and unlocked the screech from inside. Ever since his dad died Jason had begun ringing the doorbell. He was used to walking in and announcing his arrival. Now he felt he was a visitor rather than family member.

"Mom, Jason and Kristy are here," the excited voice from behind the door announced. The screen flung open and Jason was greeted with tight embraces from Matt and Ryan that confirmed a love between brothers.

"Ahem" Kristy chimed-in, her arms stretched out, her eyes crossed looking pointed to the sky.

"We couldn't forget you," Matt squealed as he bear hugged her waist. Ryan followed and she enjoyed each tender moment with the two boys who were an extension of the man she loved.

"Why are all the kids home?" she asked.

"Teacher in-service," Matt responded matter of factly.

"More like a do nothing day if you ask me," Sandy yelled from the kitchen.

"And close the damn door! You're going to let every fly and mosquito on Lejeune in this dump." The hugs and smiles ended quickly, Sandy was on the war path.

"Guess we need to go in," said Ryan, his head bowed down.

"Hurry up, guys. Close the door."

"Man, she knows how to make you feel welcome," Jason whispered.

"Be nice," she said, her eyes squinting to get her point across.

"We're in. we're in," Jason assured hoping to avoid the confrontation even before he had to time to talk to her. He pulled the door shut. Matt walked with Kristy, holding her hand tightly and swinging it back and forth, his bright green eyes looking up at hers. She smiled back. Ryan walked ahead of the group briskly and without a word went right down stairs to the family room.

"Bout time, thought you'd never get in the door with these two knuckle-heads hanging all over you," she joked with a grin.

"Nice to see you too," said Jason.

"And these two can hang on me any time," Kristy said with a smile.

"Mathew, honey, let go of Kristy and go do something. You too, Ryan. You've been under foot all morning." Matt stopped swinging her arm and looked down.

"Oh he's fine," Kristy reassured.

"No he's not," demanded Sandy. "I told him to go find something to do. So c'mon, let's go!" Matt's eyes welled up with tears but he refused to let go of Kristy's hand.

Ryan skipped away and headed down the steps. Mathew stood firm.

"Mathew. I said go. You can visit more later." Matt stood his ground, not moving at all.

"Now!" she ordered, annoyed by his defiance.

"It's okay, buddy. I'll come see you in a minute," Kristy whispered to him. Matt slid his hand down Kristy's never looking up. He turned and slowly slinked away down the steps to the family room. The sniffles of little boys crushed feelings could be heard as he stepped out of view.

"Was that really necessary? He wasn't hurting anyone," Jason said.

"Yes he was. He's been under foot all morning and needs to learn what is and is not socially acceptable when meeting company; family or otherwise. And he needs to learn he cannot hang on people. We've been through this."

"But we're his family."

"And I'm his mom and when you have two special needs children you'll know what I mean. In the meantime, I'll parent them how I want to." She turned and in a huff stormed out of the room and into the kitchen.

"Fair enough," Kristy snapped. "Just don't parent them like you did Jason." It seemed Kristy wasn't going to waste time and ease into the conversation.

Sandy opened the fridge and grabbed a Diet Coke from the top shelf and popped the tab.

"I wish I had some rum," she grumbled as she slammed the door shut.

"It's like eleven o'clock," Jason said.

"Well it's five someplace. And what the hell is that supposed to mean?" she asked turning her attention to Kristy. "Like I did Jason?"

"You know damn right well what I mean." Kristy's tone was short and crisp. Her body tensed and she stood straight up. Maybe

Jason wouldn't have to say anything at all. Kristy had this.

"You never gave him the time of day, and still don't."

Flabbergasted Sandy looked at Jason. "I raised you good; the best I knew how anyway. You had it better than most. You never went hungry, did you?"

"Well, I never went hungry but...."

"But what? What the hell is this anyway? You walk through the door and attack me? Your dad's gone; I'm leaving, so you come over and tell me what a crappy step-mom I was and what a crappy mom I am now? That I'm a whore or something like that? Is that what this is? Cause if it is, I don't need it. So you might as well go."

Jason's jaw tightened, his face got hot. He could feel himself tremble inside ready to explode.

"You know what? Stop it, just stop it. I can't do this anymore with you. It's stupid and ridiculous." Jason's anger took over the room.

Frozen in place, Sandy looked at him. "What do you mean?"

"You heard me. I came over here today to finally clear the air between us. I wanted to know why we can't get along. What I did wrong as a kid; as an adult. Why you never liked me or why I feel like you never loved me. What I could do if anything to better our relationship. Even before I open my mouth we're right where we always are; yelling, threatening, and getting nowhere. I can't do this anymore."

"And like I can?" Sandy scoffed.

"I don't know, can you? It seems like you don't even care. I want to know you and for you to know me."

"Oh please since when? You never wanted to know me. You were too busy comparing me to your mom that you mourned through puberty. I was an outsider."

"I was allowed to be in mourning and I'm still allowed to mourn her; she was my mother."

"You're right, you were allowed to mourn. But you took advantage of it and with it took advantage of your dad; always making him think I was against you and me feeling like I wasn't good enough. Hiding in your room and closing off every attempt to be close to you. So I gave up and just let you be."

"So you just gave up? You were the only mother I had."

"I couldn't be a mother without being a friend first. I never felt that way even though I wanted to."

"Then why didn't you try?"

"I just gave up. I figured I would always be compared to her. I had no clue how to be a mom, and an instant one at that. I tried to be a friend and that didn't work either"

"You seemed to do a good job with the boys."

"So is that what this is about; I love the boys more than you? It may sound stupid, but I learned how to be a mother from scratch. From day one it was learning; what to do and what not to do. And I did it with two; count them two with special needs children no less. With you, you were set in your ways. I could never replace your mom and I never tried. I could only be a friend to you. You had a mom and I would never have tried to take her place. You don't think I wanted to be closer? To be in the click like you and your dad had? I was on the outside for a long time until the boys came along. Every time I tried to join in you shut down and you turned away. You would start, quote 'missing your mother' unquote. Then your dad would kiss your ass for a week or two because poor, poor Jason was upset. He'd get pissed at me and say try harder, try harder. He could never get it through his head that I was trying and you were manipulating him. You always made it out to be like I was trying to take your father away, which wasn't true."

This is same thing Dr. Wilton said Jason thought as he listened intently.

"By the time the boys came, I had given up. I figured you didn't want to know me because I was some bar whore who hooked your daddy and not this perfect little person like your mother."

Jason flinched. His tense posture showed how uneasy he was feeling. She had caught him off guard with her sermon and its eerie similarities to what Dr. Wilton had said. Sandy sensed his trepidation.

"That's right, I know what you think and you too," she said shifting her eyes on to Kristy. "I know what the whole side of your family thinks. I'm some kind of floozy who'd been married a couple of times and was just looking for a sugar daddy. Well since we're having a Kumbaya moment let me tell you this: Husband number one, he used to beat me after a twelve pack which was pretty much every day he wasn't on the ship for my, as he put it, 'poor behavior' as a wife. And husband number two? He would just beat the hell out of me because he could. Then he'd want make up sex and slap me in the face over and over again if he thought I liked it. Liked it? Oh yeah, my eye is swollen shut and I have a blood filled mouth and I'm getting beat worse because I like it? Can you believe that? Maybe it was my fault. Maybe I did deserve it because I picked losers and hung out in dive bars."

"No one deserves that," Kristy counseled.

"Don't pity me, I'm long past that," she snapped right back.

"Did your dad and I get a quickie marriage? In some people's eyes yes. In ours no, never. He was the kindest, gentlest man I ever knew. He accepted my past and my faults and never once raised his voice, let alone his hand to me. He knew what I had been through, what I had done and what had been done to me and he never once faulted me or looked down on me like I was some piece of trash. And don't ever question whether I loved him. I adored that man more than you will ever know. I was always faithful through every deployment, through every duty, through every single day of our marriage.   I wasn't perfect, never will be. But I was a damn good wife to him and I've been a good mother. Great? No. Hell, I don't think there is such a thing. But I was good; I am good. I miss your dad more than you will know." Her voice began cracking.   "I loved him so much, I miss him so much. I never have loved anyone like him and never will." Tears trickled down her face.

"And as for your brothers? While you may think I'm some mean old witch who mistreats them and talks down to them, let me tell you this. They have to be kept on a tight schedule and their manners always kept in check so they learn what is and isn't appropriate in public. They are special needs!" she said.

"One day I'll be gone too and they'll need to fend for themselves. To do that they need to know what is and isn't right. It may seem to you I treat them like crap, but you're not here when we watch a movie, play a game, or when they climb in bed with me at O-dark-thirty because they miss their daddy. You're not here for the rides to the park, trips to the mall, arts and crafts and cookie making. No, you blow in here once every couple of weeks playing the role of big brother and perfect son it makes you feel all warm and fuzzy and then have the nerve to judge me? I play the role of mom and dad all day long. I see their pain, I feel their pain."

"I feel their pain too, Sandy. Maybe I have the same pain."

"I wouldn't know, Jason, you've never told me."

"You've never asked."

"Maybe I should have. But again, I don't know where I stand with you, let alone know where you stand with me."

Kristy cut in, "So it sounds like to me the real problem here is communication. Maybe you just need talk more."

"Look, honey," Sandy protested to Kristy. "I don't want to hear any psycho-babble. I got enough of that from the douche bag Walstad guy who spent more time trying to get in my panties than he did going over Daddy's benefits."

"Wait, you mean you're not moving to Florida to be with him?" asked a stunned Jason.

"Are you kidding me? See, you do think I'm some kind of slut. Your dad's not even cold and I'm off to Florida with some idiot? I'm not damn it." Tears dripped off her chin and into the carpet.

"That's not it at all. I just thought...."

"You just thought. See what I mean? Why not ask me? Ask me why I'm moving."

"Well, why are you?"

"Because it's too much to be here. I miss him. I miss his smell, his laugh, his face. I miss him as a dad, a friend, a protector. He made me feel so safe and so loved. Add to it that you both think I'm some horrible bimbo; we don't talk; the boys are miserable, and I guess I just want to escape my pain and my life without that wonderful, beautiful man." Sandy began to cry harder, convulsing her words through her heavy cries. "I, I, I, miss him so, so much."

Kristy walked over and reached for Sandy. She too had tears in her eye. Sandy collapsed into her arms and cried hard. Her shoulders bounced up and down with a rhythmic motion indicative of deep loss and pain. Jason looked on as the two women rocked back and forth in front of him. He had never ever seen Sandy like this. He never knew how much she loved his dad. And maybe him as well? It was true; he did think she was kind of slutty but she was right; she was always right there when Dad deployed; she sent goody boxes, sent cards, and made posters. She had birthday parties for all the kids and Christmas was hands down awesome. He always got what he asked for. He did spend a lot of time comparing her to his mom and maybe he did look for faults in Sandy so he wouldn't have to get close to her.

He felt like an idiot. He was wrong, all wrong. How could he have been so selfish? Had the last fourteen years been more him than her?
Damn that Dr. Wilton.

EIGHTEEN

Kristy opened the Kurig and replaced the coffee pod with a new one. She pushed the brew button and the machine sprang to life. As fresh water was pumped into the heating tank, fresh hot coffee drained into the waiting cup below in the glow of the holding tanks blue light. She placed the hot cup in front of Sandy and returned to the counter. An hour had passed since Sandy had broken down in Kristy's arms. Jason had gone down with the boys and played X-box while the two women cried away years of anger and pain. He came back up when he heard the kitchen drawer open and the cling-cling of someone rummaging through the silver ware.

"Do you want a cup Jason or maybe some tea?"

"No thanks, I'm good."

Sandy added half and half and two teaspoons of sugar and stirred. She carefully picked up the hot cup and took a sip, the sucking of the hot brew made a loud slurping sound. Her face was puffy and pale, she was sweaty, and her eyes swollen and still moist from the past hours good cry.

"I guess you think I'm some sort of nut job," Sandy said as she set the cup down.

"No, not at all," Jason said solemnly. "I was thinking you thought the same about me."

Sandy smiled. "Why don't we agree we're both a bit goofy and call it even?"

"Sounds good to me."

Kristy joined them at the table and pulled her chair in. She always drank her coffee black something Jason thought was awful. She, on the other hand, found it odd that Jason liked to add French vanilla creamer to his coffee. She called it foo-foo coffee. He called it good.

"So," Kristy began, "what's next?"

"What do you mean?" asked Jason. "Well, I think that the last two or so hours proves that there has been a lot of misunderstanding and built up resentment between you two over the years. I guess I'm just wondering what to do now."

Jason squirmed in his chair. He never liked to be put on the spot about anything. He was still thunderstruck from the melt down earlier.

"How about we just start from today?"

"Today?"

"Yeah. Maybe we could just kind of take all of the shit from over the years, put it on the back burner and start over; like the old woman at the well."

"The woman at the well?" Kristy asked.

"It's a story in the Bible," Jason interjected. It's where Jesus meets a shunned woman at a well who's carrying a ton of baggage. I don't think he told her take all of her shit and dump it though. I don't think he said it quite like that," he said.

"I'm impressed," said Kristy.

"Well he spent every Sunday in Bible class at church for as long as I can remember. That was up until he left for the Navy. They say when a kid graduates high school, they graduate church. And I guess it's true."

"Yep, that's me."

"I think it's beautiful," Kristy fussed.

Jason rolled his eyes with in a playful smile.

"Oh, and that's not what I meant about the shit and well and all," Sandy said defensively restoring the original conversation.

"I know, I'm just kidding."

"Well, what is it then?" Kristy asked.

"Basically, Jesus told the woman to leave all of her past indiscretions, thoughts, and sins behind and start over by coming to the living well, God. I don't know that I'd compare us to God or the well but I understand what you mean."

"Neither would I. But in a way, maybe we are. Maybe we need to empty all of the buckets that we've filled over the years and leave it all behind us. We'll just start over."

"You can do that? Just start over and forget about the last fourteen or so years?" Jason didn't think he could just forget everything that had happened let alone shed every emotion he had built up over the years.

"I'm not saying forget Jason, I'm saying leave it and move on. I am trying so hard to do that with your daddy dying and I don't want to do this anymore with you either. The boys need you. I don't want to waste any more time."

"And you need him, right?" Kristy pressed.

"Yes, I do. Of course I do. I do need you, Jason. I am sorry for all of this. It may seem odd how in two-hours I can apologize for however many years we've been at this, but I am sorry. Contrary to what you may think I do love you, Jason, I always have." Jason looked up and their eyes met.

"I just didn't know how to do it; to be a parent, a mom. And I guess I didn't try hard enough to be a friend and stepmom. I'm willing to take on what I have done wrong and try to learn from it. Can you?"

"I'll try I guess," he said unconvincingly.

"That's all we can ask of each other." Sweat rolled down Sandy's face. She reached for a napkin from the center of the table with an unsteady hand and rubbed her face.

"It's hot in here. I think I need to eat or something."

"You okay?" asked Kristy.

"I don't know, I feel hot. I feel sick I guess. Probably all that crying or I just need to eat something."

"Sick, how?" asked Jason his interest growing.

"I don't know, like I'm going to puke. Like I said, probably all the crying." She was now profusely sweating and still very pale. "Anything else?"

"I just don't feel well. It's like a weight is sitting on my chest and I just feel sick." Sandy began to rub her chest, her breathing labored a bit. Jason and Kristy looked at each other. The alarm bells of their combined years of medical training began to ring.

"Sandy come over here and sit on the couch," Kristy insisted. She reached over and took Sandy's hand. Without any resistance she followed Kristy in to the living room and sat on the couch. Kristy moved a box labeled knick knacks over and set her feet upon it. Jason rummaged through the medicine cabinet in the kitchen and found some baby aspirin. He went into the living room, took one out and handed it to her.

"Here, take this," Jason said reaching out his hand.

"What's this?" she said cupping her hands and taking the little orange pill.

"Aspirin? For what? You think I'm having a heart attack or something?"

"I don't know, but you look like hell."

"More than usual?" she chuckled popping the pill in her mouth. She began chewing.

"Ah, want some water?"

"Nah, water's for sissies."

"How do you feel now?" Kristy asked.

"Terrible."

"Kristy, call 911. Sandy, you need to go to the hospital."

Apprehensive, Sandy replied,

"Hospital? There's nothing wrong with me, I'm just upset with all of this, that's all."

"Well, we'll let the doctors decide that," Jason said. Sandy sat stoically and didn't put up a fight. Although she chewed up some aspirin, she couldn't hide her fear that something was wrong. As the echo of the sirens bounced of the houses in the neighborhood, the boys came up over the steps.

"Momma?" Matt asked, "What's wrong?" The distress in his voice was clear.

"Oh nothing, sweet baby. Just a bit of indigestion. Momma's stomach is upset so I need to go to the hospital and get checked out," she said reassuringly.

Jason greeted the Camp Lejeune Paramedics at the door and ushered them in to the living room. They moved quickly and began to take a history of what had been going on. He asked a bunch of questions while the second paramedic hooked Sandy up to a heart monitor, oxygen mask, and started an intravenous line. Ryan came into the living room. "Momma?"

"It's okay," came Sandy's muffled response from below the plastic mask hissing fresh oxygen. Both boys began to cry.

"Come on boys," Kristy coaxed.

"Let's go down stairs while they get Mommy ready to go to the hospital. She'll be fine," Kristy reassured them, and herself.

In a matter of a few minutes the stretcher came through the door and Sandy was packaged up to go. Her color had gone from pale to beige but still complained of a crushing sensation on her chest.

"We're going to the Naval Hospital," the paramedic announced. "You can follow us or ride with us, your choice."

"I'll follow you guys."

Jason took Sandy's hand. "I'll be right behind you, okay?" Her eyes were closed but she nodded her approval. Fear gripped Jason. This was his fault. He stressed her into having a heart attack? How could he do this to her and to the boys?

Sandy was briskly rolled down the walk and loaded into the ambulance. As they drove away the siren cleared the streets of lookey-loos. Kristy came up over the steps.

"Well?"

"I don't know. God, I hope I didn't just kill her."

"Jason, this is not your fault. Don't start doing this to yourself, okay?"

"Yeah."

"Hello?" a voice shout out from the front door. It was Mrs. Rainier from across the street. She was married to a Sargent Major from 2nd Marine Division.

"Hey, Mrs. Rainier," Jason said with a sigh of relief.

"Everything okay?"

"I'm not sure if Sandy's sick or just stressed. I need to get over to the Naval Hospital though."

"Is it serious?"

"I don't know right now. We'll see."

"Well you two go," she said pointing to them, her finger waving back and forth to the door, "I'll take the boys to my place. Lord knows they don't need any more trauma in their little lives. Plus they love playing with my Billy."

"Are you sure?" asked Kristy. "I'll stay with them."

"I'm sure. It's no problem at all. Matt, Ryan," she called. "Want to go over to my house, have some pizza, and play some X-box with Billy?" The boys barreled up the stairs.

"Yes, yes!" they exclaimed seemingly forgetting their mom had just been taken away by ambulance. The resilience of children is amazing, Jason thought.

"Are you sure?" Jason asked again not wanting to be a burden.

"Yes," she demanded. Fran squeezed his arm reassuringly. "Now get going, she needs you, Jason."

She needs me? How it is that everyone but me feels that way, he thought. She needs me . . . me?

NINETEEN

Even though they were only a few miles from the main base it had taken over an hour to get to the gate because of I.D. checks! Military I.D. checks slowed traffic to a crawl and considering it was the height of lunch time, an hour seemed like a blessing. Jason had screamed, yelled, and used every known word in the profanity handbook as he impatiently made his way to the gate. Kristy just sat in the passenger seat letting him blow off the steam she knew had built up and was now being released on the multitude of vehicles making their way on base. Jason, rarely if ever, cursed so she knew he was upset and for that reason she let him rant.

"Finally," he snarled as he sped away from the gate towards the hospital. He pushed the old Honda to its limits as they roared up the hill to the Emergency Room parking lot. Jason braked hard and the car rolled to a quick stop. They hurried in the old sliding doors only to be greeted by multitudes of people. The line of marines, sailors and their family members clogged the passageway with their week old knee pain complaints, coughs, colds, and boo-boos.

The Emergency Room at the Naval Hospital was like any other in the country; too small, too over worked, but mainly used and abused for routine care, not the emergent care like it was designed for. Jason waited patiently while a woman with arm and shoulder pain complained at the window. As the clerk explained the delay, she lifted a Sprite using her maimed arm that was wrapped in a homemade sling and took a long drink. She then began a tirade that she had been at the ER for over forty-five minutes and needed to be seen so she could get home in time to make dinner for her marine husband. When she didn't get the answer she was looking for which was come right in, she started yelling about how she knew General So-and-So, and her uncle was an admiral, she was entitled to care, and how her husband defended this country, and how this and how that. When her rant didn't faze the clerk she threatened to go see the Commanding Officer and tell him that his ER sucked.

"Go right ahead, ma'am," the polite and antagonistic civilian ER clerk said. "He's on the first deck by Records."

"This is crap," she said as she turned, grabbed her paperwork and Sprite and stormed off.

"Thought your shoulder hurt?" the clerk mumbled under her breath. Jason stepped up to the window.

"Can I help you, Sir," she asked Jason with a smile and a sigh.

"I'm HM2 Miller, my mother in law was brought in by ambulance."

"Name?" the clerk asked.

"Sandy Miller." She typed it into her computer.

"Hey HM2" came a friendly voice from behind. Jason turned and saw a familiar face. It was Chief Daniels.

"Hey, Chief."

"What's up?"

"They brought Sandy in; I think she's having a heart attack or something. I'm trying to get in to see her."

"Come on, come with me," he said.

"I got this, Emma," Daniels said waving at the clerk. The clerk waved back not caring one way or another.

He walked to the security door, entered his code and the door popped open.

"Why does he get to go?" shouted the woman with shoulder pain.

"Because he has a real emergency," Daniels shot back.

He waved Jason and Kristy through and followed behind them down the hall. At the main desk Chief Daniels walked up past them.

"Can I help you?" the Corpsman asked standing up to greet the Chief.

"Yeah, I'm looking for a Mrs. Miller, brought in by ambulance a bit ago."

"I'm sorry and you are?" he asked.

"I am Chief Daniels from Patient Admin and this is HM2 Miller her son-in-law."

"Let me check, Chief," he said looking down at his computer screen.

"She's in trauma bay one. CDR Welch is in there with her. He's the cardiologist on call."

"Thanks, man," Daniels said and turned towards the bay. They walked a few steps away from the desk and slid open the curtain just a bit to peek inside. CDR Welch looked up as he heard the wheels slide across the curtain's track.

"Hey, Chief, What's up?"

"Hey, Doc," Daniels replied taking and shaking the doctor's hand.

"Sir. This is HM2 Miller, her son-in-law."

"Hey, Sir," Jason took the doctor's hand. "How is she?"

"Well, she has had a mild heart attack. I think we're looking at taking her to the cath lab and putting in a stint."

"Stop talking about me like I'm not here," came the muffled complaint from a drug induced Sandy.

"We're not talking about you like you're not here," Dr. Welch spoke loudly over the ding-ding noises of the machines and hissing of the oxygen that flowed from the wall.

"You're fine, Mrs. Miller, your son-in-law is here." Sandy raised her hand and nodded her approval.

"We've given her some morphine for pain and to take off some of the anxiety. I think we have gotten to this in time and with maybe a stint or two if needed, she'll make a full recovery. We'll know more when we cath her. As for damage to the heart muscle itself, I think it's minimal, but we'll better be prepared to answer that question after some additional tests and some more time. There's always a risk with any procedure, but she's young and I think she'll do fine."

"When will you do it?" Kristy asked.

"In about forty minutes," he said matter-of-factly.

"Sounds good to me," Jason replied.

"All right then." Dr. Welch turned to Sandy and spoke loudly to drown out the hum of the machines. "I'll see you upstairs, sweetie and we'll get that ticker of yours all better, okay?"

"Sure, I have nothing better to do tonight. Hey, and if you're single," Sandy mumbled.

"Happily married, thanks," he said with a grin and chuckle. "You can have a minute or two and then we need to go," he said his eyes darting back and forth between Jason and Kristy.

"Yes, sir. We'll be out of here in a second."

"Okay, I'll see you in the waiting room outside the OR in two or three hours or so." He pulled open the curtain and walked over to the counter and began to write out his orders.

"If you don't need anything else I'm rolling," Chief Daniel's blurted out.

"Thank you, Chief, again," said Jason.

"No sweat, dude." He peered by Jason, "Hang tough, Sandy," he yelled.

"Oh yeah," came her lethargic response.

Jason took her hand in his and looked at the woman he felt no connection to for so many years. Yet in the last three hours he had found out more about her, her life, and her feelings than he had ever known before. He stared at her laying there and he thought of how his dad just lay there before he died. He couldn't help but feel a sense of guilt and that this was his fault even though Kristy tried to reassure him it wasn't. What would he do if she died too? What would happen with the boys? He had visions of some lawyer announcing, "It's twins" at the reading of her will. How could he raise them? How could he ask Kristy to raise them? He felt a panic set in. Calm down he thought, you're getting ahead of yourself. The metal balls holding the privacy curtain rolled along their old worn track with a loud tearing sound that startled him out of his trance.

"Okay, we're here for Ms. Sandy. It's time to go," a compassionate voice offered as a group of nurses and operating room technicians appeared.

"You need to say your see-you-laters."

"We don't say good-byes," she whispered.

Kristy leaned forward and took her hand from Jason.

"We'll see you in a bit, Sandy. Love you," she said kissing her hand and setting it gently back into Jason's hand. Jason just stared at her, he had never said I love you to her and as far as he could remember today was the first time she had ever said it to him. He felt awkward just saying it and not knowing if he really meant it. Maybe she needed to hear it. Or maybe not; at least not right now.

"See you soon," he said quickly rubbing her arm and laying her arm across her chest. He turned to the nurse. "Take good care of her, would ya?"

"Always do."

Kristy called Onslow Memorial and told them she would not be in for her shift. The nursing supervisor was not too happy, but she assured her she'd be in tomorrow.

"I hope nothing else happens or I'm going to get fired," she said after hanging up the phone.

"It's all good. She should be fine and you're not going to get fired," Jason said.

Jason called Fran and checked on the boys and gave her an update. The boys we're fine and having a blast playing with Billy. Her husband was corralling them all for a trip to the Dairy Queen.

"I'm praying for her."

"Thanks, Fran."

They sat on the vinyl sofa and held one another. They spoke no words and just let the tick-tock of the wall clock speak for them as they nodded in and out. After about two hours Dr. Welch popped through the door. He had traded his military uniform for blue surgical scrubs and a light green surgical mask that dangled from his neck. Jason and Kristy hopped from their perch simultaneously and intently awaited his assessment.

"Looks good. Looks real good! It went great!" he announced. "She had a small occlusion in only one artery. We cleared it, put in a stint and the blood is flowing really well. Her blood pressure is great and she's been extubated and breathing on her own. She'll be here a few days, and then home to rest."

Kristy squeezed Jason's arm and smiled broadly with joy and liberation.

"Thanks so much, Doc," Jason said as the air left his body. He caught himself hunched over in relief and grabbed for Dr. Welch's hand. He took it and shook it vigorously.

"Hey, I'm just glad we found it now. Another year or two, give or take, and she was possibly looking at a massive M.I."

"When can we see her?" asked Kristy.

"She's in recovery. Give them a bit and they'll come get you, okay?"

"Yes, Sir and thanks again."

"You're more than welcome," he said trying to free his hand from Jason's uncomfortable grip. When he finally freed himself he daintily shook Kristy's and headed out. As the door closed behind him Jason and

Kristy embraced. The day's events had taken its toll and Kristy wept silently against his chest. He could feel her body tremble. He stood with her silently stroking her back as she let it all out. After a few minutes she pulled back.

"I'm sorry, babe, I know I'm crazy."

"Nonsense, you're not crazy. You're just honest with how you feel. Something I admire about you." Kristy reached for a tissue and blew her nose. She sat down on the couch and took another one from the box and wiped her nose.

"Damn, these things are like sandpaper," she fretted staring at the wad in her hands. Jason smiled broadly. "God I love you!"

She looked up to see Jason's smile, "I love you too. What's so funny?"

"Nothing, nothing at all. Get you another tissue?"

TWENTY

After visiting with Sandy for a few minutes, they decided it was time to go. She was heavily sedated, in stable condition and in the best possible place she could be.

"There is nothing more we can do here. Let's go home," Jason told Kristy. They left the hospital and went to get the boys from Fran's.

"How is she?" she asked as the screen door creaked open.

"Good. They put in a single stint and she's going to be just fine. A few days in the hospital and she should be home."

"Oh, thank God. Just in time I guess?"

"Yeah, it seems that way."

"Well, you know you can bring the boys over whenever you need too. I'm more than happy to watch them."

"Thanks, Mrs. Rainier, I really appreciate it."

"It's no problem."

They collected Matt and Ryan, made some additional small talk with Fran and then made their hasty retreat to the car. Jason told the boys how Sandy was doing and reassured them she would be okay.

"Where would we live if Mom dies?" Ryan asked out of nowhere.

"With us I guess," Jason said a bit taken aback his straightforwardness.

"You don't need to worry about that, though," Kristy chimed in, in time to save

Jason. "Mommy will be fine, you'll be fine and all be together again shortly."

"Until we go to Florida," Matt said solemnly.

"Let's not worry about that right now either, okay?"

"Okay," he said content on the blunt ending to the conversation.

They drove in relative silence all the back to Richlands. Jason went through the drive through at McDonald's and got Kristy and himself something to eat. The boys weren't hungry since they had indulged on chips, cookies, pizza, and the ice cream cones. Jason unlocked the door and ushered the boys in. The smell of his own home hit his nose and he savored the security and safety of his own place. The boys turned on the TV and sprawled out on the couch. They loved staying with Jason and Kristy. She spoiled them and enjoyed doing things with them in the kitchen, baking cookies, making pies, and letting them make their own grilled cheese. She was going to be a great mother someday, Jason thought. After the make-shift meal of greasy fries and burgers, Kristy excused herself to make up the second bedroom for the boys. A good night's sleep is what they all needed and since tomorrow was Saturday, sleeping in was in order. Jason puttered around the kitchen finding busy work to do to keep his mind off of Sandy and the horrible events they had that morning.

"She's lucky," Dr. Welch had said.

Maybe Jason did save her by pissing her off so much she had her heart attack now rather than later. Too much to take on right now he thought.

The boys came into the kitchen. "Kristy said it's time for bed," Matt whined. "She said we could watch TV in the bedroom though," Ryan said happily on the compromise.

"Good night, Jason," Matt said grabbing him by the waist and squeezing.

"Good night, Mattie," Jason teased in return. "Love you, buddy," hugging him firmly and securely. Ryan slipped in as Matt slipped out. A big bear hug greeted Jason.

"Night," he mumbled.

"Good night, Bud, love you."

"Love you too," he said holding on. Jason released his grip, however Ryan did not. He needed more, the safety and security of his brother's hug. He was very much like Jason; he rarely if ever showed emotion and hid his feelings from the world.

With confidence Jason held him closer, "It's going to be okay, Ryan."

Kristy appeared in the doorway and leaned against the jam, her arm folded her head resting on her shoulder. A small smile lit up her face.

"I know."

"So what's wrong?"

"I just miss Daddy today. You smell like him; your shirt anyway."

"I miss him too. Would you like to wear this shirt to bed? You could use it like a night shirt like they wore in old days."

Ryan released his grip and looked up at Jason nodding yes.

"Well here you go," Jason said stepping back. Ryan let his grip go. Jason unbuttoned his shirt as he pulled it from his jeans and slipped it off revealing his tee-shirt.

"Here, buddy." Ryan's eyes lit up as he pulled the shirt to his nose. He took in the smell of Bruit after shave. His dad wore it for years and Jason had taken on the little green bottle as well. It reminded him of his dad and the smell wasn't half bad either.

"Thanks!" the brightly lit face exclaimed.

"You're welcome, buddy."

He turned and grabbed Kristy's waist. "I love you too. You're the best brothers' wife lady I could ask for." She smiled broadly.

"I love you too, now off to bed. I'll be up to tuck you in, in a few minutes." Ryan bounced down the hall and they watched him turn and head up the stairs.

"God I love them boys," Jason said.

"I know you do. You're a great brother to them, a great father figure too."

"I don't know about that. Brother yes, father no."

"I disagree. You take good care of them and you always know what to say to make them feel better."

"I just say what I think."

"But you don't do it with anyone else like you do it with them. They're your comfort zone. You don't even let me in like you do them."

"That's not true," he teased.

"You're right. You did the other day and you did with Sandy today. And see, honest open communication saved her, reassured him, and turned me on."

"Oh really?" he said with a devilish grin.

"Really!" she growled.

"Unfortunately we have four ears that are quite the busy bodies, so I'll take a rain check," he said letting her down quickly.

"Ah, shucks!"

Jason smiled at her and leaned in for a kiss. Her lips were moist and warm. Her tongue was soft and wet. He felt himself getting turned on, but he really wasn't in the mood. Kristy's hands slid down his chest and across his pants. He felt himself getting more and more aroused. Pulling back he tried to insist, "Sorry baby, you'll need to wait."

"I'll make it worth your while," she whispered.

A surge came over him. "You are so hot," he blurted out as he pinned her in the door jam.

"Thought you were on a rain check?" she gasped in between the passionate kisses.

"I got an umbrella. Come on, let's go upstairs." With no resistance and a growing excitement between them they jumped up the stairs two and three at a time hitting all of the light switches off on the way up. The boys were in the queen blow up bed and both already sleeping soundly.

"Sweet!" Jason squealed with excitement.

They closed and locked their bedroom door, engulfed each other's bodies and made love. Their bodies arched with the pleasures that come with making love with your soul mate. They were young and in love and shared their passion with all they had. They fell asleep exhausted, satisfied and secure in one another's arms.

As the first rays of sunlight peeked through the mini-blinds, their bodies lay intertwined in a mass of crumbled sheets. Jason awoke to the boys laughing and playing across the hall. He rolled out of bed, slipped on some boxers, sweat pants and an old tee-shirt. He kissed Kristy on the head.

"I love you, baby." He popped open the door and was greeted with a pillow to the face. The boys burst in to laughter.

"Pillow fight!" screamed Ryan. And with that the three of them swung, swatted, and laughed their way through the pounding of down pillows. As Jason swung left and right, he was hit from behind with a thud on the head.

"Get Kristy," Matt screamed. She had heard the ruckus and wasn't going to miss out on this kind of fun. The four of the pummeled each other and laughed. After being bombarded with multiple head shots, Jason called a truce.

"Who wants pancakes?"

"Me, me, me!" came the excited chants.

"Me too," Kristy said, smirking.

"Well let's go. Last one in the kitchen cleans it." The boys jumped past them and ran down the stairs pulling each other back so they could be first.

"Careful, boys, careful!" Jason ordered. They just laughed and kept running.

"Morning," he mumbled.

"Morning to you too," she said.

With a slight shove, Jason fell back on the bed. "What the..." he blurted out.

"You said last one cleans. It isn't going to be me," she said with a wink and a smile. She ran out the door. Jason smiled, sprang up off the bed and followed right on her heels. They laughed as they came into the kitchen, Jason tickling her sides.

"I win," she announced.

"It's a tie."

"No way," she said laughing.

Pancakes, pancakes, pancakes," chanted the two hungry boys.

"Okay, okay, I'm on it. Why don't you two turn on the boob tube and we'll get it ready?"

"Oakaly-doakaly!" Matt replied eagerly. The boys skipped into the living room and jumped on the sofa pulling the blanket down and covering themselves up.

Jason and Kristy turned on the radio and worked in silent tandem mixing, cooking, and frying up some peppered bacon. They had K-Love on and sang along with some of their favorite Christian rock bands. It added additional spirituality to their lives and the music was good too. This was another reason they bonded so quickly.

Jason had read somewhere that couples who share their faith and Christian values with each other and their children had a healthier and more satisfying marriage. They attended church regularly in Jacksonville at the church Kristy had been raised in. Jason had been very active in the churches he had attended at his father's different duty stations. He could never deny that his father had not given him a spiritual foundation. Because he moved around so much they never had a consistent church family. Now he did. Jason tried hard to live a Christian life, but he was human and made mistakes.

A Navy Chaplain once told him that going to church didn't mean you were going to heaven. And as far as his using profanity, Chaplain Tony told him, "It's not the word, it's how it's used. Cuss words like damn, can mean nothing except social stigma. However, if you call someone ugly or fat it can hurt and be more damaging than any cuss word."

That seemed to give Jason a sense of deliverance so when he did curse he didn't worry about offending God or going to hell. He didn't curse much if ever but when he did, he didn't worry about sin. God would forgive him.

As promised Jason was the one who cleaned up the kitchen while the boys changed and brushed their teeth. He finished just in time to catch Kristy finishing her daily routine of primping. She looked as beautiful as ever.

He slipped by her and kissed her on the neck. She clutched her neck to the side squeezing his cheek as she sniggered.

"You smell good enough to eat," he said.

"You're such a dirty bird!"

"I know," Jason said as he pulled the shower door shut. The rush of the cool water felt good. He stood under the rushing water and let it refresh his body and mind. There's something about a shower. A person can be cross-eyed tired but a shower magically peps them right up. It's a natural high courtesy of H2O and Jason loved it. He was wide awake and he was feeling fantastic. Life is good, he thought. Life is good.

"Jason!" The identifiable yell from the bedroom echoed in the bathroom. He turned off the shower so he could hear.

"What?"

"The hospital called, Sandy's awake."

"Alright. I'll be right out."

"She was asking for you."

"Say that again?" he said in disbelief.

"She wants you."

"She must be delirious?"

"Jason!"

"What?" he responded with a chuckle. Jason turned the water back on and laughed. He placed his face back under the shower head. The sound of the rushing water trickled in his ears blocking out any other noises.

She wants me? For what? he thought.

TWENTY-ONE

They left the house, the boys racing to the car excited about seeing their mom and excited too about the impending road trip even if it was simply down Highway 24 to the Naval Hospital. As they left Richlands, Jason stopped at the Scotchman Station and purchased a pack of Marlboro Gold Seventy-Twos. He didn't smoke, but always bought a pack when HM3 Beaz was working on duty.

HM3 Beaz had joined the Navy two days after his seventeenth birthday; his mom signing the permission forms to let him enlist. He went to Corps School and then to Field Medical Training Battalion to be a Fleet Marine Force Corpsman. He graduated top of his class and went to 1st battalion, 2nd Marines. Two months later he was in Iraq and three weeks later he was shot twice, once in the chest, the other shattering his left arm while pulling a wounded Marine out of a burning HUMVEE. The chest shot went around his SAPI plates and somehow missed his heart. He was MEDEVAC'd back to the States and was recovering pretty well. He had a purple heart and had been nominated for the Bronze Star for valor. He was a good kid. Even through all that though he couldn't buy cigarettes. He's still only seventeen and in North Carolina you have to be eighteen to buy cigarettes. What a bitch Jason thought; you go to Iraq, save a Marine, get shot not once but twice, and so sorry you can't buy cigarettes? A total injustice Jason thought. So every time Baez had duty, Jason bought him a pack of smokes. It's not something he would normally do; help someone develop lung cancer, but he felt the law was stupid for a kid who had given so much.

They pulled into the parking lot which was almost empty. All of the clinics were closed on the weekend except the Emergency Room. It was as usual, packed. They strolled into the hospital and Jason approached the front desk. HM3 Baez was there.

"Jason, what's up, buddy?"

"Not much, man, I brought you something," he said tossing the smokes to him.

"Oh God, thanks, man. One more month, than I can buy them myself. You believe they wouldn't sell me a pack at the exchange? It's not right."

"I know, dude, but hey it will be all over soon."

"Yeah, I guess. So what's up? I know you didn't come by just to bring me some smokes."

"Actually I am looking for my mother, stepmother I mean," Jason quickly corrected himself. "Sandy Miller. She was admitted last night."

"Let me check. Sorry to hear. She okay? Nothing serious is it?" his concern seemed genuine and Jason appreciated it.

"Nah, she's going to be okay. A little heart issue, that's all," he said not wanting to say too much.

He looked up from the computer screen, "She's on the multi-purpose ward, Room 323."

"Hey, man, thanks." Jason extended his hand. Baez took it.

"No sweat, anytime."

Jason turned back to Kristy and the boys standing by the door. "She's on the third floor. Let me pee real quick, and we'll go up."

"I need to go too," Ryan blurted.

"Alright, you guys go and we're going to start on our way."

"What's the room number?"

"323."

"Okay, we'll see you up there."

Jason and Ryan marched off to the head directly across from the Quarter deck while Matt and Kristy headed down the passageway past the pharmacy to the elevators. Matt ran ahead and eagerly pushed the button. The door opened and they both filed inside.

"What button?" he asked eagerly.

"Three, kiddo."

"Which shape is that one?" he asked confused.

"Oh, I'm sorry sport. The top button is number three."

With a wide grin he pushed the button for all it was worth. The door closed and with the hum of the gears to the elevator jerked with a thud and sprang upwards. Just as fast as it stared it stopped. The door opened on the second floor and a woman waited to get in. Matt looked up and blocked her entry.

"Move over here, Matt." Kristy was embarrassed and her tone showed it. She tugged on his sleeve and he begrudgingly moved to Kristy's side.

As she prepared to enter the elevator, a deep fear erupted in her stomach and shot up her throat. It was him. Look away.

In an instant she was outed.

"I know you," Matt announced in a long proud drawl.

"No, you don't," came the stern reply that bounced off the small elevator walls. So much for playing it cool.

"Matt don't be rude. I'm sorry," Kristy said, even more embarrassed.

Matt turned and looked up at Kristy. "No, it's true; she is the lady that talked funny. She was in the kitchen; she gave me ten dollars."

"I have no idea what you're talking about," she growled staring straight ahead.

"You should teach that boy some manners."

"And you should turn and face people when you speak to them, that's proper manners," Kristy snapped right back. As always, she was one not to shy away from a skirmish.

"You're her," Matt implored again.

"Matthew Miller that's enough!" Kristy's tone was sharp and stern. Matt was not used to this and quickly put his head down, his bottom lip quivering while tears welled in his eyes.

"You're just like your loser father," she whispered to herself much louder then she had thought.

"What did you just say?" Kristy demanded.

Off guard and flustered she fired back, "Nothing, mind your own business."

"Lady this is my business. Who are you, how do you know us?"

She ignored Kristy's demand as she pressed her full figured body to fit through the sliding door. She moved swiftly down the hall.

"Come on, Matt, let's go."

"Hey! Who are you? Hey, I'm talking to you. How do you know his father?"

She kept walking, not looking back. She had screwed up and screwed up big time.

Kristy picked up her pace. Several patients and staff members' had come out into the hall to see what the commotion was.

The mystery lady reached a door and fumbled in her pocket for the key. She unlocked the door, squeezed through an opening big enough to get in and quickly pushed the door closed. But it didn't. She looked up to see Kristy's face only inches from hers. Her foot was wedged between the door and the jam preventing its closure.

"Who you are?" she demanded.

"Get away from my office, or I will call security," she ordered.

"Go ahead, and you can explain to them how you know a nine year old special needs child and his dead father."

"I work here; I know a lot of people."

Kristy glanced over her shoulder to the top of a bookcase against the wall.

"Where did you get that piece of pottery?" she demanded.

She glanced behind her and saw the red ashtray sitting prominently on top. Her war trophy had been discovered.

"None of your damn business."

She scowled and the tone of her voice became violent and aggressive. "Now get your foot out of my door, or I'll break it you witch."

"I told you she was at the house in the kitchen," Matt cried.

Kristy turned to see Matt's face. He was crying and rocking back and forth in fear. Looking past him she saw a dozen or more patients and staff watching the show. She realized she needed to go to Matt, this woman could wait. She turned to the door and snapped, "This isn't over. I'm coming back."

She pulled her foot from the door. With a loud crack the door slammed shut. Kristy reached for Matt.

"Oh, honey, I'm so sorry." She went down on one knee and took Matt in her arms as he sobbed. "Its okay, sweetie, I'm not mad at you."

"I know," he howled. It's just . . . it's just I'm not special needs. I'm just special."

"I know, baby. Shhhhh, it's okay. You are special, honey."

Kristy realized she had called out his disability directly in front of him. Sandy and Chris had always made sure Matt and Ryan we're never labeled and never excluded because of their delays. They always called the boys special like a special gift from God. They were never referred to as special needs.

"Excuse me." A deep voice approached her from behind.

Agitated, she turned. "Yes."

"I think I can help you?" he replied cautiously.

"No thanks. I do not need any more help."

"No, ma'am, I mean maybe I can answer the question you got."

"And what would that be?" she angrily demanded.

"How she knows your pops," he said rather matter-of-factly.

"And you are?"

"A friend. My name is HN Louis and I knew your pops. I did him a favor once. Look, take my number and call me. I can't talk to you here there's too many people around. Plus I got patients to take care of. I'll tell you everything I know. Now I got to go." Kristy took the yellow post-it-note with a number on it. Just as casually as he walked up, he walked away.

A few moments later Jason and Ryan appeared.

"What the hell is going on?"

"What's wrong with Matt? Why's he crying?"

"The lady, the lady was at the house," Matt wailed.

"Who? What lady, what house?"

"Come on, I'll explain it to you later. Let's go see Mommy, huh?" she said to Matt giving him a reassuring hug back and forth.

"Okay," he said sniffling.

"Here, use this tissue." She took one from her purse and handed it to Matt. "Blow your nose real good." He wiped his nose and blew it hard.

"This tissue is hard," he said. "It's all scratchy."

"We know," Jason said looking over at Kristy with a smile. She however, wasn't smiling. They all started down the hall to room 323.

He looked over and whispered, "What's going on?"

"Let's get through this visit and I'll fill you in, okay?"

"Okay," he agreed reluctantly.

TWENTY-TWO

"Mommy!" the shrieks of excitement came from the both the boys as they ran to Sandy's bedside.

"My babies!" she yelled back in a raspy voice as they all embraced. "I missed you so much, my little men."

"We missed you too, Momma!" Ryan exclaimed.

The boys pulled back and Kristy stepped up leaned over the bed and reached to Sandy. They embraced.

"It's so good to see you; you scared the hell out of us."

"It scared me too," Sandy said laughing.

Jason moved forward. "Hey you," he said reaching for her hand.

"So you come and see me after a near death experience and all I rate is a hand shake? Get yourself over here and give me a hug," she demanded.

Dumbfounded, he cautiously obliged and leaned down towards her. Sandy grabbed his neck and pulled him in tight causing him to lose his balance and almost fall in the bed with her. He caught himself on the rail and regained his balance. Sandy planted a big kiss on his cheek.

"It's so good to see you here. Thank you so much for looking after the boys and for taking care of me." She kissed him again and let go of the death grip on his neck. He lifted himself off of her and smiled and uneasy smile.

"I'm glad you're feeling better."

"Me too!"

What the hell has happened to the real Sandy? This is awkward. Why is she so damn happy? Maybe this was the honey-moon period following a mid-life near death experience. And you know what they say; honeymoon's always come to an end.

Kristy ever so the prepared foster mother had brought some crayons and paper so the boys could draw a few pictures if they got bored. Let's face it; kids can only handle a hospital for so long.

Jason stood back by the window as Ryan and Matt talked and laughed with Sandy. They told her about pizza and X-Box at Ms. Fran's house and how she let them order their own ice cream cones. Matt told her about the pillow fights and Ryan got her laughing with the last in line for pancakes contest. It was so nice to see the boys laughing and carrying on. Jason could not remember Sandy ever being so free spirited. As they talked and showed off their art work, Sandy's eyes darted up to meet Jason's. She smiled at him. It was sincere and honest. He tried to smile back, however his defenses were still up and he only managed a small smirk. When or how do you let them down, he thought? He couldn't afford to get hurt again.

After an hour Matt started to get a bit whiny. "I'm hungry," he said. "Can we have lunch now?"

"I'll tell you what," said Kristy. "How about we go down to the Light House Café and get a burger?"

"I want to go too!" shot Ryan from across the room.

"How about us three go and Jason and Mom can have some time to talk?"

"It's okay I'll go," Jason insisted not wanting to be alone with Sandy.

"No, Jason," Sandy interrupted. "Stay. I'd like to finish our talk."

"What talk?"

"The one that got me here. Hopefully not to that degree."

"Okay, we'll go then," Kristy replied as the boys leaped off the bed and ran to the door. "Maybe we'll see the lady again," Matt said.

"What lady?" asked Sandy.

"It's a long story for some other time," Kristy assured.

"Be good."

"They always are. You want anything, Sandy?"

"No, no, I'm on the lettuce diet. No more of that fat slop for me."

Kristy gave Jason a quick kiss and told him she'd bring him a burger and fries.

"Sounds good. Extra onions please."

The three of them headed down the hall and a weird silence took over the room.

"So where were we?" Sandy asked.

"I think we were at the 'I was a bad son, you we're a bad Mom' junction."

"I think you're right," she said pulling herself up in the bed.

"Now Jason, I'm not sure if Kristy told you but I was asking for you this morning."

"She did."

"Did you want to know why?" she tempted.

"I guess, sure?"

"You we're right. You were right when you said we can't do this anymore. I agree I can't do this anymore either. Jason, I loved your father very much and whether you chose to believe it or not I have always loved you too."

"What's the point of all of his? Are you going to say you had some sort of near death experience and now we should be all buddy-buddy?" he snapped.

Calmly, Sandy continued, "No. The point is, is you're right. Maybe this is some near death trip or maybe it's just how I always felt. You calling me out made me think. I've been wrong and I don't want to do this anymore. Maybe this is my entire fault, I don't know. What I do know is you hide behind a wall and you don't let anyone in."

"So now you're analyzing me?"

"No Jason, I'm telling you I do the same thing. I hide behind walls. My life was hell at one point. I let your dad in and no one else. I

need to drop my wall and let you in. I'm
asking for the same thing from you."

Without warning, Jason's eye welled
with tears. Not again he thought. Of all
people, not in front of here.

"I know you hurt, Jason. And I know
that maybe I caused it. I'm sorry, I really am. I
just want to start over. The boys need you and
Kristy both. I can see that. And now more
than ever. I guess what I'm trying to tell you
or better yet asking you is if you could please
let me in."

A tear ran down his cheek and flowed
over his top lip. He licked his lips and the salt
flavored liquid engulfed his mouth. He licked
them again.

"Jason?"

"Jason?" she asked again humbly.

Staring at the New River in the distance
Jason spoke.

"Look, Sandy, maybe you can just start
over and go on like the last thirteen or fourteen
years never existed but I can't. Okay? I just
can't. I need time to figure this out."

"Time to figure what out?" her tone
sounded irritated.

"To figure out everything!" he
exclaimed. "Who I am today has been defined
by my childhood. I'm me because of you and
Dad. I can't just wake up and change my
whole profile or my whole life because we had
an argument. I need time to get all of these

feelings in check. Give me time and let me grow into this. Please?"

"Now who's analyzing?" she said.

"I mean it, I...."

"You what?" she asked. "You're saying you're you because of me? No way! You're who you are because that's who you are. Maybe we influenced you when you were younger but let's face it, you're old enough and wise enough to make your own decisions and accept the responsibility and accountability that comes with them. Leave it behind at the well and move one. Don't pin this on your father and I."

Wow, did she just paraphrase the Bible, he thought? His mind returned to the topic at hand.

"I'm not pinning it on anyone. I just need time to find me and to tell you the truth, I need time to find you in here as well," he said rubbing his hand across his chest.

"Find me in there? Like you're a drone or something?"

"No, it's just I'm so confused. Twenty-four hours ago you we're just as short tempered and mean as ever spilling your guts and your whole life's story on me. Today you're all lovey-dovey."

Sandy thought for a second. "Okay. I can see that. Maybe you're right. Maybe I am asking too much too soon and not just from you, but also of me. And maybe me spilling my guts was me reaching out and letting you in, I don't know. What I do know is I'm not this awful person you think I am. I'll lie off of you. But I want you to know that I am willing to work on this with you. Fair enough?"

"Fine, but answer me one question since we're so open and honest all of the sudden," Jason replied.

"Sure, what?"

"Why did you sell all of Dad's stuff and not even give me a chance to get anything from the house, or nothing for the boys?"

Sandy stared at Jason and took it all in.

"Jason, come here and sit down" she said scooting over and patting the bed. "I'll tell you."

With a hint of apprehension he moved slowly over to the bed. He sat down on an angle, his right leg tucked under his body, his left leg dangling from the side of the bed.

"Fact of the matter is we're broke."

"Broke?" he asked looking at her puzzled.

"What about the SGLI and death gratuity."

SGLI, or the Serviceman' Group Life Insurance is a low cost life insurance for active duty members and other qualifying members. It comes in increments of $50,000 up to $400,000. In addition to the SGLI, the next of kin is given lump sum death gratuity of $100,000 to offset immediate expenses a family might have.

"Well—," she hesitated.

"Well what?" he asked.

"Your dad, he was going through a lot."

"I know."

"I guess you knew he was drinking very heavily and having some PTSD issues. Not to mention when he got the cancer, he became more and more withdrawn."

"Yeah, I knew," he said solemnly.

"Well, we did get the death gratuity, but I used it to pay off all of our bills and to help pay for family to get here for the funeral. We we're heavily in debt, Jason," she said with shame. "We were floating in a sea of debt. We had the truck and credit cards out the wazoo."

"What about the SGLI, it's like $400,000 right?"

"Normally it is. But your dad only elected to take $200,000.

"What?"

"I know. I felt the same way. Why he did it I have no idea. With that he put $100,000 in trust for the boys. He knew they would need lifelong care and didn't want them to be a burden on you, me, or who ever had to take them in someday. Then unbeknownst to me, he took an advance of his SGLI when he found out he was terminally ill and I guess drank it all and blew some at the casino."

"How much?"

"It was close to $50,000."

"Holy shit!" Jason exclaimed.

"That's what I said. I guess he forged my signature and had a buddy do the notary.

As for the other $50,000 he left me $25,000 and had $25,000 put into a trust for you and Kristy."

"He what?" Jason couldn't believe his ears.

"You heard me. He wanted you to have some money for a new house or maybe for when you had kids. So we're broke. I will get his Navy pension and I know the boys will qualify for Social Security, and I have already contacted the Veteran's Administration for help. But let's face it, we will be living on a fixed income at a time when the economy sucks and our future is uncertain."

"Why didn't you tell me?"

"Couldn't. We didn't talk much, I thought you hated me, you thought I hated you and so on," she said waving her hands frantically above her head. "When I found out, I didn't say anything. He was going through so much and he had so many demons I just couldn't do it to him or you for that matter. I didn't want your last memories of him to be bad or to be tense; with the drinking and all. I wanted him to die feeling loved and adored by his children. I never wanted to have any of you kids to have a bad memory of him, ever."

"You were looking out for us kids?"

"Don't sound so surprised, but yes I was. I know how much he meant to you and I didn't want to ruin that."

"So why tell me now?"

"Well I was going to wait, hoping we would be older, wiser and on better terms. After everything that's happened I felt it right to tell you now. And, I didn't sell everything. There is stuff put away for you and the boys."

"Really?"

"Really, there is. I did sell a lot of things, things that he never liked or wanted. But I also saved a lot of things for you. I was broke and I wasn't sure how I was going to take care of us. I really needed the money. Maybe I should have talked to you first, I just didn't know how. I don't let many people in and I was afraid. Hell, I can't believe we're talking now but so happy we are," she said grabbing and squeezing his hand.

"He loved you, Jason, he loved all of us. Don't let his cancer, his drinking, his PTSD, his demons, or any of the decisions he made change your memories about him, okay?"

There was a slight hesitation. Jason nodded. "Okay," he said as a tear streamed down his face. "I won't."

"Here, have some tissues," she said holding up the blue box. "These things blow, no pun intended, but they're better than nothing," Sandy complained. "It's like a damn piece of sand paper."

"That's something else you could work on" Jason said as he reached for the box.

"What's that?" she asked.

"Your language; It's pretty vulgar and embarrassing. Not to mention you say a lot of stuff in front of the boys that they don't need to hear."

"So, you're telling me how to raise my kids now, right?" she said. Jason felt his tension level take over the room. He looked up from blowing his nose and met Sandy's scowled face. She smiled a big smile and winked at him.

"Got yah!" she joked. Jason shook his head. Good God he sighed in relief. *She's gone nuts* he thought. She's truly gone nutty. What the hell is going to happen next?

"I'll tell you what, Jason; I will work on it if you work on something for me."

"What would that be?" he asked nervously.

"Work on Jason."

"What do you mean?"

"It means you take a lot on for other people; Dad, me, the boys, your work, Kristy and everything else. But when was the last time you took time for Jason? You need to take on something for you that means something to you. That's all."

When did Sandy get her Ph.D. in Psychology? And where the hell was I when she was getting all this weird psycho-babble training, he thought?

"Fine" he said appeasing her. "I'll do it, or at least try to anyway."

"Good, now go sit in the hall, I got to go pee and have no panties on."

"Whoa, TMI, TMI, la-la-la-la-la" he repeated as he jammed his fingers in his ears sprang from the bed and headed towards the door. It was a visual Jason didn't need.

"See I kept it clean, I didn't say piss," she said with a grin.

Jason smiled and shook his head side to side as he left the room. Now that's the Sandy I know and love. Love? I said love.

TWENTY-THREE

The drive back to Richlands' was like another bad dream of information that seemed would never end. The car was starkly quiet and the air still. Kristy told Jason the whole story of what happened on the elevator. Jason was incensed.

"Why didn't you tell me when I asked?"

"Because I knew you would react this way and I wanted you to be okay when you talked to Sandy. Not to mention the boys were there and Matt was already freaking out. I'm sorry. I wasn't trying to hide anything. I was just trying to do what I thought was right."

Jason sat silently and thought about everything she said. He reached for the stereo turned it on and changed the fader so only the rear speakers where on. He wanted to talk to Kristy without the boys hearing them. He was fixated on the ashtray Kristy had seen on the shelf.

"If it's the same one, it was my dad's. He made it when he was in grade school."

"I'm sure it is," she said confidently. "I remember it being out in the living room curio cabinet."

"How do I get it back?" he asked himself aloud.

"Can you? I mean if she bought it at the garage sale it's hers."

"Maybe I'll just ask her. Ask her how she got it, tell her who I am and ask if I can buy it back."

"I wouldn't buy anything from that cow," Kristy snapped.

"Whoa! Someone's got her kitty cat claws out."

"Damn right, she ticked me off. And to make matters worse it got Matt all riled up."

"I wanted to ask you about that," Jason said. "Why was Matt so freaked out?" The boys heard nothing except the music coming from the rear speakers.

"Well, part of it was the whole commotion that was going on and part of it was my fault."

"What do you mean?"

"I referred to Matt as special needs."

"You did?"

"Not directly. But when I was screaming at that cow I asked her how she knew a special needs child. He got really upset, more than I was. I told him I was sorry. I just feel so bad."

"It's okay, babe. He would have heard it sometime in his life. We can't hide it from him forever," Jason said as he looked in the rear view mirror.

"In fact I think he already has."

Matt was playing with an action figure on the seat and singing along with the radio.

"I just feel bad," she said solemnly.

He reached for her hand. She took his and squeezed it. "I know. But it's okay." "I love you, Jason."

"I love you too," he said raising her hand to his lips. He kissed it.

Once home, Kristy got ready for work while Jason got the boys settled in to a late afternoon's routine. He'd order a pizza, got a movie off of Netflix and just settled in to relax with his brothers. He was happy to have this time with them and would miss them terribly when they moved to Florida. It had occurred to him that this move would probably be the last time he'd see them for a long time. It would bring finality to his family and his dad's death. Even though his dad was gone, the boys were a connection and an extension of him that he could find comfort in. Now he'd be alone; everything Miller gone.

He kissed Kristy off to work and spent the night watching movies with the boys as his mind wandered. He spent more time thinking then he did watching. He really wanted to talk to this guy who had approached Kristy and when he did she wanted to be there. He called the number several times and left messages but he never called back. Jason was growing impatient but his hands were tied until he called back.

He woke up at seven thirty on Sunday morning on the sofa. The boys were lying all around him, body parts hanging in every direction. He wiggled his way free of the arms and legs and made a pot of coffee. While it brewed he showered and shaved.

He called the number and left and fourth message. "Look, man, please call me. I really would like to talk to you."

Kristy got home around eight thirty. It was an unusually cool morning and Jason met her with a kiss and a cup of coffee on the porch. She sat down on the front stoop as the steam billowed over her face. She took a sip. With her eyes closed she absorbed the aroma and flavor of the fresh brewed coffee.

"You read my mind. I was hoping you'd be up and made coffee."

"That's me, the great Kreskin. How was your night?"

"Good. Busy as all get out. I think all of Onslow County is admitted to that place. It made the night go quicker, but I'm tired."

"They give you any heart ache for calling out Friday?"

"Not really. Just a verbal warning letter in my mailbox."

"How can it be verbal if it's a note in your mailbox?"

"Who knows, I think the Charge Nurse Mrs. Alverez doesn't like confrontation or is afraid of me."

"I think she's afraid of you," he joked.

"Oh yeah, I'm so naughty."

"Yes. Yes you are," he said with a devilish grin.

"Not now, pretty boy, I need some sleep."

Jason laughed. "I know baby, go to bed. I'm going to take the boys to the movies I think and then to the park."

"Not going to visit Sandy?"

"Nah, not today. I need a break from all of this drama. I figure I'd call her later let the boys say hi. She'll understand, I hope."

"I can see that," she agreed.

"Maybe that guy will call back. What's his name again?"

"Louis, I think. Did you call him?"

"Only like four or five times."

"Jason!"

"What?" he asked defensively.

"Stop calling the guy; he'll call."

"How do you know?"

"I don't, but he said he would. And it's not like we can't find him if he doesn't, he works there, dah!" bumping into him with her body. "Now stop calling him and enjoy your day with the boys, okay?"

"Okay."

"I mean it, Jason."

"Okay, okay, I'll leave it alone. Maybe you should call him. Maybe he'll like your voice better."

"Maybe," she agreed. "Now," she said as rose from her seat "I'm going to bed. Give me a kiss." Jason leaned forward from where he was standing and took in a long warm kiss.

"Sleep good, baby, I love you." She smiled and ran her hand over his face. "Night-night," she said turning and going into the house. "Tell the boys I said hi and have fun today."

"We will, babe," he said with a smile.

Jason waited for the boys to get up and got them ready to go out for the day. It was hard enough sleeping during the day, the last thing she needed was two boys rough housing through the house all day. They needed to get out burn off some energy and forget the spectacle going on around them. After checking the papers and realizing there was nothing playing that the boys could see, Jason came up with a brilliant idea. He walked into the kitchen where the boys were scarfing down Trix cereal.

"Who wants to go to Jungle Rapids?" The boy's heads shot up to meet Jason's face. Bright, brilliant smiles came over their faces.

"Me, me, me!" they uttered through a mouthful of colored cereal.

"Alright then, get your bathing suits and I'll pack us a bag." The boys just stared at him.

"What?" he asked.

"We don't have one here."

"Oh crap, that's right."

"So we can't go?" Matt said

"Ah, sure we can."

"How?"

"We'll stop at Wal-Mart and get a new one," Jason said matter-of-factly.

"Really?" Ryan asked.

"Really. So go get ready. Brush hair and teeth and be quiet as you can, Kristy's sleeping."

"Okay, Jason," they said in unison as they ran out of the kitchen. The excitement they had was evident in the way the bounced and bobbed down the hall and up the steps. Before leaving, Jason had the boys call Sandy. Although she said she understood, there was a hint of disappointment in her voice when he said they weren't coming to see her.

"I'm sorry, Sandy, I just need a break."

"I understand it's okay. Isn't it nice thinking of Jason for once isn't it?"

"Thank you Dr. Sigmund Freud. It is," he said with a grin.

They spent the day riding every water ride in the park, in what seemed like fifty times. Then they hit the go-carts and the Jungle golf and Jason had had it. It seemed the boys did too. The excited shrieks and laughter had been replaced by burnt cheeks and tired eyes. They piled into the car for the hour-plus ride home. The boys were asleep in minutes, leaning against their respective windows. Jason smiled and just took it in. He was happy, really happy. And tired, really tired. He fought to keep his eyes open and finally reached the house.

"Boys, wake up we're home." Nothing; not so much as a peep. A bit louder Jason said, "Boys! Matt, Ryan get up we're home, let's go, get up."

They slowly awakened from their deep sleep stretching and yawning like a bear waking from a winter's hibernation. They all piled through the front door in a stoic silence of tired. Kristy was in the kitchen and came out to greet them.

"Here come my men!" she exclaimed. "And boy don't you guys look wiped out." The boys grunted and nodded as they slinked by her on their way to the laundry room to put up their things.

"Hey, baby, how was it?"

"Good. We had a blast. But, I'm so tired I can't even see straight."

"You look it," she said sympathetically.

"I can't wait to get to bed."

"Well, I have something that may perk you up."

"Right now?" he said with a tired wink.

"Not that. Get your mind out of the gutter," she said winking right back.

"Louis called me."

Jason sprang back to life. "He did? What did he say?"

"He's going to meet us tomorrow morning at the Lighthouse around eight-thirty. I told him I had to work and so did you, so we needed to meet earlier, rather than later."

"Did he say anything?"

"No, and honestly I didn't ask. I wanted him to tell it, whatever it may be to both of us. It could be nothing, but we'll see."

"I know," he said. "I guess I just want to know what was or is going on."

Kristy reached over and rubbed his face. "It will all come out somehow, someway, someday. You'll see. It'll be fine, babe."

"I know," he said his face falling into her hand absorbing he soft strokes.

"Now get your butt in the kitchen, I made pork chops!" she ordered with a smile and a giggle.

"Yes, ma'am!" he said proudly.

The four of them sat around the table and shared stories about the day's events at the water park with Kristy. They all laughed and carried on; Matt even doing an impression of Jason screaming down one of the speed slides. It was a lot of fun but Jason caught himself drifting away and thinking of his dad. He missed him today, a lot. He missed not being able to do these types of things with him.

Dad was never a touchy feely guy and family fun days were few and far between. When they did have them dad would wander off to get beers and sit in a chair watching bikinis walk by. He rarely got in the pool or went on rides. That is, unless he was drunk. Then he'd show off for all of the ladies, but wind-up embarrassing his family. Then the fights would start. Sandy would tell him he'd had enough, Chris would tell her to mind her own business and all hell would break loose with the screaming and the yelling.

Jason hated that about his father. Why couldn't he just be like normal dads? But then he'd defend him. What was a normal dad he'd ask himself in his dad's defense. Jason resigned himself to the fact that his dad loved him the only way he knew how. Jason needed to accept his love his way and not try to change it to what he wanted it to be or what he thought it should be. He came out of his trance. This was a mind battle for another day he convinced himself as he returned his attention to the dinner table chatter.

Dinner ended and before Jason could finish clearing the table with Kristy, the boys were fast asleep on the couch. Jason was semi relieved. He could use a good night's sleep himself. He was tired and his mind was racing back and forth between Sandy, his dad, the mystery woman, the unfinished letter, a woman dad loved years ago and on and on and on. Sleep was his priority too. The last thing Jason remembered was kissing Kristy off to work. It was the beep-beep-beep of his alarm clock that brought him to.

He dropped the boys at Mrs. Rainier's so they could get to school that morning. She'd get them off the bus too which was one less worry Jason had that day. He strolled into the Naval Hospital and headed to the Light House Café. He smiled when Kristy appeared from around the corner. As they embraced, the sweet smell of her body broadened the smile across his face.

"Been waiting long?"

"Nope, just got here."

"Me too."

"Well, let's go see what this Louis guy has to say, shall we?"

"Let's," she said.

They both got coffee and settled in a booth. Neither one was in a talkative mood. That was fine. Jason's dad had told him once that if you can sit with a woman for a long time and not say a thing, it proved your relationship was natural. You didn't need forced conversation. It was the ones you had to entertain that you needed to keep away from he warned. There was no need to entertain Kristy; she was Jason's keeper.

The tall slender black kid strolled into the café. His sneakers were untied and his shorts were pulled down exposing his boxer briefs. A NC State tee-shirt and light wind breaker completed the ensemble.

"Wuz up," he said and nodded at them as he plopped down beside Kristy. She slid over in the booth and turned to her right to better see him.

"Not much," she said. "Thanks for coming."

Jason just stared at him.

"Hey no sweat. I liked your Pops, he was a good dude. Helped me out. And taught me a lot in the little time I knew him."

"How did you know him?" Kristy asked.

"I was his Corpsman when he was here. I was the night guy, nineteen-hundred to zero-seven hundred. We talked a lot at night, wasn't anything else to do. Plus like I said he was cool."

"Cool, how? Like he was some kind of clown?" Jason snapped at him.

"Whoa, what's up with that attitude?" Louis asked, his voice changing to a higher octave as he spoke.

"What's up with that," Jason mocked "is you stroll in here looking like some kind of thug, talking like you and my dad were drinking buddies and that happens to rub me the wrong way. That's what's up," Jason said accentuating his punctuation.

Louis just stared at him, their eyes meeting. After a few tense seconds Louis busted out in a belly laugh. He sat back, grabbed his stomach and belly laughed, over acting his amusement by leaning forward and smacking the table with his hand. This was a first, a guy laughing in his face. Stunned, Jason sat back and looked over at Kristy who was just as shocked. She looked over at Jason and just shrugged.

"What the hell is so funny?" Jason demanded.

"Dude, your Pops described you to a tee. He said you were hot headed, all military like and man he was right. And for your information, he told me to call him Chris. I didn't out of respect." He continued laughing and slowly it tapered off to a broad smile. "He showed me a ton of pictures of you all. That's how I recognized you the other day," he said, nodding at Kristy.

"My dad talked to you about me?" Jason asked in disbelief. His tone had changed to interest.

"Yeah, man. I mean it was never anything bad, just chatter more than anything."

"What did he say — ?"

"Jason," Kristy said reaching across and grabbing his hand.

"No," he said pulling his hand back, "I want to know what he said."

"Know what he said about what?" Louis asked the smile leaving his face. "What he said about me, his wife, his family, him dying."

"Yo man, this isn't going to be some Dr. Phil moment is it? I mean I thought you wanted to know the story behind nurse coo-coo-for-cocoa puffs and your pops. I didn't know you wanted to find out who loved who and why."

"That's not it at all," Jason said. "I just want to know what was going on in his head."

"Dude, didn't you ever talk to your own pops?" a stunned Louis asked.

"I did, but we weren't close."

"Jason, you we're too," Kristy chimed in.

"No we weren't," he said sharply still looking at Louis. "Not like I thought we should be anyway. I guess I just want the independent version."

Louis and Jason stared at one another. The genuine anticipation in Jason's eyes was unmistakable to Louis. He didn't know much, but what he did he would share.

"What do you want to know?" Louis said as he looked down on the table. He bounced his legs up and down and slid his fingers across the table. He was suddenly nervous.

"Everything from the first day you met until the day he left to come home to die," Jason said."

"That's a lot."

"Look, I'm sorry I snapped. It's just I need to know for reasons I can't go into right now. So much has happened in the last year. I just need to know. Please," Jason implored. Kristy reached and took his hands again and squeezed them tight.

Louis let out a sigh and began to tell the tale of his brief yet meaningful relationship with Chris Miller. After forty-five minutes Jason had heard enough.

"No offense but I know all of this!" Jason blurted out as he sat back shaking his head.

"Look, you said tell you everything. This is everything," an agitated Louis shot back.

"I know, but I'm looking for something more specific."

"Dude, make up your mind. I don't got time for this. What?"

"I found a letter in my dad's things when I was cleaning out his house, it was addressed to someone named...."

"Charlie, right?" Louis interjected.

"How did you know?" he asked, shock visible on her face.

"Because your pops gave that letter to me and asked me to deliver it for him, but before I could part of it disappeared."

"There's more?" Jason asked anxiously. "It was a whole letter? And disappeared how?"

"It was a whole letter. I was going to make a copy for him. He wanted one just in case something happened and I needed it."

"What would he need a copy for?" Jason asked.

"I don't know. It just seemed like it was so important to your pops to have another copy."

"Did you read it?"

"Hell no!" Louis said emphatically. "It wasn't my place to read it."

"But you looked at it?" Jason snapped.

"Look, I wasn't snooping; I wasn't getting in his business; I just was making a copy. I can't explain why. It was obvious that this wasn't some random thoughts he had. He worked on this letter day and night until the very end when ya'll took him home."

"So what happened?" Kristy asked.

"I went to the copier the night he gave it to me, put it in, hit the button. It spit out like five or six blank pages and then stopped; it was out of toner. When I got back the first few pages in the discharge were gone. The only thing left were the last couple of pages in the feeder never copied. I looked all around, but never found the missing ones so I gave up on making a copy."

"Did you tell my dad?"

"I wish I did. But I just couldn't disappoint him like that. So I took what I had." "So there is no copy?"

"Nah man, sorry."

"Do you know who took them?" Kristy asked.

"Nah. I have my suspicions though."

"Who?"

"Your girl," Louis said turning and nodding to Kristy.

A puzzled look came over her face and Louis knew he had to help her along.

"Old girl on the ward."

"You mean that cow from Saturday?"

"The one and only."

"Who is she?" Jason asked.

"Her name is Lieutenant Shriver. She and your pops hated each other with a passion."

"Why?" asked Kristy.

"Because my dad caught her taking advantage of the junior guys and basically turned her career off," Jason said, the memory of the story his dad had told him flooded his mind. "She got a terrible fitrep and now she's just buying her time until they kick her out."

"That's her," Louis pointed out.

"So why do you think it was her?" Kristy asked.

"Well she hated your pops, she hates me and the only one around the nurses' station was her. Plus, your pops caught her snooping through his book one day. He never reported it he just bitched her out. He did ask me to hide it if he was asleep or off the ward floor. Told me I should watch my back with her too, so I did."

"Obviously, not good enough."

"Dude, that's messed up!" Louis snapped sternly. "Your pops...."

"Stop calling him pops," Jason snapped back.

"Fine. Chris," Louis said antagonistically, "was a good man. I admired him and liked him a lot. He wasn't just my patient; he was my friend so get off my back."

"Alright, stop it both of you!" Kristy ordered. "We need to find out if she took it and if so where is it. And where is the rest of the letter."

"Well, I can tell you where the rest of the letter is," Louis said.

"Where?" asked Jason.

"I gave it to the Doc, just like your po--, I mean your dad asked. I told him I only had half, the other half was stolen or disappeared and he said okay, took it and that was that."

His heart began racing, and his stomach began to twirl in a tickle. "Who? What doctor?"

"Doc Wilton."

"Doctor Wilton from Mental Health?" Jason roared. "Are you frigging kidding me?" Jason's shock and disbelief took over the table.

"Yeah, that's him. Your dad wanted me to hand deliver it to him. He said it was really important."

Shocked, Kristy turned to Jason. "You talked to him didn't you?"

"I sure did and he didn't tell me anything. Now I find this out. I can't believe this." Jason sat in silence staring down at the table. The white Formica top was worn and stained and it absorbed the anger Jason had building inside him. All this time he's been looking and searching for answers and they were right upstairs on the second floor. Patient confidentiality or not, Jason wanted answers and he was going to get them one way or another. Kristy's soft reassuring voice broke his trance.

"It was her," she said still staring at Jason.

"It was her what?" as he shot his eyes towards her.

"She stole the letter."

"How do you know?" asked a puzzled Louis.

"Matt, Jason's brother saw her. Saturday when we were here, Matt said that she was in the house. He saw her in the house. That's how this whole thing with her started. We were in the elevator and he recognized her. She stole the letter, slipped into your dad's house during the garage sale and planted it so we'd find it. She wanted to hurt Sandy and you guys to get back at your dad. The only way to do that was to plant this letter, let someone find it and have them think what you thought; that you dad had this secret life while he was married."

"That's deep," Louis speculated.

"But it makes sense."

"Think about it; she was snooping around his room; was the only one at the nurses' station and Mathew remembered her."

"She even has the ashtray," Jason blurted out.

"And she got it at the garage sale which puts her at the house. She could have snuck inside especially with all the people."

"So that's had to be when she did it. While everyone was busy buying his stuff she snuck in the house and planted it. Matt caught her and she gave him some B.S. and got away with it," said Jason.

"She didn't get away with anything; I'm going to see her. I want the ashtray back and I want her busted for burglary, robbery, whatever."

"Gotta prove it though," Jason shot back.

"Okay, a bit too deep for me, y'all," Louis concluded as he slid out of the booth and stood up. "I can't get any more involved and in fact I don't want to get involved. I told you what I know and anything else that happens is on you. I don't want to get involved no more."

Jason slid out of the chair and stood to face Louis. "It's all good, man. No one will mention you or drag you into anything. I just appreciate you talking to us."

"Even though you called me fifty-million times and then got all uppity?" Louis interjected.

"Yeah, even after all that. I'm sorry, man, I didn't mean to be ungrateful. I really appreciate what you did, taking care of my dad, delivering the letter."

"Or parts thereof," a smiling but embarrassed Louis added.

"Parts or no parts, you helped him and he needed someone and you were there," a somber Jason said.

"Is that what this is?"

"What?"

"You don't think you were there for him do you?" Louis asked as he leaned back.

Jason was stunned and caught off guard. He was not expecting this line of questioning. Hell, he wasn't expecting any questioning.

"Um, I guess I. . ., well what I mean is I...."

"Dude, your pops loved you a lot. I don't want to get all mushy, but he talked a lot about you, her," he said pointing at Kristy, "and your brothers and moms. Like I said we talked a lot. He was proud of you and he was happy that if anyone would be there for his family after he was gone, it would be you. Now I don't know why you feel the way you do, but if you think about it you were there for him. Still are."

"Oh yeah, how's that?" Jason questioned.

"Simple, man, you're here. The way I see it is you're still there for him, clearing his name, protecting him, and his family too. And that's something a lot of people can't say. Take care, bro." With that Louis turned and slowly walked to the door, pushed it open and left.

"You okay, babe?" Kristy whispered.

"Yeah, I'm okay," he said staring at the door. I got to get going."

"Okay." Kristy slid out of the booth and grabbed Jason's hand. What do you want to do?"

"About which part?"

"All of it."

"I don't know, but we'll figure it out. We can talk tonight when I get home." Jason's voice was dull and his mind seemed to be somewhere else.

"You sure you're okay?" she asked.

"Fine, baby," he said planting a kiss on her forehead. "Now I've got to get going. I'll see you at home, okay?"

"Okay, sweetie." Kristy said trying to reassure herself that Jason was really okay."

"Love you."

"Love you too," he said as they walked out of the café. He headed down the passageway. In a matter of moments he was gone in a sea of military uniforms and patients clogging the halls.

Kristy turned and headed for the staff entrance and exit. It was a familiar voice that made her stop. She hesitated. Should I, she wondered? Damn right I should! She walked to coffee shop at the end of the passageway.

TWENTY-FOUR

He stormed into the Clinic on a mission. It was now or never. He couldn't wait any longer and was going to find out one way or another.

"Can I help you?" came the pleasant voice from behind the protective glass. The Mental Health Clinic had installed a locking glass widow and a security door ever since a patient had beaten the snot out of one of the psychiatrists. They had been asking for more security but the command didn't think was an issue. It's funny how it became an issue after the smack down took place. There was no way in unless they buzzed you in. The front desk was completely incased in security glass, cameras and panic buttons that went right to hospital security and the base police.

"Hi, I'd like to see Dr. Wilton."

"Do you have an appointment?" she asked.

"No, sorry I don't."

"Is he expecting you?" Again so pleasant.

"No, he's not," he said now agitated.

"Well, I'm sorry then, he's booked solid and right now he's in a conference call with the staff. Do you have a referral? I can make you an appoint...."

"No I don't have a referral," he snapped. "I'm not here for care; I'm here on a personal matter." His demeanor had changed.

"You're going to need to calm down," the receptionist said calmly trying to defuse the situation. Her pleasant voice and innocent vibrant face so full of empathy and support was now red with fear.

"If you can't control yourself, you're going to have to leave or I'm going to call Security. Do you understand?" she demanded gaining more backbone.

With that said, the door to the clinical area opened a young marine stepped out. Jason saw his opportunity and leaped over to catch the closing door and ran through onto the office space.

"Hey, you can't come back here!" came the screams from the front desk. "Stop him!"

"Call Security, call Security!" the receptionist yelled.

"I just want to see Doctor Wilton, that's all," Jason shot back. "Now where is he?"

"Stop! You can't go back there!" a psychiatric technician yelled as he emerged from a different office.

"Where is he?" Jason demanded.

"Get out!" came the response. "We've called Security, get out."

The commotion Jason had started, forced open several doors from various offices. Psychiatrists and social workers peered at the angered sailor storming down the passageway. Jason continued on his crusade. "Where is Dr. Wilton?" he demanded again.

"Get out! We're calling Security!" came the response.

Jason kept charging down the hall, looking in each office as he went. He reached the final door on the left and swung it open. A group of naval officers and civilian doctors all darted their eyes to the door; Dr. Wilton's was one set of them.

"There you are," Jason barked.

"Who the hell do you think you are? How did you get back here? What are you doing here?" came the response from a tall well-built Navy captain. It was Captain Gray, the Director of Mental Health Services. His booming voice and large physic captured Jason's attention.

Oh no, Jason thought. *What have I done?* His sudden burst of adrenaline turned into fear. *Well, too late now*, he thought.

Jason regained his composure and his military bearing, "I need to see Dr. Wilton, Sir. It's important."

"No, you need to get out," he ordered.

Jason didn't move, frozen in place.

"Now, sailor!"

"But Sir —," Jason implored.

"But Sir nothing, get out!" he ordered. With that several other people in the room stood up and Jason could hear the sounds of people running down the passageway behind him.

"Please!"

"It's okay, Captain, I'll see him," came a small voice from in the crowd.

"Lucien, you don't have to."

"I know, Sir. It's okay though. I've sort of been expecting him," came the reassuring response.

"Are you sure?"

"Yes, Sir. I'll see him."

Jason's risk had paid off. Suddenly he was grabbed from behind and jerked into the passageway. His body was slammed up against the wall and his arm bent way up behind him. The two Masters-at-arms fumbled with a set of flex cuffs to secure Jason's hands.

"Ouch, ouch, ouch, you're going to break my arm," Jason moaned.

"Do not resist, do not resist, you're under arrest, do not resist!" came the firm and growling order.

"Petty Officer, Petty Officer!" Dr. Wilton yelled. "It's okay, he's okay. I'm going to see him. It's a bit of a misunderstanding that's all."

"Misunderstanding? Are you serious? We got a call and a panic button alert that some guy had broken in and was after you."

"I'm not a patient," Jason mumbled, his face planted firmly against the wall.

"You should be," came a shout from the crowd that had gathered.

"No, no, it's fine. Really it is. Now you can let him go."

"Stand down MA1, it's okay," Captain Gray ordered, his voice calm but strong.

MA1 Laverne stared at Captain Gray and then shifted his eye to Dr. Wilton.

"It's fine MA1," Dr. Wilton said patting his shoulder. "Let him go."

"Let him go," MA1 ordered. With that order MA2 Jones and MA3 Kelso let Jason go, dropping the flex-cuffs to the floor.

"Damn it," Jason yelled as he turned around to face the crowd. His uniform was disheveled, his arm was throbbing at the shoulder, and his face was stinging from its scrapping against the textured wall paper.

"You about broke my arm!"

"You're lucky you're not going to the brig you putts," Laverne shot back.

"That's it, we're done. MA1 thanks for you quick response. Dr. Wilton why don't you and HM2 go talk in your office. Everyone else, thank you but the show is over. Everyone back to work please. Thank you," Captain Gray said.

The hordes of people began to return to their offices and work spaces just as Captain Gray had told them too. Jason felt a sense of relief; however it was quickly dashed.

"Before he leaves," Captain Gray began "I want his name, department head's name, and where he works. You may not be under arrest, but your ass is mine. This HM2 is not over."

"Yes, Sir," Jason replied smartly. He was in some big trouble. But he didn't care right now. He wanted answers.

Dr. Wilton walked past Jason with his head down and a stack of papers in his hands. He motioned to Jason. "This way HM2, let's go up to my office."

Jason turned and saw the people out looking at the commotion. They were returning to their work spaces as ordered, however Jason could feel their eyes burning through his uniform and into his head. He was embarrassed that he had let his emotions get the best of him. Never let your personal feelings get in the way of your professional responsibility his dad would tell him. It seemed Jason had screwed that one up, and bad.

Dr. Wilton stopped at the first office on the left, turned and faced Jason who was coming up behind him. He stood to the side and waved him in.

"Come in, Jason and have a seat over there," he said pointing to a set of small recliners separated by a cherry wood round table. Jason went in and took a seat in the old leather recliner that faced the office. He had his back to the wall and studied the decorations and furniture in the room.

The room was small but cozy. The recliners made it seem relaxed.

Closing the office door behind them, Dr. Wilton went over to a filing cabinet opened it and grabbed a manila folder. He pushed the drawer shut and placed the folder under a stack of papers he had carried up from the conference room. He joined Jason in the corner taking a seat in an adjacent recliner.

"So," Dr. Wilton began, "you wanted to see me. What about?"

"Cut the bull, Doc, you know why I'm here and what this is about."

"No, actually I don't. Why don't you tell me what I think this is about?"

"Alright, first stop the soft spoken psycho-babble crap. Second, I'm not here for a session, and third I know that you have the rest of the letter my dad wrote."

"You mean this one," Dr. Wilton replied calmly. He reached into the manila folder and pulled out several pages of paper. He held them up. They were stapled together along with a legal sized envelope hanging vertically to the papers.

"Oh, I'm sorry," Dr. Wilton said as he noticed that Jason was staring to see the words. He turned the envelope horizontally and flipped it over so Jason could read it. It read: To Dr. Wilton; From Senior Chief Miller. I think I found the missing piece to my puzzle, happy reading!

"You had it all along, I came and saw you and you didn't tell me."

"You didn't ask," he replied matter of factly.

"Oh, don't give me that, you knew what I was looking for and you held on to it."

"I had no obligation to give it to you. It's patient confidentiality HM2, plain and simple. As a Corpsman you should know that. I also told you, you would need primary next of kin authorization to read it. Legally, my hands were tied."

Jason took a deep breath leaned forward and put his head down. Dr. Wilton was right legally. If Jason wanted a moral victory he had come to the wrong person. He wasn't giving up after coming this far. He looked up.

"I know that. And while it may be a legal obligation, there's also the moral obligation and the human factor here. He was my father."

"HM2, there is no moral obligation to do anything for you at all. Legally I have to protect my patients which includes his thoughts, his dreams, his fears, and in some cases his demons. As far as the human factor, what exactly is that?"

"Don't analyze me, Doc!"

"I'm not. I just want to know what you mean."

His calm demeanor and gentle voice was really irritating Jason.

"It means give me a break," he said as his voice cracked and his face got hot. "I need closure. And from what I see he got it by writing the letter."

He leaned forward and pulled a clump of folded papers from his digital cammies.

"This is the second part to the letter. It must in some way given him peace. He needed closure, and that letter gave it to him."

"You mean since your father has died he has closure on what ever bothered or debilitated him, right?"

"Yes I'd think so."

"Do you really think so?" Wilton asked sincerely.

"I don't know for sure, but maybe it did."

"And maybe it didn't," Wilton shot back.

"So what's the big deal then?" Jason asked, almost pleading.

"The big deal is you went about this all wrong," a sternly voiced Wilton began. "The big deal is a Hospital Corpsman violated HIPPA rules; the big deal is an HM2 embarrassed himself and his family's name and father's memory by barging into a meeting ranting and raving. And the big deal is because you're on staff at this command doesn't mean you get special treatment. You we're wrong, period." Dr. Wilton slammed the file down on the coffee table. The loud crash startled Jason. There was a brief moment of quiet.

"So you have the first part of the letter?" he asked looking at the worn pages in Jason's lap.

"Yes, I do."

"Do you want to read it?" Jason asked.

"Do you want me to?"

"Jesus. Can you stop with the question on question crap? Do you want to read it or not?"

"I would like to, yes considering it was meant for me. You need to realize that this was a very important step for your father and his mental health."

Jason looked at Dr. Wilton curiously. "What do you mean by mental health?"

"You had to know your father had some issues, right? Didn't your dad ever talk about Iraq, the war, anything?"

"No."

"How about his nightmares, his drinking, his visions?"

"No, not directly. I mean I knew something was going on but I never really went looking for it. My brothers are special needs so I can't really rely on them for information or put them in a position to spy or anything. So I guess I did but didn't."

"You didn't want to know, right?"

"I guess."

"And you don't get along with your step mother is that correct?" Dr. Wilton asked. He was pushing Jason and he knew it. He just didn't care at this point.

"True. We didn't get along."

"Didn't? Why the past tense description?" Dr. Wilton asked.

"I think things are starting to improve."

"Why do you think that, Jason?" Dr. Wilton asked, his face showing intense interest in the response.

"I don't know. Maybe I misunderstood her and where I stood or stand so to speak."

"And where would that be?"

Jason was getting irritated. "In the way. In the way of her the boys. In the way of my dad."

"I see," Dr. Wilton went on, "However, in reality you're discovering that those feelings are false? Is that a fair assessment?"

"Yeah, I guess so."

"And they were false because?"

"Because why?" Jason responded sarcastically. "Why don't you tell me because obviously I don't know and you're the doctor," Jason scoffed.

"Because. . . ," Dr. Wilton pressed with a hint of impatience in his voice.

"What?"

"Because she took over. Sandy took over."

"Took over what? How? What the hell are you talking about?"

"Sandy took away your dad; your only other parent. You had already lost your mother and then you felt you lost your father to her. You felt alone, abandoned, and while you may have grieved your mother you could not grieve your father because he was right there living a new life in front of you. And you had no one to grieve with. So you internalized. You labeled yourself the black sheep and lived the role to the tee. You have held on to this 'Oh woe-is-me' attitude for so long you believe it. You have developed an anger and hostility towards Sandy and in some cases the world, especially when you don't get your way. All brought on by you. I think you're a time bomb; tick, tick, tick," he said tapping the crystal on his watch. "It's only a matter of time before you blow-up unless you get yourself together."

Jason broke in, "So, you don't count today as an explosion?" He turned his head and looked out the window.

"I think today was a preview. I think there is more to come unless you can come to terms with your life and focus on the future and not the past."

Sandy had said something similar he thought. He looked at Wilton.

"And how do I exactly do that?"

"Well for one, I tell my patients that yesterday's achievements and yesterday's failures are gone. Do you know why a wind shield is so big and a rear view mirror so small?" he asked.

Dr. Wilton waited a moment and gave the answer himself, "It's because the future is wide open and the past is a small and fading memory. It's the fool who looks for so much in an area so small. You need to get yourself together or everything you hold dear will someday slip away."

They stared at one another, a soft hum from the vent the only sound audible in the room. Dr. Wilton picked up the folder.

"Do you know why I got the letter out when you came into the office?"

"No."

"It's because of this," he said leaning forward and handing some papers to Jason. "It's authorization allowing you access to your father's records."

"How? How did you....?"

"I went and spoke with her in her room. I told her the truth. Well, enough of it to protect your family and enough to get you a signature. I told her you were struggling with your father's death which is true, and that there might be some closure in his records for you which is also true. However, I did not tell her about this letter and its contents. It could cause more harm than good. After talking with you in the passageway, I felt it important that you have access so you can get the closure you need." He picked up the letter. "Just like this letter gave your dad the closure he needed. Here, take it. Take it," he said thrusting it forward.

Jason just looked across the table in stunned silence, the authorization form still clutched between his fingers.

"Here," he insisted, "take it."

Jason set the forms down and took the stapled papers and envelope.

"Take as much time as you need, you just can't leave with it."

"Alright," he muttered inaudibly.

"Can I read the part of the letter you brought?" he asked. Jason nodded his head yes, still in disbelief he had made such an idiot of himself. Maybe he had misjudged Sandy and Dr. Wilton. Everyone he thought was against him might have been really been out to help him. He took a deep breath and looked down. The answers to so many questions lay in his hands. He took another deep breath and began to read picking up exactly where he had left off.

TWENTY-FIVE

. . . the world was against us. Your mom's dad totally freaked out. She was Muslim and I was Catholic, so that didn't go over well. Especially since all of the problems in the Middle East. Even my mom, your Grammie freaked out. She was so mad and disappointed in me. Pre-marital sex was a no-no in both religions, but I didn't care though. I loved you and your mom more than I anything else in my life. And I know your mom loved me as well. There is something about true love; you just know. It's not acquired, it's not learned, but it's just there. That was your mom and you. It was just there.

When I found out I could not see your mom anymore I could feel this sick twisting fear in my stomach. It's hard to describe, but it's like a nausea that tickles if that makes any sense. I tried and tried to see your mom, night after night and day after day. I even had some guy show up at the door at Grammies asking me to forget about you and your mom. He said that she had been sent back to Pakistan and I would never see either of you again. I wanted to kill him, but that wasn't to be. You and your mom being sent away was never an ending for me, but rather a beginning. One that leads me here today to this paper, with this pen.

I think the day he came to the house helped shape me into who I am today both good and bad. It was the beginning of endless searches, dead ends, and literally thousands of hours on the internet looking for someone I could never see, touch or hold. It was that emptiness I think that led me to so much self-destruction. It's what haunts me about never finding you. I built up a lot of resentment and anger during that time, something I can only now admit. I drank too much, smoked too much and alienated myself from everything and everyone. It built up and built up to the point where I accepted it as my normal everyday life.

When I was in Iraq I would see all of these children running and playing. They were so innocent and for that few hours of play time they were unaware of the war raging around them. Their faces were like any other from that region with a pretty olive tone. Everyone had thick black hair and dark brown eyes. I would go and play soccer with them, give them the candy from my MRE, and pass out goodies from the care packages I got from home. Then one day it all changed.

We were in the RAS when the call came in that a car bomb had gone off in Haditha, a city in the western Iraq province of Al Anbar. Within ten minutes they started to arrive. There were no Marines, no soldiers, no military at all. It was all civilians mostly women and children. To put it mildly, it was a blood bath. There were kids with missing limbs and with gaping holes from shrapnel wounds. They were crying looking for their mothers who had been blown to bits right in front of them. One kid had several of his mother's ribs embedded in his face. It was such a mess. As the mayhem continued air crewman carried in a hazmat bag.

"What's in the bag?" I asked.

"A couple of rag heads. Mostly parts so we just scrapped up what we could. Where do you want it?"

He held it up like it was an old bag of dirty laundry. An orange bag? That's what these beautiful people had been reduced too. That's when out of nowhere it hit me. You and your mother were these beautiful people I was watching you die and in some instances killing you.

You were every one of those children with thick black hair and those beautiful brown eyes, just like your mother. One minute you were playing and laughing and the next minute bleeding, crying and dying. I went from one extreme to the other that night. I went from die hard kill them all to why are we even here? Don't get me wrong, I still had and to some degree still have an anger towards the insurgents and criminals that tormented and tortured innocent Iraqi's and coalition forces. But I guess my perspective changed on the real reason we were in Iraq and the real reason two-plus-thousand American died there. My mind started playing tricks on me and it got to the point where all I saw was the blood and death of women and children.

I used to think you were one of the kids all mangled up and blown to hell they'd brought into the RAS or the FRSS. Voices in my head would tell me it's you. My child was bleeding out and dying right in front of me. Your mother was the stately grandmother screaming for her dead grandchildren and their maimed and disfigured mother. The orange bags would move and my Grandchildren would reach out to me. What if the girl the Marines were accused of raping was you? And what if I am killing my son-in-law, my daughter, and my grandchildren every time I pulled the trigger or watched a raid live in the Combat Operations

*Center? When they reach out their bloody hands
from the operating able, were they reaching for me?
Do they know I'm their grandfather? I see faceless
bloodied bodies in nightmares so vivid I can smell
the blood. They're all telling me to go now. Go
where? Where was I supposed to go? It would be a
long time until I figured out where to go and how to
get there. And now as I pen my final letter in this
life I think I'm there.*

*I've never told anyone this Charlie, but I've
come to believe and accept that I have Post
Traumatic Stress Disorder. This letter to you is the
final part of my treatment, but not my cure. I am
dying and there are no more options for me. I don't
want to die unhappy. This is the most important
step I can take so I can finally say I got my head
fixed before I died.*

Head fixed? Jason read that before. In
the first part of the letter, Dad wrote something
about fixing his head. He wasn't talking about
his cancer getting fixed; he was talking about
his battle with himself getting fixed. Jason
read on:

*I look back on my post 9/11 life and think
how I screwed it up not on purpose, but by happen-
stance. The war played like a movie over and over
in my mind and I have spent many nights drinking
myself to sleep only to be woken up by the same
movie with the same crummy actors. I tried to
numb my self-induced pain and suffering by
alienating myself from all of my friends and my
family. I spent a lot of time making up excuses as to*

why I can't or won't be going here of their blocking out the disappointed faces of my family. I found myself crying for no reason with it just kind of coming over me. I'm still hyper-vigilant to almost everything around me. Whenever I went out I had to sit facing the whole room making sure I can see the comings and goings of every patron and employee although I'm not as jumpy. I took out so many of my frustrations and pain on my family. I was happy one day, sad and miserable the next. PTSD ruined my life because I let it and my inability to let go of you and your mom only fed it. If I had recognized my own daemons before I went to Iraq and got treatment maybe I would never have gotten PTSD. Maybe I would have recognized it or my own symptoms and done something about it. It robbed me of my children, my wife, and my life because I let it. Well no more. I cannot be a prisoner to a condition I can control.

I never thought that my life would end up this way; where I would be putting all of myself onto a piece of paper in hopes of making myself better. Better? That sounds odd since I'm dying. But I look at it this way: cancer is killing me. I will never be cured. But writing this letter is releasing me and with that I will finally be saved. Like I wrote earlier it's not a cure. It's saving me from me.

I don't want to die a bitter person mad because they got cancer. But since I have to I choose to die happy. I have taken so much granted and dwelled on the most frivolous things. But, I have looked at so many aspects of my life and I realize how lucky I have been.

I have a great wife who is good to me and the kids. She has always been faithful to me and always been there when I needed her. Long nights, weekends, holidays, and deployments you name it she was there. I love her and even though so many people said I was crazy to even think of marrying her, she has been one of the greatest pillars of my life.

I have great kids; Matt and Ryan are so special to me and I believe whole-heartedly a gift. I know only special children wind up with special parents. I worry about them, but Sandy has always been so good with them and I know she will guide them to a very good life.

I especially don't need to worry about Jason. I'd like to think that we've always had a special bond. I know there has been a lot of times he has needed me and I haven't been there. Some of it was beyond my control however a lot of it was because I mistakenly thought he was okay. I always could count on Jason; good grades, good behavior, keeping himself out of things, he even passed the driving test first try. No matter what the case Jason was never an issue. Then it dawned on me one day: Jason was never an issue. How could I have been so stupid? All of his life I thought that the good grades and good behavior were because he had no issues. The truth is, I think he had so many issues that I was blind to them. It was easy to ignore them. Out of sight, out of mind I guess. But I realize today that all of the silence, all of the introverted behaviors, all of the times he never came out of his room wasn't because he had no issues, it was because he had issues. Sadly it took me to this point to figure it out. He needed me to be a dad and ask him about his day or take him out and play ball. He needed acknowledgement for his grades and not just taking it for granted he'd get them. My mistake with Jason was thinking Jason was okay even though I think I let him down most of his life. I hope I haven't realized too late to get up the nerve to tell him how proud I am of him, how much he has meant to me as a friend, a son, and a Sailor. And maybe before they plant me, I'll get up the nerve to tell him how much I love him and how much he reminds me of his mother. His mother.

Teresa was an incredible woman who gave me a new sense of life at a time when I had no life left in me. When she was taken from me I became so self-absorbed in my life for me that I forgot about so much about others. I tried my best, but I know I could have done better telling him more about her and about how much she loved and adored him.

"You just did Pop," he whispered. A small tear fell from his eye and dripped on the page.

I told her about you and your mom and she was so supportive. I think that's why we got along so well. She didn't judge me she just accepted me. I never told Sandy though; she is a totally different woman. Not to say she wouldn't have supported me or understood me. I was just a different person after Teresa died. And speaking of different, there's Kristy! Your sister-in-law. That girl is a piece of work.

A smile came across Jason's face.

I could think of no other woman I'd want for a daughter in law. She reminds me of Teresa; so full of life, so pretty, so out spoken, and she doesn't take crap from anyone. They say you marry your mama, I think the boy did just that.

So you're probably wondering where I'm going with this now and how this all relates to you. It's time. It's time to close this chapter of my life and move on. I won't forget I'll just simply accept you as a part of my life that I have come to terms with.

You have been my lie on and off for 20-some odd years and my escape from reality full time for quite a while. I have used you to forget my pain, used you as an excuse to get drunk and fall asleep on the couch. You were the one I would blame when I couldn't go to back to sleep at night, when I screamed at the kids, or sat outback and just got smashed. You were my lie, my fantasy, my crutch, and my excuse. Now I won't lay everything on you; I take the blame.

The normal thing is for people to take responsibility for their own actions and behaviors. However, when you're trapped in a cycle of PTSD, alcohol abuse and depression the blame game becomes normal. I think they call it denial. You were my normal and you were my denial. I have seen and sadly taken part in things I will never be proud of. But I've worked hard so I could be proud again and be normal; whatever that is.

I want my memories and daydreams of you and your mom to be the exception. I want to be free.

I want to be free to live, to love, and to face the transition from this life to death with open sober eyes. The time has come to let you go. You need to go on and be a memory in my life. A dear friend of mine asked me once if I knew why a windshield was so big, and a rear view mirror so small. His answer was simple, "Because the future is wide open and the past is a small fading memory like the one seen in a rear view mirror."

Jason's smile broadened and he glanced over the letter to see Dr. Wilton reading just as intently as he was.

All my life I have lived a lie in what you looked like, what your voice sounded like, and what type of young woman you have become. Hell, I even gave you your name. The truth is I don't know what happened to you, where you are, or what you've become. Are you alive or dead? Alone or with your mother? Are you happy and do you miss me. When I am honest with myself I know the answers to these questions. You are dead but only God knows where you are in flesh. I think you're in heaven and Lord knows I will know soon enough. The not knowing is what has haunted me for most of my life and in fact made me dead in a way. But I can't use you as an excuse any longer. It's not fair to your memory and it's certainly not fair to me. I know I will see you someday and we will be together. I have accepted God's plan with a clear mind, open heart and a renewed vision of life.
I was able to sleep last night. Maybe not like I did when I was twenty –five, but certainly not

like I had been in recent years. And I did it without any help from the pharmacy. A personal accomplishment since I have had so many different drugs for this damn cancer.

Jason noticed his father's hand writing had changed. The neat legible penmanship had been replaced by elongated letters. Some words were accentuated in their form while others written above or below the ruled lines.

Hey it's me. Who else right? I been gone a few days and I feel weak. My time is getting closer and I am going home tomorrow to die where I want to be and make sure my final days are with kids and Sandy.

I have put a lot on you during my life. If I hadn't I guess wouldn't be where I am today and that is saved. If there is any positive of me dying of cancer it's I am living again. You gave me life as I face death. I'm really happy. I feel today like I did so many years ago when I found out you were going to be part of my life. I will never forget that feeling or the genuine quality of my emotions.

It's not about quantity of life. It's about quality. I love you and will see you soon.

Daddy

TWENTY-SIX

Jason sat stoically as tears streamed down his face. He couldn't believe what he had read. The side of his father he remembered as a little, little boy in Great Lakes was again alive on the pages he had held. He didn't want to let them go, but after a moment he reluctantly leaned forward and set the pages on the table, envelope side up.

He looked up to see Dr. Wilton sitting and staring at him. His legs were crossed and he was resting his left elbow on knee. His head was cupped in his left hand.

"Well."

"Well, what?" Jason asked.

"What did you think?"

"Holy shit comes to mind."

"He was someone I knew a long time ago but I guess I didn't know. I mean, he had so many things going on in his mind I never knew about."

"And if you knew, what would you have done?"

"Maybe I would have helped him or talked to him about it. I don't know. I do know that I'm pissed or maybe hurt at him for telling a dead kid this but not me."

"Would it have made a difference?"

"I might understand him better."

"Jason, we have both read the whole letter and I must tell you it's remarkable. This was not the Chris Miller I initially knew. I knew a very damaged and fragile man with PTSD, depression and alcoholism. It took a while until he trusted me to tell me about Charlie which was huge for him. The admission paved the way for this meeting right now. There's a saying, 'you don't know, what you don't know'. Do you know what that means?"

"Yeah, my grandpa used to say it."

"Well, if there were ever a case where this rang true this is it. Sandy does not know this letter exists. She doesn't know what she doesn't know. Her memories of your dad are what they are. She only speaks of him as strong and loving. She doesn't think of the arguments, the drinking, the alienation. Having her read this letter would simply add questions and resentment to an already overwhelming situation.

"But it was okay for me to read it?"

"Yes, you knew about it. You had dug around for it and wanted to read it. No one put a gun to your head. This was a choice. Don't blame me, Sandy, or the world. Or for that matter your father. This letter is the opposite for you than it is Sandy. You need this letter to realize you think and act only on the negatives that happen in your life not the positives. Just like your father did."

"I'm just so confused I guess. I mean he never told me any of those things he wrote."

"Did he need to?"

"Maybe I wanted to hear them. Maybe having him tell me he loved me. I missed my mom so much, it would have…"

"Would have what? Made you a better husband, son, brother?"

"I don't know. I guess I just wanted to know he loved me."

"You did know you just chose to look at the negatives. And if you think about it, he did tell you."

"Oh come on."

"Jason, 'I love you' are three words we are programmed at a very young age to say and receive. It doesn't necessarily mean anything. Do you think a father saying 'I love you' to the nine-year old he just got done putting a cigarette out on means anything to that baby? It means nothing. To that kid, I love you means more pain and abuse. Actions Jason speak louder than words. My parents have been married fifty-two years and have never said I love you, at least not in front of me. But they do and they show it to one another each every day."

"But he drank himself stupid in the garage and forgot about us."

"To a point maybe yes he did. But those were his demons. From what I gather he rarely if ever lashed out at you kids or Sandy. I know at times he did. But for the most part would you agree he was easy to talk to?"

"Yes."

"And did you go on vacations and have some really good times?"

"Yes."

"Finally, would you agree if you really thought about it for a minute, that there is honestly more good memories in your mind about your father, Sandy, and your life than bad?"

Without hesitation Jason responded, "Yes?"

"See, you didn't even hesitate. You do know he loved you. He was difficult at times, even a bad father. But he loved you very, very much. No one is perfect and there is no perfect parent. I didn't see an instruction manual fall out of my wife when my son was born. If you look inside yourself you will see he loved you the only way he knew how, not how you wanted."

This sounds familiar, Jason thought.

"If everyone had their way we would be loved how we wanted to be no ifs ands, or buts. Just this perfect vision of how we think things should be. Jason, that's not love, that's death. The same death you mourn each and every day. If you have never found this letter and never jeopardized so much to find the rest of it you would have only known that your father loved or didn't based on your life with him. You wouldn't have known about Charlie, his underlying mental illness, and how he really thought about things. This should be an awakening for you too."

"Oh, so it should be like the cure he babbled about? I'm cured, he's dead?"

"Jason, you're missing the point about what he meant about cured versus saved. Your dad wasn't cured; he was saved."

"What the hell does that mean?"

"He saved himself from himself. From the demons that controlled his life for so many years. He was saved from the pain of war, the pain of losing not one, but two women he loved not to mention a child he never knew and the guilt that came with it. He managed to save himself from being what he thought was a pretty crappy father. So many of our men and women in uniform are never saved; some of them your friends. They have this false sense of being cured. They never get around to being saved. Some doctors cure symptoms with this prescription or that one until they find one that works to cure the symptoms. In your dad's case his cure was a bottle of J.D. Some cure an abusive marriage by getting a divorce, but go right back into another abusive relationship. They never get to the underlying reason. You can run, but you can't hide. It will follow you and will someday catch you unless you turn around and deal with it head on. Your father was one of the few who were able to do that."

"A bit too late."

"I don't think so. It's never too late. Read the last paragraph again where he talks about quality of life versus quantity of life.

The fact the he was able to find life while facing death is an incredible achievement. It proves it's never too late. Do I wish all my patients could be saved earlier in life, or find a way to maybe prevent it all together? Sure. So why not treat someone for PTSD before they get it."

"What?"

"Jason, I have been searching for a way to prevent PTSD before it can happen. I want to regress and re-expose these marines and sailors to the most traumatic experiences they've had prior to going to combat and have them relive them, in depth."

"The point being?"

"The point being this: You're an eight year old boy when a family friend sexually abuses you. You live your whole life with this built up anger and rage for the man who did these horrible things to you. You never dealt with them, they just built up. Fast forward 11 years and you're now a marine thrust into combat. Your best friend in the whole world through boot camp, School of Infantry and so on is blown up. In a heated firefight you move closer to a village. Your adrenaline is running high and your pissed. You want the guys responsible for your friend's death to pay. All of the pent up anger and rage you felt from your childhood unexpectedly manifests itself. You want to kill everything and everyone for killing your friend. But for also abusing you as a child. You're a time-bomb; tic, tic, tic."

"What if though we had dealt with that anger and rage of abuse before going to Iraq or Afghanistan? What if you could recognize your anger and put yourself mentally back in check because you've already dealt with it and you have the tools to be saved from your own actions. Actions based solely on events you've never dealt with years ago. We could eliminate PTSD or at the very least prevent some of the most serious cases. Because let's face it, war will always have PTSD causalities."

"So their past would be in the rear view mirror and their tour the windshield, right?"

"In a way yes. And that's why we chose you."

"Chose me? Who? What do you mean?"

"I mean we chose you. Your father and I chose you."

"Chose me for what?"

"We chose you to be my first real case in which we would attempt to stop PTSD before it started. Your dad told me so much about you and your life. He talked about you losing your mom, your relationship with Sandy, and your brothers. He knew it weighed on you and that you had a lot of anger. He even said so himself in the letter that he wished he could have gotten treatment before he went to Iraq. He thought it could have changed his life earlier. He came a long, long way and he worked hard but even still he regretted not having been saved sooner."

"It was you. You put the letter in Sandy's house. You made sure I found it. You used me?"

"Your dad wanted the letter there; a copy of it anyway. But it seems his young friend on the ward screwed that up, inadvertently it seems. Jason, I provided the guidance he needed and I did help him work out his issues. But he did all of the work himself. As for you. Yes I did, we did. I'm sorry."

"Sorry? I'm an experiment and you're sorry?"

"Yes if truth be told."

"What?" His anger became palpable and Dr. Wilton leaned back in his chair.

"I'm a lab rat for some stupid idea of how to stop PTSD?"

"Not stop it, but prevent..."

"I don't care for what reason you want to believe in your twisted mind this is insane. I've been sitting here for God knows how long listening to your snake oil sale and this is an experiment?"

"No it's not!" Wilton yelled back.

"Everything up to this point has been the truth. Everything. I saw the anguish in your dad and after months and months he realized it. Together we needed to see if we could stop just one kid from coming home and blowing their heads off, or from beating their wives, or drinking themselves to death. And were almost there. Jason, he didn't want you to wind up like him, he wanted better for you. Take your selfish head out of your selfish ass and think about someone more than you. We are almost there. Hell we've made incredible progress in all of thirty minutes. A few months of intense therapy before your first deployment and you can know that you have the tools to come home and be okay. Love you? You wonder if he loved you. He did this for you and if that's not a sign of a father's love I don't know what is."

Dr. Wilton's ringing phone broke the tension in the room. He scooped it up, the anger tangible.

"What!"

"Yes." His eye shot to Jason's.

"She is, huh? And demanding to see me? Okay, bring her down to my office."

He hung up the phone and stared at Jason. Damn it, this is not how he planned it.

TWENTY-SEVEN

Kristy waited outside the coffee shop door, her head turned away so her face was obscured to the regulars inside. She passed her on the right side and headed down the passage way towards the Quarter Deck. Kristy waited a few seconds and followed her. She was just as she remembered; extremely loud and obnoxious as she scolded the barista, "I wanted decaf mocha," in that horrible nasally voice. She was about five foot three inches, a hundred and maybe eighty pounds. She wore dark rimmed glasses and had straight oily black hair. Her complexion was greasy and she had small black-heads and pimples around her nose and chin. She had on red scrubs and a white dotted smock. She turned the corner and went towards the elevators. She's going back to the ward Kristy thought. She peeled off and headed for the stairs. She bolted three steps at every stride until she reached the third floor. The elevator doors opened and she walked past Kristy oblivious to her even being there. The hall was empty except for food carts that blocked the view from the nurses' station to her office door. She turned and looked behind her. The fire doors were closed. There was no one there. Kristy began to fast walk behind her.

As she pulled the key from the lock and pushed opened the heavy wooden door, Kristy grabbed her from behind and applied all of her body weight and momentum on top of her lunging them both forward. The door slammed shut behind them as fried eggs and hash browns flew through the air. Landing on top of her, the wind was knocked from her lungs. She gasped for breath and tried to scream but no air came out. Pouncing on top of her, Kristy quickly gained total control. Lieutenant Shriver tried to scream as she took in her first breath, but Kristy quickly covered her mouth with one hand and with the other took her left arm and bent up behind her applying heavy pressure. Her head was turned to the side and the shock and fear on her face was intense.

"If you make a sound and I'll break it. Do you understand? Blink once for yes."

Shriver blinked once and winced in pain. Kristy was in-fact close to breaking her arm.

"Now you listen, and you listen good. I'm not in the Navy so I have nothing to lose by being here but you do. You know there's a lot more you can lose, right?" Shriver blinked. "I'll loosen the grip a bit, but if you even think of screaming or trying anything, I swear to God I'll break it off. Understand?" Again Shriver blinked.

As promised, Kristy loosened her grip on her arm. The interrogation began.

"You stole Chris Miller's letter, right?" A blink. "And you planted it in his house so his wife would find it so you could screw up his family, right?" Another blink.

"I said one for yes,"' she said as she applied more pressure to her arm. Shriver winced; a tear ran down over the bridge of her nose and dripped on the carpet.

"Now again you planted it right?" Again, three blinks.

"Jesum Pete. I'm going to take my hand off your mouth. You scream, you'll be in a cast forever. Got it?"

One blink. Kristy slid her had away slowly. Shriver wiped the tears and snot on her smock.

"Well?"

"I did put it there—," she said through tears.

"Lower your voice!"

"I'm sorry, please don't hurt me."

"Be quiet! What were you saying about putting it there?"

"It wasn't my idea. I was going to mail it. I tried to steal the whole letter, but couldn't. So I took what I had to mail it. I didn't want to go to his house. But I was told I had to take it and put it in a place where he'd find it. It was a treatment. The son, not the wife had to find it. I wanted his wife to get it, but he said no, I had to take it."

Kristy was confused. "Treatment? He, who?" Kristy pressed. There was a pause as Shriver thought about her answer.

"He'll be mad at me," she cried.

"And I'll break your arm. Would you rather be kicked out of the Navy or never be able to lift a doughnut to your face. Who?" she demanded.

"It was Dr. Wilton!" She sobbed. "He's the one that made me do it. He found out I stole the letter. He came to my office and told me to deliver it to Senior Chief Miller's house. I was to make sure that your husband found it, not her. He said if she found it, it would be all wrong. I thought why not I'm already getting kicked out of the Navy."

"So why did he want Jason to find it?"

"I don't know, he just said I had to do it this way, some kind of treatment."

"And the ashtray you stole?" she hissed as she applied a bit more pressure.

"I didn't steal it; I paid a dollar for it."

"Before or after you planted the letter and took advantage of the boy?"

"After. And I didn't know he was special. Ouch! You're really hurting me. Please loosen up a bit. I promise, no trouble."

"Consider the ashtray donated to the estate effective today?" she said, loosening her grip a bit.

"That's fine. Take it, it's all yours."

"One more question; how did he find out you stole the letter?"

"Someone from the ward must have told him."

Louis, Kristy thought.

"I never found out who. I swear he wouldn't tell me who, he just told me I he needed me to do it."

"Now, I'm going to let go of your arm and get off of you. If you so much as move one muscle before I am out the door, I'll beat you over the head with that ashtray. Do you understand me? Do you?" she snapped as she applied a brief pressure to her arm.

"Ouch, ouch, yes, yes, I promise, I won't move!"

"And I was never here, because I will find you, you can bet on that."

"No you weren't here. Nothing happened. Its okay, I promise. Just please go. I'm sorry."

"Yeah, I bet you are. Just like you're sorry for manipulating a child with special needs so you could plant some stupid letter, right?" she snarled as she reached up and took the ash tray from its perch.

"My son. He has Down syndrome. I would have never done it had I known your was special needs. I would have taken my chances had I known."

"He's not my son, he's my brother-in-law." Suddenly Kristy had an overwhelming sense of pity.

"I'm still so sorry," she sobbed. Shriver lay crying even harder than before compounding Kristy's guilt. In front of her laid another woman, another daughter and mother who somehow got her life screwed up.

"Hey," Kristy said apologetically.

"Hey," she said again nudging her with her foot. "Hey, get up. Stop crying." Shriver turned over and looked at her.

"Come on, get up." She reached out her hand.

"Don't hurt me."

"I'm not going to. Come on, get up."

"Why? Why are you being so nice all of the sudden?" a dazed and confused Shriver asked.

"Because I don't think anyone's ever been nice to you," came the sincere reply. And because I wasn't very nice to you."

Shriver took her hand and got up off the floor and sat down at her desk. She lifted her hands to her face and began to sob. Kristy looked at her and set the ashtray back on the file cabinet. She moved around Shriver and picked her glasses up off the floor and then sat down in the high back chair across from her. With her left hand she slowly and sincerely rubbed the back of a very sad woman.

TWENTY-EIGHT

The knock on the door broke the staring contest between the two men. "Come in, it's open."

Jason sprang up in shock as Kristy walked in carrying the red ashtray.

"What the hell? Why are you here? And where'd you get that?"

"I could ask you the same question," an equally shocked Kristy said as she moved past Wilton and over to where Jason was standing. They embraced. Jason held her tight and she could feel his sense of needing her.

"And this old thing?" she said displaying it proudly. "An old friend of Dr. Wilton's and a new friend of mine gave it to me."

"Please why don't we all sit down," Dr. Wilton interjected uncomfortably. "We should talk."

"Yes, I think we should."

"About what now?" Jason asked. Confused and dismayed he sat down and pulled on Kristy's right had signaling her to sit in Wilton's old chair. He moved over to his desk and sat down across from them.

"I think I know why you're here," he asked directing his eyes at Kristy's.

"Oh do you now?" she barked back.

"What the hell is going on?" he said looking at Kristy. "And what do you mean you know why she's here?"

"It seems, Mrs. Miller —,"

"My name is Kristy. Mrs. Miller is around the corner on the ward."

"Excuse me," a flustered Wilton said. "It seems Kristy has been doing some investigative work."

"I have indeed."

"What?" What is going on?"

"What's going on is that the good doctor here is the one that had the letter planted in the house. Well not him, he got a very weak and easily manipulated nurse to do it for him. It seems he wanted you to find it, not Sandy. For what reason I do not know."

"I know."

"What?" Now it was Kristy who was flustered.

"What I mean is I know he wanted me to find it. As far as Shriver putting it there, that I didn't know." Jason was disillusioned by the whole thing. "You had that Lieutenant plant that letter so you could run your experiment?"

"It's true, I did it," he said.

"What experiment?" Kristy asked forcefully.

"Why not tell her about our talk," Wilton interjected.

"What talk?"

"Tell her, she should know."

"Know what?"

It what seemed like an eternity Jason told about his last half-hour with Dr. Wilton, the second half of the letter and the weird and, what he thought was, a cruel experiment.

Kristy sat back overwhelmed by everything Jason had told her. *Wait until I tell him I just committed kidnapping and assault.*

She turned to Wilton, "Are you some kind of nut case?"

"No, not at all," Wilton said with a slight chuckle. "On the contrary I am pretty sane. Whatever the definition of that is."

Resentful Jason pressed him, "Why? Why should I believe anything you say?"

"Because I have never lied to you and never will."

"Jason, this was all a big mistake."

"You're not kidding," an annoyed Kristy snapped.

"You were always meant to see the whole letter, but in a controlled environment."

"What does that mean?"

"Like we talked about earlier, it was to be an experiment. Your father and I talked a lot. He wanted me to find you after he died and have you read the letter, have us talk, tell you about it and go from there. When it was stolen I had given up hope of that happening. And then one day the young man who delivered it came back and told me he thought the good Lieutenant had taken the letter."

"HN Louis, right?" Jason asked.

"You have been doing your homework haven't you?" an impressed Wilton said with a smile. "Anyway, I went to her and had her deliver it. I had no clue she'd go in the house, which was just an extra."

"An extra? That's sick."

"No it's not actually. There's a lot you don't know about LT. Shriver."

"Like what?" Kristy asked.

Wilton hesitated. "I don't do this often if ever but considering the circumstances, I think it best you know. Having Lieutenant Shriver deliver that letter was very good therapy for her."

"Really?" a skeptical Kristy asked.

"Yes, it was. For many years she had been in a very abusive and controlling relationship. Soon after her son was born the violence escalated to include her son. She found the courage, left him and had him arrested. He's serving five years in a North Carolina prison. I have been working with her for a while on assertiveness and self-esteem. She has lived in a cocoon for the last ten or so years. All of the things she did; the having her laundry picked up and dog walked by the junior enlisted was so her husband didn't beat her or her son. She was afraid to speak up, to tell your dad or even the Nursing Director. She's made a lot of progress, so much so I think she should be given another chance. She's the poster-woman for battered woman's syndrome. Having her deliver that letter got her out of her comfort zone and made her face her own fears of doing something independent and risky. She had been controlled for years and in effect brain washed. I will admit I did take advantage of her but it was beneficial to the three of us. And just to be honest, she did go a bit over board."

"How?" asked Jason.

Wilton sighed. "It seems while she was there she was caught by one of the boys, Matt I think. She came up with some cockamamie story about being sick; even used a British accent. Anyway, seems she gave him a ten-dollar bill she had taken off the counter."

"She stole ten-bucks from my dad's house."

"Are you kidding me?"

"I wish I was. Her stealing is a whole other issue that I'm working on. Anyway, she gave it to Matt. When she got back she was very upset about it. Her son has....?"

"Down syndrome?"

"My, my we have been busy."

"How'd you know that?" Jason asked.

"Where do you think I got the ashtray," she said with a smile turning towards him. "She's not a bad lady, Jason. Weird, but not bad. But I guess I'd be weird too if I had endured the last few years of her life."

Dr. Wilton leaned forward in his chair. "Jason, your dad was very afraid you had his addictive tendencies. His biggest fear is that you would go to Iraq or Afghanistan and see all of the horrors that war inflicts on the mind. Your dad didn't want you to wind up like him. He didn't want you to come home with PTSD and screw up your life or her life," he said pointing at Kristy. "Not to mention the lives of any kids you may have. This letter was meant for you and me to talk about one day so we could unearth any demons and old skeletons in your closet and take a proactive approach to maybe preventing you from getting PTSD."

"But there is nothing saying he would get it. You can't make that diagnosis yet. He hasn't been anywhere!" Kristy shot back.

"You're right. But based on his father's behaviors, his tendencies and his addictions, Jason is a prime candidate for it. There is scientific proof that children of alcoholics are at greater risk at becoming alcoholics. There's also a genetic-environmental linkage to mental illness meaning children of the mentally ill are susceptible to mental illness. So why not believe that children with a parent with PTSD could be more susceptible to acquiring PTSD?" Wilton leaned on his desk, hands folded in a praying stance.

"Jason, your father. . . I mean us, did this for you and for every other of the hundred-plus-thousand folks going off to or coming back from war. It wasn't meant to trick you. I did it for him to help you and to maybe help others. He was more than a patient, he was my friend."

"Were you ever going to tell me about this?"

"Yes. I had hoped it would have gone much smoother than this, but it obviously went a bit wrong."

"A bit?" Kristy barked. Jason took her hand and gave it a reassuring squeeze.

"I was simply a messenger. If I'm guilty of anything its poor judgment and..."

"And taking advantage of weak and easily manipulated woman."

"Point taken," he said somewhat self-consciously. "Probably not the best way to do it, but hind-sight as they say is twenty-twenty."

"God, no more analogies, please," Jason implored.

"Fine. I sent you that half of a letter because that's all I had. I hadn't planned on only getting part of it. I sent it in hopes of helping you. I went about it the wrong way and for that I apologize. Your father wanted you to know everything about him; it was another way of being saved. His dying wish to me was that you get that same feeling of freedom. The only way to free you I believed was to do this. I screwed it up. Had I went down and picked the letter up maybe this would not have happened. But your father had a great fondness for the young man on the ward and wanted him to bring it to me."

"He screwed that up," Jason interjected.

"Not his fault."

"Why should I believe you, or believe anything you have to say?"

"Because I told you, I have never lied to you and never will. If you don't believe me, than maybe your father will get you to believe," Wilton said rising from his chair.

"What?" Jason asked.

He walked to the file cabinet, opened it and rummaged through the hanging folders until he found what he was looking for. He pulled the envelope out and sat back down holding the envelope to his chest.

"I was only supposed to give you this when and if I thought your life was spinning out of control. With all that has happened the last few weeks and more recently the last four or five days I thinks it's time. I wish it could have been under better circumstances." He reached out to Jason. On the envelope it simply read 'Jason." He took it.

He sat back, looked over at Kristy and slid his finger under the lip. The slow tearing of paper echoed in the silent office. Kristy moved closer and locked her arm with Jason. She stroked his arm in a reassuring manner. He lifted the heavy paper out and unfolded it. The penmanship was crisp, clear, and as straight as could be:

TWENTY-NINE

My Dearest Jason,

If you're reading this there has been a huge shift in your life. It's one that I thought might happen, but somehow held out hope it wouldn't. I asked Dr. Wilton to give this letter to you if he thought you needed it. He has done so much for me, that I thought he might be able to help you. I guess he thought it was time.

I am not there to know if it's the war or the just everyday life that is causing you pain and trouble right now. However, I bet if you look deep enough you'll find buried pain and anger that has festered for many years. A lot of it I bet can be traced back to me while the rest is strictly the daily pitfalls life brings. I don't know, I'm not there. What I do know is the shift is ruining your life and without help it will destroy it. I should know, it did me.

I carried a burden of guilt and resentment for twenty-some-odd years that deprived me of a fulfilling life with my family and friends. I don't want that for you! I am grateful we were able to make peace with one another. In our own way, we forgave each other's faults. We laughed at old stories and I hope solidified that we really did love each other. I know I knew. What's interesting, is we never took time to point out each other's faults, ask why, and come to real terms with the things I might have done wrong as a father. I guess when someone's dying you don't want to rock the boat. 'Let them die in peace' people say. I'm lucky because I did die in peace. If you live another fifty or so years, do you really want to do to your kids, your wife and yourself what I believe I did to all of you?

I think my life overall was good and I came to believe I am a good man. But the war changed me. It intensified all of the negative feelings I had carried my whole life. It pulled me further and further into my own world of self-pity, denial and alcohol abuse. It was only after my diagnosis with cancer and my chance meeting with Dr. Wilton that I realized that if I wanted to get better it was me that needed to get better. No one was going to do it for me.

I had to take the first steps to get honest and open; I had to make peace with me and all of the wrongs I thought I was dealt. I focused on the bad and wallowed in self-pity and self-destructive behaviors that made me miserable for many, many years. Doc Wilton helped me realize I wasn't dealt a hand worse than anyone else, I just played my cards wrong. Maybe if I had the opportunity that you are being given I wouldn't have become the person I did.

I want you to find peace in life before it's too late. I am fortunate that I found peace and acceptance with myself. But I admit I am disheartened that I didn't have more time to share it with my family.

I was the best dad I could be given my own life and the things that happened in it. Some days I was able to give one-hundred-percent other days I gave nothing. Maybe I wasn't the dad you wanted me to be, but is anyone who we really want them to be? I think not. You have to accept that I was the way I was. Look past my faults and look ahead with your own vision. You need to accept the way you are and come to terms with your life up to this point. You have an opportunity to do something that as far as I know has never been done before; preventing PTSD with therapy prior to deployment. We are preparing a Marine or Sailor to fight a debilitating condition before it has a chance to manifest. If they can free their own mind, and use techniques to recognize the stressors associated with symptoms of PTSD it could save countless lives, marriages, you name it. This continuing therapy and early intervention in Iraq or Afghanistan means that if someone is exposed to traumatic events they have the tools in place to recognize it, deal with it appropriately, and combat it. It potentially makes them less likely to act out negatively. Think of it as new type of PTSD called: Preventing Traumatic Stress Disorders. Take the help Dr. Wilton is going to offer you to learn from your mistake and walk with integrity as a man. Through your selfless act you will have saved yourself and set in place a program that could save countless Marines and Sailors, their families, and innocent people from one of the most diabolical aspects or war: PTSD. I love you son and always have. I hope you can feel me in your heart.

You're my hero,
Dad

He folded the letter and stuffed in back in the envelope.

"Wow. Thank you," he said shaking the envelope at Wilton." A single tear slid down his face.

"Thank your dad. I don't know the contents of that letter. It's personal between you and him. Based on your reaction it seems to have hit a nerve. Am I right?"

"Yes," he said and Kristy nodded yes too. She had read the letter over his shoulder and understood the message. Kristy pulled her arm from under his and wiped his cheek dry. He leaned forward of her and looked down to the floor. Instead of the voice saying, "no not here," it said nothing. Tears streaking down his face, he was able to let it out freely and it felt good. He held nothing back. The urge to hide from people was gone. For the first time in his life he was able to freely express his emotions without fear.

Wilton reached for a box of tissue.

"Here, take one," Wilton said.

Jason sat up and reached across the desk. He plucked a few tissues from the box. He wiped his eyes and blew his nose not embarrassed by the noise of it made.

"Are they the sand paper brand?" Kristy asked.

"Nah, nice and soft," he muttered through tears.

"Yeah, we get the good ones up here. We get a lot of crying. Guess they didn't want people leaving from here and heading to the ER with abrasions on their face."

"All jokes aside, am I the guinea pig?"

"No, first and foremost you're a patient, because let's face it you do have some things that you would like help working through, right?"

"Yeah."

"Second, if this process helps another person that's great but its worthless if it doesn't help you. Your well-being is first and foremost. Third, your father brought you down this path for a reason. He loved you and needed you to know you're worth more than you think."

The room was silent again. Jason stared at his hands neatly folded in front of him. Kristy sat on the couch rubbing the back of his neck. She was in it for the long haul and Jason could feel it.

Dr. Wilton just looked ahead at both of them, letting them digest an incredible morning's events.

Jason sat up. "You're right, Doc. He did guide me here. He wanted me to find this entire mess and figure it out somehow. He wanted me to find Charlie and myself." He paused and looked up at Dr. Wilton, "I'll do it. I mean I'll try. Not for him or you but for my family and me."

He turned to Kristy, "I love you so much and I'm so sorry for all of the crap that's been going on lately," as he began to cry again.

"It's okay, baby, I understand so much more now. Come here. I love you too," she whispered as he fell into her chest and a rhythmic motion of sobs and kisses. Dr. Wilton rose from his desk and walked to the door. He opened it and slid the sign on the outside to read 'In session, do not disturb.' He pulled the door shut behind him as he stepped into the hall.

THIRTY

"Are you sure you want to do this? I mean really sure?"

"Yeah, I'm sure," came the nervous reply.

"You can back out if you want to, it's cool."

"No, let's do it before it's too late."

"Okay then. The microphone is in this pen. It's a flash digital voice recorder that we have hooked up to a transmitter so we can hear what's going on from here. Like we talked about this morning; try to get them to tell you anything without leading them into it. You can't put words in their mouth it won't stand up in court. The important thing is to have whoever your talking to in front of you. It sucks picking up people behind you. Your body acts like a muffler. Okay?"

"Okay."

"And try to take it slow, build a rapport if you can."

"You're kidding right? This guy wanted to kick my ass a week ago."

"Here they come," came a voice from the back of the van.

"Right on schedule," Detective Loza replied checking his watch. "You're on, good luck."

Jason stepped out of the van and strolled into the Lotto-Beer and walked directly to the counter. Mr. Umar was perched on an old bar stool, his face buried in the Delco Times. It was 8:05 a.m. and Mr. Umar and his brother had just flicked on the opens sign. It appeared they were the only ones there. The Upper Darby Police thought it would be better that Jason goes right in when they opened. They didn't want the younger more aggressive guys there out of fear it could escalate into a real mess.

A lump suddenly appeared in Jason's throat, he swallowed hard. Maybe he should have Listened to Detective Loza and bailed. Too late now.

"Mr. Umar?" No response.

"Mr. Umar," he said a bit louder.

"Yes, yes, who is there?" he grumbled not looking up from his paper, his glasses resting on the top of his nose.

"It's me, Jason Miller."

"Who?" he asked more annoyed.

"Jason Miller, I was here a few days back about my dad Chris and Fathiya.

"You!" The quiet man was suddenly fully enraged. He flung the paper to the floor, leaped from the stool and charged towards Jason. The only thing separating them was the counter. Jason watched his hands for a weapon or broom handle. None. That's good, he thought. He'd gotten within five feet of Jason and stopped. His sudden stop hurled his glasses off his nose and sliding across the floor.

"Get out of here, you son of a bitch!" he

screamed. I told you to never come back here, get out!"

"Where is Fathiya?" Jason shouted back.

"Christ, I thought you said take it slow?" Captain Westbrook asked listening from inside the cramped van.

"Yeah, this kid's going right for the jugular," Loza said, chuckling as he moved the head phones away from his ears. The transmission was coming through loud and clear.

"How dare you, that's none of your business! Get out or I'll....."

"What? Call the police? Go ahead." Jason taunted. "Call them. Maybe you can explain where Fathiya and my brother or sister is."

"Brother or sister? There was no brother or sister just a bastard carried in the womb of a whore. You know nothing and neither does your so called police. They found nothing. Your incompetent so-called police never will find anything. Now get out," he yelled.

"So she was pregnant?" Jason persisted.

"Get out," came the reply and began walking slowly towards Jason.

"Where is my sister, Mr. Umar?" He stopped walking in the direction of Jason and leaned back on the cigarette rack. A self-assured grin came across his face.

"Where is my brother, Mr. Umar?"

"Make up your mind, is it brother or sister?" he provoked. "Now, get out."
Jason was losing him, he was losing it all. Umar seemed to be too smart and too smug to tell him anything. He needed something to burst his bubble. He took a deep breath, reached into his pants pocket took out a piece of paper and took the leap.

"You killed them didn't you?"

"Oh crap!" Loza stammered.
He began reading. "Isn't killing a believer a sin with the punishment being hell. Isn't murder considered the fifth greater sin..."

"Oh big giant crap! He's reading from the Koran," Loza screamed.

"And whoever kills a believer intentionally, his punishment is Hell; and he..." The paper was torn from his hand as Umar jumped forward, his grin now a glare.

"You did it, you killed them and for it you will burn in hell."

"Get out, get out!"

"You killed a believer, Mr. Umar."

"Should we go in?" came the SWAT leaders' voice crackling over the police radio.

"No, not yet. Let him go a minute more."

"But he could...."

"I said let him go! That's an order!"
Loza listened intently for anything, anything at all.

"You killed a believer, Mr. Umar and her unborn baby."

An uncontrollable rage came over
Umar. A large vein in his neck swelled and his
face
turned a deep red. The words left his mouth in
violent secession.

"She was not a believer she was a whore
and it was not a child it was a bastard.
Believers
do not associate romantically with non-
Muslims, do not fornicate out of marriage
especially with the likes of you. They do not
bring shame by getting impregnated. She was
worth nothing to me soiled and impure.
Nothing!"

"You killed your daughter," Jason
yelled.

"Get out," he yelled back, spit spewing
from his mouth.

"Say it," Loza coaxed. "Say it."

"You did it. You killed your daughter,"
Jason shot right back just as angry.

"I killed a whore and the bastard she
had poisoning her womb."

"Got you, you piece of shit!" Loza
screamed with delight.

"Get him now?" the SWAT officer
begged.

"No! We need everything we can get,
especially a body."

Umar went on. "I would kill her again if
she stood here much like I wish I could have
killed your father!"

Aaack-puuuuuh! A large wad of phlegm landed on the floor in front of Jason's feet. "I spit on his grave! A daughter's dowry is worth one hundred or even one hundred thousand fifty-times the amount if she is educated in this pathetic and stupid country. How could I ever send her back to Pakistan and expect to get anything of value for her when she was a whore. He stole everything from me."

"It takes two to......"

"Don't give me your Western philosophy excuses and propaganda. She was a whore and he stole my dowry from me. But I would get my revenge. I knew the lustful man wanted her. He came looking for her, calling for her. I could see his pain but it was not enough for me. I wanted him to suffer forever like my family would suffer in shame! I did kill her! I took her and I cut her throat. I stabbed and stabbed the devil growing inside her polluted womb. I pray to Allah that he spent a lifetime in pain and died a broken man.

"I spit on her grave and if I knew of his, his too." Aaack-puuuuuh! Another large wad of phlegm landed on the concrete floor.

"Where is she?" Jason demanded.

"In hell where she belongs," he taunted. And just like that his tone changed instantly from anger and rage to self-assured arrogance.

"You'll never know and it will torment you. It will bring me great joy knowing you suffer like that bastard."

"That's it, take him," Loza ordered. With that order a group of SWAT members charged the front door. One pulled the door open and jumped behind it. Another threw in the grenade. Before the two men could turn around there was a BOOM! The loud thunderous explosion did its job. Jason dove into the aisle away from the counter and the rush of SWAT members. They seemed to come from every direction through the front and the back doors weapons pointing. Lasers traced their target through the white smoke the grenade had produced.

"Police, police, police!" came the screams. "Get on the floor, get on the floor, do not resist, do not resist."

Umar was caught completely off guard. Stunned and in shock he was thrown to the floor before he knew what time it was. Several officers leapt on him and secured him in flex cuffs. Flustered he began yelling, "What is going on? I did nothing wrong, you can't come in here like this. Who are you?" he demanded.

Once the area was deemed secure, Loza came through the front door with his eager young detectives in tow. They had found Umar's brother hiding in the beer cooler. He too was arrested on a concealed weapons violation; no permit.

He stopped to check on Jason. "You okay, you alright."

"Fine, fine. Did we get him, did we get him?" Jason asked eagerly.

"We did. Watch this." Loza turned and stepped over to Umar.

"Mr. Abdullah Ibn Umar?" Loza asked.

"Yes. Who are you? What is this about?"

"I am Detective Anthony Loza with the Upper Darby Police Department and you are under arrest for the murder of Fathiya Tahzib Umar."

"And you are crazy!" he boomed bursting into laughter. A huge smirk came across his face. "You have no proof, you have no body. For all you know she is living in Pakistan with her bastard."

"Mr. Umar, we're not that incompetent as you may think." Loza held his arms up and bent his fingers to show the exclamation. The smile trickled out of his face and he stared stoically at Loza. How did he know I said that?

"You see, in this country we use things like transmitters and recorders. Just like the one Mr. Miller had on."

"Lift up your shirt please, Jason," Loza motioned. Jason did as instructed and pointed to the wires taped to his chest up to a small hole in his shirt where the pen had been placed neatly.

"In this pathetic country it may take a week or a year. Hell it may even take twenty some odd years but we never stop until we get justice. Justice for a young woman and her baby. Now get this piece of shit out of here. He gives good beer a bad smell."

Umar said nothing. He was for once speechless. He was paraded out the front door, SWAT officers surrounding him in a show of force and accomplishment. They placed him in a cruiser to finalize his transport to the station. People scurried into the store in droves to do forensic work, interviews and all of the other intricate detail that comes with this type of operation. Within a half-hour news crews were everywhere and police tape lined Long Lane and Market Street. Relatives of Umar and his brother were starting to show up and demanding answers the patrolman could not, nor would not answer. Before all the commotion began Jason slipped out of the store and walked over to the cruiser holding Umar. He knock on the passenger window, the officer cracked it.

"Yeah?"

"Can I talk to him for a second?"

"And you are?"

"He's with me," came Loza's familiar voice.

"No problem, Detective."

He cracked the back window enough for Umar to hear. He looked up to Jason from the cramped back seat.

"I'm sorry to say your prayers weren't answered." Umar looked confused.

"My dad died happy and pain free. He saved himself and freed himself of you a long time ago. It's something you won't be able to do when they strap your ass to that gurney and slowly inject the poison you deserve. Isn't it ironic to think that this pathetic country, as you call it will show a coward and heartless murder like you mercy as you die?"

He turned and walked away.

THIRTY-ONE

Jason kept vigil outside the store with the news-crews as the police and forensic guys dug up the office floor. Loza had offered him a seat in the command center with fresh coffee and a chance to catch some much needed sleep. He politely declined and stayed to himself. The night air felt good and kept his mind fresh.

He blended in not wanting to alert anyone that he was so deeply involved or that they were digging for his sister or brother and his father's first true love. He wanted no fanfare. He just wanted the closure daddy had longed for and Jason hoped to give him.

Abdullah's brother, Ali filled in all of the blanks he had left out. Loza's detectives had grilled him for hours. When they broke the news to him that he could be executed if he helped kill her he quickly changed his tune. He spilled his guts. The confession was overwhelmingly graphic and given in great detail:

Abdullah had lured her to the shop after hours on a Friday telling her he needed her to help stock shelves. When she arrived he ambushed her. He forced her to the basement and began to beat her. He slapped her and punched her in her face and chest. Overwhelmed with fear, she tried to fight back but he quickly overpowered her. Ali sat on the steps as a spectator and guard. He made sure she could not get up the stairs to escape. He stabbed her once in the abdomen cursing her in his native language of Urdu calling her a whore and a shame to her family. She put her hands of her abdomen to protect the baby but he continued to stab her. The huge buck knife slicked through her hands and entered her abdomen.

The interview slowed. Ali stopped and began to sob. He leaned forward and set his head on the table crying. Loza was playing good cop. He was compassionate and caring. His tone was reassuring and supportive. It was a good tactic but just that; a tactic. In reality Loza wanted to bash his head in. It had to be done this way though, they needed the confession and to get it you had to play the game.

"What's wrong?" he said reaching over and touching Ali's arm. "What? What's the matter?"

Ali sat up. He grabbed a napkin left over from the sandwich, chips, and coke he had requested and devoured earlier. He dabbed his eye and blew his nose, tossing the soiled napkin back onto the table. Loza was trying to hold it together.

"What's wrong, Ali? Let it all out, man. The truth will set you free."

He looked to Loza. "While he cut her she cried and screamed. I sat not knowing what to do. She begged me to help her. I just sat. Then she looked at Abdullah." His voice trailed off and was filled with a subdued cry.

"What happed when she looked at Abdullah? It's okay, Ali you can do this. What happened?"

With his voice cracking and tears streaming face he replied, "She asked him, 'Papa, why Papa? I love you, Papa, why?' And then...and then..."

"Then what?" Loza pressed.

He pulled the knife from her stomach and held her face close to his. He said 'You are a whore and an abomination.' He spit in her face and then slid the knife across...across... across her throat slowly so he could see her reaction!"

With that Ali let out a defining wail and threw himself on the table, his head making a loud thud. After more than twenty-minutes of coaxing with kid gloves the interview continued.

Ali waited on the stairs until Abdullah was sure she was dead and then had Ali help him dig up the basement floor. They worked all night and most of Sunday until her body fit in the hole. They set her inside, covered her with dirt, and then entombed her in fresh concrete. They were done by eight a.m. Monday morning, no one the wiser. Because they were such a secretive family and never associated with anyone her disappearance went un-noticed by everyone except Chris.

It was after three-thirty the following morning when Detective Loza waved for Jason to come over to the command center. He knew what it probably meant but it didn't make it any easier. They had found her.

She was lying face up in a small blue dress covered in dark earth and dried blood. Her arms were stretched out across her and her hands rested across her stomach protecting her baby even in death. Under her body they found the knife described perfectly by Ali. They were sure it was used to kill her. Jason asked to see her but the forensic team said no. It was a crime scene and she was evidence as morbid as it sounds.

Her body was remarkably preserved considering it had been entombed for over twenty-three years. A combination of cold dirt along with the sealed concrete help preserve her. Later that morning Loza went to the cell that held his prisoner. He told Abdullah they had found her. He reacted just like he thought he would; he simply pulled the blanket over his head with not so much as deep breath of acknowledgement.

Jason demanded but Loza refused to let him attend the autopsy. He didn't think it was such a good idea.

"I just want to see what she looked like," Jason said.

"Not in this condition, you don't. Trust me on this."

Jason sat in the Delaware County Medical Examiner's Office impatiently waiting for the autopsy to be finished. Hours later he sat down with the pathologist, Dr. Greenburg and Detective Loza.

Greenburg went over the obvious cause of death; multiple stab wounds but what Jason really wanted to know was about Charlie.

"Doc not to be rude but can we skip this for now? Did I have a sister or brother? I have been waiting a long time. I just need to know."

The answer pierced him like a bolt of lightning. Nothing prepared him for this

"You have to be kidding me. Twins?" Jason asked in disbelief.

"No, I'm confident. The fetuses were very well developed and quite well preserved. She was more likely than not in her early second trimester; probable twenty to twenty five weeks gestation. As far as I can tell they we're fraternal; a boy and a girl." Greenburg's voice was cold and monotone.

"A boy and a girl?" Jason asked again, stunned.

"You sound surprised," Greenburg said.

"I am, actually. I wasn't sure how far along she was and frankly never could have imagined she could be carrying twins. My dad probably didn't know based on what I was able to find out. He never made mention of it."

"I'm sorry. I hope I didn't do anything to tarnish your father's memory."

"No, Doc, you're good. It's all good."

"When can I take them for burial?"

"Well that's up to the District Attorney. My work is done. Because I have ruled it a homicide the deceased is considered evidence. It's their call."

Jason looked over at Loza, his eyes imploring help.

"I'll make some calls," Loza reassured.

"Thanks."

They stood and they all shook hands. As they walked out of the building together a large gathering of gray-ashen clouds caught Jason's eye. *Funny how the weather knows exactly how you're feeling*, he thought.

"By the way, Detective, is Umar going to be charged for killing the twins as well?" Jason asked.

"Sorry Jason," Loza huffed. "The laws back then didn't cover fetal homicide. The first laws didn't hit Pennsylvania until '97. Can't charge him with anything, just the one count of first degree premeditated murder and all of the other felony charges that go along with it, use of a weapon in the commission of a felony and so on. He'll fry, don't worry about that."

"I'll be at my grandmother's if you need me or when you find out when I can take them home."

"No problem," he said taking Jason's hand with a firm handshake.

"Thanks, Detective, I appreciate it."

"No thank you. We would never have been able to close this case or get justice if you hadn't been involved and did all the leg work you did. We owe you."

"Thanks but I've been paid . . . in more ways then you'll ever know," Jason said smiling appreciatively.

After the collection of all of the evidence the Coroner released the body. No one who had the legal rights to the claim Faith's body did. In fact her mother relinquished all rights. She was left to the state to dispose of and discarded again like a piece of trash.

It took just ten minutes of testimony for the judge to sign the order giving Jason the rights to Faith's body and that of her babies. The judge agreed that he was the closest living relative to the fetuses.

Dr. Greenburg identified Chris as the father with DNA testing.

"It is with a 99.8% certainty he was the biological father," he testified. The next day he stood outside the Donahue Funeral Home as the silver coffin was placed in the hearse.

"You're going home," he said quietly. An hour later they were on a plane for the trip back to Jacksonville.

THIRTY-TWO

The decision to tell Sandy everything about his dad, Faith, and the twins was strictly Jason's. Kristy and a reluctant Dr. Wilton agreed with his decision and felt she should know especially since Jason was planning a funeral. It would be hard to hide that. He sat down with her at the house and over the course of an afternoon told her everything. He began by reminding her that we all have a past. The day of her heart attack she had told him so much about her past and if anyone could understand, he thought it would be her.

He told her about the letters and offered to let her read them. She declined. He told her of his adventures in Pennsylvania over the last two-weeks. Sandy's reactions would have been surprising to some but not Jason. She was calm and listened intently and as told her about Faith's murder, his father and the search for the truth. She seemed to take it well or at least the best someone could under the circumstances. She asked a few question but really didn't say too much. She changed her mind and wanted to read the letter. Dr. Wilton let Jason take it to the house. She went to her bedroom to read it alone. After a short time alone reading and crying; she returned them and thanked him with a firm embrace. The letters answered a lot of questions Sandy had on her mind for many years; Chris's drinking, crying spells and so on. When Jason pressed her to maybe talk more about it she politely said, "Jason, we all have a past." With another firm embrace and an 'I love you' whispered in his ear, she had the closure she felt she needed.

His aunts and uncles were very supportive and did everything they could to help Jason and Kristy plan a decent yet reasonably priced funeral. Kristy's parents had generously put up the money for a new headstone and the guys at the Clinic had a bake-sale to help raise money to defray the costs.

Jason returned the next day to the Naval Hospital and gave Dr. Wilton back the letter. He spent a few hours going over everything with him and told him he needed reassurance that he was doing the right thing with the funeral, the burial, publicity, etc. The media coverage was intense. The national morning news programs kept calling for interviews. There was even a call from a movie producer about rights or something.

"Ask yourself this," he began. "What exactly is the right thing to do? If you believe it's right, then it is."

Jason's grandmother disagreed with everything and was not so supportive. She felt it was too much to take on and even threatened to boycott the funeral. Jason pleaded and she finally relented. He had pushed the Catholic doctrine of forgiveness and mercy.

"Fine, I'll do it for your dad and for you and for those innocent babies," she grumbled.

Jason knew his Catholic Grammie could never turn away from a church she adored.

Jason wanted a Catholic funeral Mass but with all of the news media he decided it would be impossible. Some religious groups had already cried foul over some of the news coverage and wanted to know why they were referring to Fathiya as Faith and why Jason hadn't followed Muslim laws and rites in burying her. In the only interview Jason did on Good Morning America, he emphasized that it was not about religion or Gods. It was about murder pure and simple. He questioned why the same groups that chastised him never mentioned the two innocent babies who were nearly to term. Somehow with that one interview any negativity of the case and any reference to religion were dropped.

Jason decided that Faith would be called be her given name; Fathiya. She was Muslim and he would respect that the best he knew how with help from a Muslim Chaplain. He also decided that Charlie and Charles would be baptized Catholic at the funeral home. The priest sat stone faced with his mouth open in total disbelief as Jason told him the story of his new older brother and sister conceived but murdered so long ago.

It was a simple yet cherished moment. Father Murphy prayed with Jason and Kristy as he baptized the tiny bodies all covered up except a tiny grayish colored face. The entire family attended and cried tears of joy as the trickles of holy water ran down their foreheads and into the shiny brass basin.

Most people would have seen just two weathered, worn and mummified bodies but to Jason they were beautiful. He had not seen Fathiya and chose not to. Detective Loza was able to get him a picture of her when she was in high school and that was the memory he would cherish. She was just as beautiful as he thought she'd be and he chose to remember her like his dad had described. The picture was all he needed.

The grave side service was held at the Coastal Carolina State Veterans Cemetery. Chief Daniels was able to get Charles and Charlie, as they had become formally known, added to his dad's Defense Eligibility Enrollment Reporting System (DEERS). How he pulled that off will remain a mystery forever thus making them, at least on paper his dependents.

Much to everyone's surprise including Jason's, Sandy was insistent they all be buried with Chris. She wanted him to have the final closure in death which he never had in life. Special permission had to be granted by the North Carolina Department of Veterans Affairs to allow Fathiya to be buried with them and at first they denied the request. But when CNN started to asking questions around the VA's regional office in Winston-Salem, they suddenly made an exception to policy. They even paid to open the grave.

Matt and Ryan had been told enough to satisfy their curiosity of another funeral at Dad's grave. As they got older and could maybe understand they would tell them more.

THIRTY-THREE

As the three coffins arrived by hearse, Jason felt his throat tighten. He could do this he thought. Mourners began to cry quietly and respectfully. Even though no one knew who Fathiya, Charles, and Charlie were, the brutality of their death, the fact their father was a Senior Chief Petty Officer in a military town and the senselessness of it drew a large crowd. Some estimated more than three-thousand people. News media from around the country were hovering on scaffolding the city had erected inside and outside the cemetery.

He was touched by how many people from his command had come. The Commanding Officer, Executive Officer, Command Master Chief, and the whole Chief's Mess were there. The senior Marine staff, General Arthur and his Chief-of-staff. And all of his friends and co-workers from the Clinic, so were all of the nurses Kristy worked with.

As he scanned the crowd he saw her way in the back.

"Is that Lieutenant Shriver over there?" he whispered to Kristy with a nudge. She looked up.

"I invited her."

"What?"

"She needed to see this. She needs to see how families love each other and grieve with each other no matter what. She needs some sort of peace."

She turned away and looked back of the coffins as they were being carried to their final resting place. There was nothing more to say, Kristy had this one.

Scanning the crowd again he spotted Dr. Wilton and Captain Gray. Detective Loza came as well. He stayed at Chris' house and both knew they would become lifelong friends now. After helping arrange the transfer of the bodies to North Carolina, he had reached out to the Jacksonville Police Department, telling the Chief there the whole story. They provided an escort and all the traffic control around the cemetery. To top it all off, Chief Daniels had even arranged for three honor guards to carry the coffins from the hearses to the grave site. The Navy did take care of its own.

The Muslim Chaplain, Imam Yusuf Ali-Abdulla began the service and went through the proper rites and rituals for the burial of Fathiya. Her remains were handled in accordance with Muslim tradition; she was bathed, wrapped in a plain white cloth, and mourned with traditional funeral prayers. She was to be laid perpendicular to Mecca as required under custom. Jason wanted to ensure her beliefs and that of her religion were respected.

Father Murphy went next. He went through the proper Catholic rites and rituals for the final resting of Charles Matthew Miller and Charlie Sandra Miller.

Jason was holding it together very well until the priest began to read Psalm 23:

"The Lord is my shepherd; I shall not want. He makes me to lie down in green pastures: he leads me beside the still waters. He restores my soul: he leads me in the paths of righteousness for his name's sake. Yea, though I walk through the valley of the shadow of death, I will fear no evil: for thou art with me; thy rod and thy staff they comfort me. Thou prepares a table before me in the presence of mine enemies: thou anoints my head with oil; my cup runneth over. Surely goodness and mercy shall follow me all the days of my life: and I will dwell in the house of the Lord forever. Amen."

Jason's tears came hard and so did the clutch Kristy had on his arm. He didn't care. To her left sat Grammie. She wasn't able to stand long so one of the Corpsman had gotten her a chair. She wept into a napkin as she reached out to softly stroke the little pink and blue coffins the honor guard placed at the grave site in front of her. Although the services took forty minutes it seemed to be over so quickly. Much like the last three-weeks that now seemed like a blur.

Jason stepped away from Kristy's grip and reached into the basket and took out two white roses. While planning the funeral Aunt Maria had suggested the family place white roses on the caskets of the children since the white rose signified purity and innocence.

"There's no better definition of purity and innocence then those babies," she told Jason.

"That would be really nice, Maria but I don't know that we can afford it."

"I'll pay for it," came the voice from behind him. It was Uncle Frank.

"It's the least I can do. Okay?"

Overwhelmed, the only thing Jason could say in a broken voice was, "Okay."

As Father Murphy sprinkled holy water on the caskets and prayed silently, Jason placed a single rose on the light blue casket. The small brass placard engraved Charles; son of Chris and Fathiya. He moved to the pale pink casket complete with a small pink bow that flickered in the wind. Her coffin also had a small brass placard engraved, Charlie, daughter of Chris and Fathiya. He placed a rose on hers. He moved between the two caskets placed head to toe of one another and stretched his arms out and reached for both of them. He lightly brushed his hands over both casket and felt the tears roll down his face, the crisp wind cooling them and giving him a chill.

"Sleep little babies. Sleep and sleep well. Sleep in peace with your Mom and Dad."

He brought his hand to his mouth and kissed his fingers and rubbed Charles' casket. He did the same lightly placing a kissed hand on Charlie's. As he filed past the caskets he reached in and took two bunches of red and white roses. Red and white roses given together signify unity and they were finally united. He moved closer and placed one on his dad's grave.

"I found her, Daddy. She's here with you now and for eternity. Take care of each other and the babies. I know I'll see you all again someday. I love you."

He moved a few feet away and placed another bunch on Fathiya's coffin a few feet away when he felt someone gently take his arm. It was Sandy. She had tears running down her face.

"They're together like they should be," Sandy said. "It's the right thing to do."

"Thank you, Sandy, thank you so much for understanding, for helping, for listening, and mostly thank you for..." Jason froze.

"For what?" she asked waiting for him to finish.

"Jason, for what?" she asked again, confused.

"For loving me. Thank you for loving me."

"Oh and I do so much!" she said reaching for his neck. The embrace was long overdue. Years of resentment, fear and anguish washed free through the tears he cried deeply into her shoulder. He could feel her hands squeezing his neck and back. He felt her warmth overtake him and he felt whole again. This chapter in Jason's life was closed it would fade into distant memories as he traveled forward with life. He was in no way done closing chapters, but this one was closed.

He lifted his head from her shoulder and took her arm. He waited for Kristy to place her roses and she took his other arm. They walked out from under the tent that covered the graves arm in arm. The bright Carolina sun and fresh morning air greeted them like an old friend not seen in a long while.

Damn if the sun doesn't know how you're feeling.

THIRTY-FOUR

The last box was placed in the U-Haul and the door pulled shut. Sandy and Kristy had walked the house one more time to make sure nothing was missed. Matt and Ryan rolled around laughing and wrestling in the freshly mowed grass. She was really doing it he thought. After everything that's gone on over the last month she's doing it.

"Hey there good looking," came the cat call that roused him from his trace.

"Hey baby," he said planting a kiss on Kristy's lips.

"Gross!" came the shrieks and giggles from two grass covered boys rolling back-and-forth.

Jason shot them a smile. "Did you get everything?"

"Yep, it's all here. You okay with this?"

"I am. It's not like I didn't know it was coming moving day and all."

"Okay boys, let's go," Sandy yelled out. She had Norman in a small cat carrier oblivious to the fact he was alive let alone moving.

"Yeah, we're moving, we're moving," Matt squealed. The boys jumped up and headed for the truck.

"Thanks for helping me, guys," Sandy said. "And for helping me do a do it your self-move, following me to the new place and everything."

"No problem, that's why we're here," he said.

Jason would drive the U-Haul with the boys. Kristy and Sandy would follow in the Honda with Norman and his litter box. Lucky them. Let the road-trip begin.

He opened the driver's door on the U-Haul and prepared to get in when a brilliant white shine caught his eye. He moved his head and as he did the shimmering light grew in intensity. Curious, he stepped back closed the door and took a step forward.

"What do we have here," he said baffled by its beauty.

It was a penny. A shiny alluring copper penny! Jason held it between his thumb and fore finger and smiled a giant smile. It was a 2009 and had a small 'P' which signified the Philadelphia mint.

He had wonderful images of a man he knew truly loved him.

"Daddy," he whispered thoughtfully. "I'm thinking of you too."

They pulled into the driveway of the new house. The boys were giddy with excitement and Jason had to tell them to leave their seat belts on and the door closed until he stopped the truck. As soon as he set it in Park, they were out the door like a shot. The house was a small craftsman style three bedroom. It was a cute new construction home in an inexpensive neighborhood. Jason was shocked when Sandy announced she had given up the condo and was now looking for a house.

"It's too small and not right for the boys. They need to get out and play."

"What about Dave?" Kristy joked. Jason almost fainted. He couldn't believe she brought him up again. .

"I told you already, he's a bone head. I have feelings for one man and he's right here," she said bringing her hands to her chest.

"I know, I'm just kidding," Kristy said, giggling.

"Well, what do you think," Sandy asked taking Jason's hand.

"I love it. It's beautiful. I am so happy for you and the boys. It's real nice."

"So, are you going to miss me and the boys?" she teased.

"Yeah, I am. But considering your right next door I guess I can get over it." They both let out a laugh.

When Sandy announced she was staying in North Carolina, they were thrilled and shocked at the same time. She explained how the market was better and her money could go further here. Plus all of her friends were here. When she took Kristy house shopping with her she got the itch too. Jason had told her about the trust money for a new home and it just seemed right.

They had found the two-story house on a cul-de-sac with the small craftsman next door. Jason was skeptical taking on a mortgage payment, Sandy being so close, and privacy. She assured them she would not be a bother and would respect their privacy. None of them would just stop in without calling. From there it all seemed to fall into place.

Jason and Kristy gifted her $10,000 from the money left to them. She tried to refuse the gift, but Jason insisted that he wanted her to have it. He had taken her to Navy Federal Credit Union and had her meet with a financial counselor to get her finances in order and do a budget. He assured her if she lived within her means, she would be fine.

Jason and Kristy had closed the week prior and were still getting unpacked; now it was time to get Sandy and his brothers settled.

"So what are thinking?" Sandy asked breaking his daze.

"Everything. Dad, you, the boys, our new houses, everything. I'm glad you stayed. I would have really missed you guys."

"I'm glad we stayed too. Truth is I needed to be closer to my baby."

"Your baby, huh?"

"Yes! My oldest son and his wife," she said squeezing his hand smiling.

Her son? Wow.

He had to admit that sounded good coming from...his Mom.

EPILOGUE

Chris second guessed himself again and the life he had lived. Maybe he hadn't been as good a father, husband, son, and servant as he thought. He could no longer talk, move or signal to anyone. He could hear everything, smell everything, and even feel it when someone took his hand or lightly stroked his face. He knew the end was near, nearer than ever before. The shaking of his hospital bed redirected his attention.

The boys carefully climbed into his hospital bed and lay down with him, one on either side. As they snuggled in close keeping his cold body nice and warm, Sandy gently lifted his arms and placed them over them so he could hold them one last time. He didn't have the energy to stroke the backs of his sons and cried out in anger and this new agonizing pain that had taken control of him. No one heard his cries but him as he tried in vain to sooth their sobs but couldn't. No words, no motions, no nothing. He simply laid there as the boys cried for their dying hero.

When the boys finally got up Sandy stayed by his side holding him, talking to him, and reassuring him. He blamed himself that she had to take care of him and repeatedly moaned, "I'm sorry" over and over when she bathed him, cleaned his soiled diaper, and rubbed cream on his now festering bed sore. In his final days she strove to keep his modesty even though he felt he had lost his dignity. She would hum songs and tell him how she loved him and how she was so happy that she could do this for him. "No wife should have to do this," he whimpered to himself, too weak to produce a single tear and too feeble to tell her aloud.

Through all of this, Jason would come in each day to talk even though Chris couldn't acknowledge his presence. Somehow Jason knew he could still hear him. Leaving him was hard; he was his first born and the only link to his now deceased mother. He turned out to be a fine young man and a dedicated sailor. Weeks earlier Chris had told him how much he had meant to him as a friend, a son, and a sailor and most importantly that he loved him. Any father would be honored that their son followed in the family business especially when it was shared with a nation. He could not have been prouder of him. He regretted he would miss the birth of any grandchildren he and Kristy may have, but knew Jason would be a great father, much better than he had been at times. The sadness and regrets he had flooded his mind; the missed baseball games, the excuses not to go fishing so he could stay home and stay drunk, the ignored stories a boy wanted to share, that a father simply had no time for. How he wished he had been a better father.

He didn't want to leave, however going would ease the burden and pain everyone shared. The fact that the hospice nurse had not left and was dutifully attentive was one clue he was finally dying as was the arrival of his mother, sister and brother. Most of Sandy's family had come to the house including Frank. He arrived first.

"Don't give him a dime," he thought he whispered to Sandy. In truth he had only whispered it to himself in a slow and stammered voice.

Just as suddenly as the physical pain stopped so too did the emotional pain. He had a calming and reassuring flood of passion take hold of him. The emotional pain wasn't the beginning of hell, it was the beginning of his journey. God had one final task for his servant Chris. He called him to take on the pain of those who couldn't understand it, those who missed it, and those that aimed it at themselves. As so began a flash back in Chris' mind that suddenly calmed his fears and opened his heart. He knew he had given of himself in a way no mortal man would ever know or believe possible. Only those preparing to pass through the tunnel would fully understand the overwhelming sense of compassion and sacrifice of life that he suddenly felt.

He had saved his sons years of unimaginable hurt they could never comprehend because they were special. His body and mind had taken and absorbed the emotional pain of his death freeing Matt and

Ryan from what they could never handle. Chris had been wrong. His arms so gently placed by Sandy did in-fact sooth their sobs and wrapped them in the security and safety they needed to understand their father's death. He laid there still and silent and let them hold, love, and say good bye to their father at a level they could grasp. He had eased their burden and realized he had done the same for Sandy as well.

She had agonized over the loss of her father and the falling out they had a few years before. When she found out he was dying of hepatitis she stubbornly refused to see him and by the time she finally did, it was too late and he was gone. She regretted not reconciling with him or taking care of him as he died. When faced with the reality that Chris would surely die, she committed herself to care for her husband. She eagerly accepted the daunting job and in it found a way to reconcile with her father through Chris' inability to care for himself. She was honored and proud to care for her husband and closed the void she had missed with her father. She could finally forgive herself for her father, and let the pain go. What Chris thought was a curse for her, was in fact gift. All of Sandy's painful emotion had been taken by Chris. Sandy could live in peace and so too could he and Jason.

Jason was honored and grateful to have this time with his dad to say goodbye that he never had with his mom He would think about her when he spoke to Chris and wonder what he would have said to her if given the chance. As he sat down one afternoon and took his father's hand, he was suddenly overwhelmed and realized he was in fact speaking to her. The anger and resentment he carried around year after year eased from his body each day he visited his dad. Chris felt the pain his son needed to release and took it away like any father would from their child.

He had blamed himself for failures as a father and the many sins that he had committed over the years. That burden too lifted away from his soul and was replaced by good times he had with his son. His missed baseball games were replaced by the nights driving to Raleigh to see the Carolina Hurricanes play. The fishing excuses were replaced by camping trips and lakeside fishing excursions that produced small hordes of bluegill. And the ignored stories were replaced by long talks about girls, life, manhood, and respect.

God had forgiven Chris for his sins long ago and he finally realized he did so much more good than bad. The pain and heartache aimed at himself was gone and taken on in an emotional and physically painful gift given to humanity some two-thousand years before. He could move on now free and forgiven.

His breathing was labored and his pulse weakened. He could hear the light crying and the weeps from inside the room.

"It's okay, baby we're all here," she reassured him.

"It's okay." The fight was gone from his body and he was ready to go. He was ready to slip from this great life to another. He knew his dad would be there. So would Teresa and Faith. He would meet up with his friends, sailors and marines lost in combat. The many innocent faces that haunted his dreams and nightmares would no longer be an affliction that controlled his life. Instead, they would become companions in a calming place of beauty and peace. As he took his last breath, the clamor in the room simply faded away. The darkness turned to light.

There was a bright light after all. His cold and harsh body felt young, warm and vibrant again. He entered the light and was greeted with rejoice and celebration. The dark black hair and beautiful brown eyes first caught his attention. Two children; one taking each hand. The people gathered around Chris saw none of this.

For them, Chris's life ended in no dramatic fashion. It was nothing like you see in a movie; the final words of the dying or the melodramatic final gasp of air. No, it was just over.

Chris' mouth lay open and his body was an ashen gray color. The size small hospital gown seemed two sizes too big, and the single bed was mountainous compared to his withered frame. No, it indeed was nothing like the movies.

Sandy cried harder and harder as Grammie rubbed her back with one hand and dabbed tears with the other. Sobs and muffled weeping filled the room. Emotions were high with everyone except Jason. He held it all in as usual.

"Good bye, Pop," Jason mouthed. He pulled his hand from Kristy's, turned and quickly smeared it away.

"Where are you going?"

"Bathroom," he muttered as he dashed to the downstairs bathroom to grieve in private; always in private.

ABOUT THE AUTHOR

Mike Lechette served 22 years in the Navy and retired as a Senior Chief Hospital Corpsman in 2009. He spent the final 12 years of his career in Naples, Italy, Great Lakes, IL, and Camp Lejeune, NC in the Patient Administration Department and the Decedent Affairs Program. He deployed onboard the USS Savannah (AOR-4) during the Gulf War and again with the 2d Marine Regiment, RCT-2 during Operation Iraqi Freedom. He worked closely in and with the Regimental Aid Station, Shock Trauma Platoon, and in Mortuary Affairs. He has an extensive knowledge in the interworking of Navy Medicine, Navy policies and procedures, as well as contacts and friends around the world who help validate aspects of his work to ensure accuracy.

He is married and has four children and resides in Jacksonville, NC.

www.ingramcontent.com/pod-product-compliance
Lightning Source LLC
Chambersburg PA
CBHW070735180626
46818CB00007B/2855